*S**eason* of
*S**acrifice*

Season of *Sacrifice*

A
Historical
Novel

by

TRISTI PINKSTON

Golden Wings Enterprises

This is a work of historical fiction. The characters and places are real, and the incidents are based on historical accounts. However, for the sake of storytelling, the author has taken some liberties with dialogue and certain incidents, and takes full responsibility for any errors or omissions as a result thereof. Likewise all views expressed herein are the sole responsibility of the author.

Season of Sacrifice

Published by

GoldenWings

Golden Wings Enterprises
P.O. Box 468, Orem, Utah 84059-0468

Cover image copyright © 2008 by Max Bertola

Cover and book design copyright © 2008 by Tristi Pinkston

GoldenWings is a registered trademark of Golden Wings Enterprises

ISBN 978-0-9794340-1-3

Printed in the United States of America
Year of first printing: 2008

10 9 8 7 6 5 4 3 2

This book is dedicated to:

Benjamin, Sarah, and Mary Ann

May your story be remembered,
your faith commemorated,
and your courage imitated.

ACKNOWLEDGEMENTS

I realize, now more than ever, that I'm only successful because of those who have helped me. From the moment of the first idea until the moment the book sits on the shelf, many people contribute their thoughts and ideas, support and criticism, and the final product belongs to each of those people.

Here are just a few:

My husband Matt and my children Caryn, Ammon, Joseph, and Benjamin. Thank you for believing in me, supporting me, and cheering me on.

My parents Ruthe Clark and Joel W. Norton, for raising me on stories of my ancestors and teaching me about my heritage and the value of the past.

BJ Rowley for taking this project under his "golden wings" and bringing it to life.

My readers Josi Kilpack, Tara C. Allred, Annette Lyon, Katie Parker, Anne Bradshaw, Gordon Ryan, Shirley Bahlmann (who is also my own personal cheerleader), and Sian Ann Bessey for helping me with grammar, content, and clarity. Jeff Savage, for going to bat for me time and time again. Candace Salima, for insisting this story be told and defending my right to tell it.

Max Bertola, of www.so-utah.com, for generously allowing the use of his fabulous Hole-in-the-Rock photo on the cover.

Last, but not least, all of the LDStorymakers for their friendship and advice, and for putting up with me. I couldn't ask for a better group of friends.

INTRODUCTION

Like Nephi of old, I have been born of goodly parents. As I read through the family histories and journals that have been passed down for generations, I am uplifted by the stories of those whose name I carry. Mine is a legacy of devotion and dedication that spans the globe.

We each have such a heritage when we look at the past to see all that has been done to bring us to where we are now.

This book follows the life of my great-great-grandfather Benjamin Perkins. Much of the story I will tell comes directly from family history books, journals, and letters. All of the characters are historical. Only a small portion of this story have I created. I invite you to read the chapter notes at the end of the book to see which things come from actual history and which things I invented to further the plot.

Pulitzer said:

The story of the Hole in the Rock pioneers is one of faith and courage.

Prize-winning author Wallace Stegner says in his book *The Gathering of Zion*:

For every early Saint, crossing the plains to Zion in the valleys of the mountains was not merely a journey but a rite of passage, the final, devoted, enduring act that brought one into the Kingdom. Until the railroad made the journey too easy, and until the new generations born in the valley began to outnumber the immigrant Saints, the shared experience of the trail was a bond that reinforced the bonds of faith; and to successive generations who did not personally experience it, it has continued to have sanctity as legend and myth.

Mons Larsen recalled the hardships of the San Juan expedition with the comment:

> *The handcart journey which I made from Winter Quarters to Salt Lake City was not nearly as hard as the journey through the Hole in the Rock.*

I have felt honored to spend a portion of my time studying and learning about Benjamin. His life has touched mine in ways I can't even begin to describe. His faith was ever present and strong, even in times of great trial.

The courage and determination of the Hole in the Rock missionaries never faltered. Above all else, their testimonies were iron-clad—undamaged by the darts thrown at them by the world.

I am inspired by the people they were and motivated to become a better person myself. I only hope that I can live up to the legacy and the name left to me.

I remember them with reverence and respect.

Tristi Pinkston

The Mission to San Juan

By Joel W. Norton

Rejoice! Ye saints of latter days.
    Thy flight from harm is done.
The promised valley spreads below,
    this place is right. "Drive on."
Behind thee now loom mountains high,
    and prairies without end.
Give thanks to Him for safety sure,
    in songs of gladness blend.

But wait! From Jesus Christ once more,
    to his choice and loyal seer,
The vision of thy prophet now,
    is Zion spreads from here.
Go north and south and east and west,
    pack up and take thy all.
In faith go forth to do His will,
    in answer to the call.

At last! Ye settle to the south,
    to tame a hostile land.
From forts to towns along the way,
    ye chose to make a stand.
Thy mission is for hope and peace,
    a place to make thy home,
To rear a righteous family
    and never more to roam.

And so! The land accepts the change.
    The desert's now a rose.
Ye children of the covenant
    are blessed with all that grows.
Thy first concern is towards mankind.
    Ye seek to serve with might,
Then follow in the Savior's path
    with spirits now contrite.

Behold! Ye stand, and are prepared
    to serve yet still the Lord.
Will ye to Zion now return,
    or go to preach his word?
Thy strength has come through faith in Christ,
    and willingness to share,
Thy victory o'er the flesh is made
    in showing that you care.

The call! It's clear! To leave again!
    Another flight to face.
A mission to the Lamanites?
    San Juan—where is that place?
Indians, and cowboys,
    and outlaws inhabitate the land.
And now they must give up some room,
    here comes a Mormon band.

Prepare! Ye saints late fall to meet
    with wagons, goods and teams.
A six weeks' journey you will take
    to once again find dreams.
Have tools in hand to till new ground,
    and seed to plant the earth.
Plan to share with those you find;
    thy life will then have worth.

The camps! At intervals of ten,
    in miles between each one.
From Escalante to Dance Hall Rock,
    for resting and for fun.
Is this for sure the way to go
    to reach the river side?
Explore the trail for miles ahead,
    return and then decide.

What's this! Reports from scouts sent out,
    and some dare disagree.
"It can't be done" spreads through the group,
    but those with faith still see.
Ye must go on! The call's from God,
    don't let doubt so overcome.
Thy leaders chose the course to take.
    This battle now is won!

A notch! The river seen below.
    Is this the way to pass?
Wagons too wide to get inside;
    the grade's too steep—alas!
Wales sent two of their hometown best,
    the rocks to blast and blow.
Tacked to the cliff by Uncle Ben,
    the dugway's built below.

The Hole! The only way to go—
    a road for wagons east.
Constructed as you move along
    to serve both man and beast.
The faithful say it can be done
    with focus on the goal.
Thy faith with work will thus reward
    the mission as a whole.

Behind! The Colorado flows.
    It's been twelve weeks to cross.
Unsure of what now lies ahead
    ye must make up the loss.
Building the road through land unknown,
    deep canyons slow the work.
Made strong with faith in Jesus Christ
    ye saints will never shirk.

It snows! And yet thy spirits soar.
    Thy songs of praise are pure.
The cold and wind do not deter.
    Thy trust in God is sure.
And now a detour to the north.
    A forest to cut through.
Hardships do come the way each day.
    By now they're nothing new.

The comb! A ridge without a top.
    No way to reach the sky.
On toward the river bank,
    not room enough to try.
The way is now up San Juan Hill.
    This is the final test!
Beside the river 'neath a bluff
    at last a place to rest.

No death! But pain and sickness born,
    yet not without relief.
The time six weeks became six months;
    the trek beyond belief.
Thy lives are spared all through the trial,
    the seed-grain is thy meat.
Thy joy is found in brotherhood.
    The journey's now complete.

Rejoice! Ye saints who settled there
    in Utah's last outpost.
In answer to a call from God,
    to thee He gave the most.
Endowed with power from on high,
    enabled to the trials endure.
No greater calling comes to thee,
    thy calling and election sure!

Cast of Characters

The Williams Family:

Evan   born November 15, 1827
Mary Davies   born April 27, 1827
    Mary Ann   born August 27, 1851
    Thomas   born November 5, 1853
    Sarah   born May 23, 1860
    Catherine   born April 23, 1862
    Richard   born November 12, 1865
    Jane   born July 19, 1867
    Evan Edward   born April 4, 1869
    Gwilym   born June 16, 1871

The Perkins Family:

William   born February 16, 1807
Jane Mathews   born May 28, 1814
    Mary   born July 23, 1837
    Joseph Mathews   born May 20, 1840
    Benjamin   born February 3, 1844
    Elizabeth   born January 13, 1847
    Ruth   born September 17, 1849
    Hyrum Mathews   born February 25, 1851
    Naomi   born July 31, 1852
    Martha   born February 26, 1854
    Daniel   born April 30, 1857

Due to the complexity and size of the Williams and Perkins families, I did not include all of the siblings as characters.

Children of Benjamin and Mary Ann Perkins:

Mary Jane   born November 6, 1870
Caroline Cordelia Thurston
                            born February 11, 1873
Catherine   born January 16, 1875
Naomi   born June 14, 1879

Additional children were born to Benjamin and Mary Ann Perkins, but are not included as characters in this book.

Children of Benjamin and Sarah Perkins:

Mary Ellen   born September 28, 1882

Additional children were born to Benjamin and Sarah Perkins, but are not included as characters in this book.

The Rowley Family:

Samuel   born October 29, 1842
Ann Taylor   born April 24, 1846
    Mary Ann   born March 6, 1866
    Samuel James   born January 12, 1868
    Hannah Eliza   born January 20, 1870
    Sarah Jane   born July 15, 1872
    Alice Louisa   born October 11, 1874
    George Walter   born June 25, 1877
    John Taylor   born September 1, 1879
    Maggie Elizabeth   born December 27, 1881

Additional children were born to Samuel and Ann Rowley, but are not included as characters in this book.

Other historical figures who appear in this book:

Hobbs, George B.
Jones, Kumen and Mary
Lyman, Platte D.
Neilsen, Jens
Smith, Silas
Smith, Stanford and Arabella

And many others . . .

Benjamin Perkins

PROLOGUE

Treboeth, Wales
September 28, 1859

Ben! Come here!"

Benjamin Perkins dropped his chisel and ran toward the urgent sound of his father's voice. In the dim light of the coal mine, he could barely make out William's features. "What is it?" he asked.

William reached out and grasped his son's shoulder. "There was an accident at the mine in Blongloha. They need us to help rescue any survivors."

Ben followed his father through the tunnels, his mind racing. An accident in a mine could only mean one thing—death. The mines weren't friendly to those who tunneled them.

They reached the mine entrance where the foreman stood, marking down all the workers who were volunteering. He wrote down William's name, but grunted when he saw Ben.

"He shouldn't go with you."

"He may be only fifteen, but he's one of the best men we've got," William said.

"Please, sir," Ben spoke up. "I want to help."

The foreman shook his head. "I wouldn't be sending my son, but I can't tell you what to do." He made a mark on his sheet and waved them on.

The miners piled into the back of a wagon and rode the six miles to Blongloha. The constant vibration of the wheels on the road might have lulled Ben to sleep if he hadn't been afraid of what they would face when they reached the scene of the accident.

The mines were nothing more than tunnels burrowed through dirt, the walls and ceilings held in place by timbers. If one of those timbers broke, thousands of pounds of dirt would fall on the miners beneath, burying them alive as they worked. Each collier knew to move slowly, place his chisel deliberately, or his life might be forfeit.

When the wagon pulled to a stop at Blongloha, Ben and his father dashed to the opening of the still and silent mine. Not even an echo of voices sounded from inside. One worker sat on the ground near the entrance, head in his hands. He raised his face when he heard the rescuers approach.

"Where are the others?" William asked.

The man shook his head, despair streaked across his face along with the grime. "Hundreds . . . trapped." He didn't say more, but pointed at the mine.

Without hesitation, Ben and the others walked directly in, locating the cave-in within minutes. Ben's stomach clenched as he looked at the task ahead of them. He didn't see how anyone could have survived. The other men paused a moment as well, then got to work.

They plunged their shovels into the dirt time and time again, carting out piles of rubble in wheelbarrows and coal carts. The farther in they got, the darker it became, but they lit their Davy lamps and kept on digging.

"Here!" William Perkins yelled. He threw his shovel over his shoulder and began digging with his hands. Ben came to his side and worked with him, his heart racing. They uncovered a man's legs, then torso, and finally his head. Ben winced when he saw that the man's skull had been bashed in by the falling debris.

"Let's drag him out and keep digging." William took hold of the man's arms. "Ben, get his feet."

Ben couldn't move for a moment. The corpse's eyes were open, and his face wore an expression of surprise. The miner clearly had not anticipated the collapse.

"Ben!"

At the sharpness in his father's voice, Ben stooped down and picked up the man's feet. They carried him out to the mine entrance, then turned around and went back in. Two of the other miners passed them, also carrying a body.

Ben worked feverishly with his shovel, wanting the nightmare to end. The dust in the air was becoming unbearable, the heat stifling, and he was surrounded by death on all sides. He pulled his handkerchief out and tied it over his nose and mouth, wishing he could also tie something over his eyes and heart.

The rubble near the entrance was completely cleared away and moved outside, along with the hundreds of bodies that had been trapped within. The rescuers proceeded further in to the mine. Sections of the wall and ceiling had come down in chunks through each of the tunnels. Arms and legs could be seen protruding from the debris all around them. Ben had believed that once they cleared the main blockage, the death would be over. But there was no escaping it.

He had always hated the dark of the coal mines. He didn't mind the work itself—it lulled him into a state of mental numbness where he didn't have to think beyond the placement of his chisel or the angle of his next blow. The weight of the tools and the coal sometimes caused his muscles to ache, and he was frequently sore from the strenuous labor. He took the dark home with him at night, where it haunted his dreams.

Ben closed his eyes for a minute, and his memories assailed him. His parents had joined the Mormons when Ben was a small boy, and the people in their small Welsh community had turned on them. Ben's father lost his own job in the mines and could find work nowhere else, so they were sent to the poor house—a shoddily constructed hall of cement and rotten wood where those who couldn't pay their bills were placed. Men and women were separated, and Ben was taken from his mother. His three-year-old mind couldn't understand his father's words, that it would all be over soon and that he would see her again. For six long months he stared at concrete walls of stark, heartless gray, and wondered why she had left him.

The authorities at the poor house eventually figured out that the Perkins were not lazy and would take any job they were offered. The mine officials were forced to give Ben's father back his job, and they were released from their prison. Ben's mother nearly fainted with relief when she saw her young son again. Those six months had been just as hard for her as they had for him. They clung to each other for hours.

The fear of abandonment still remained bottled up deep in Ben's heart, and although he had tried to overcome those fears as he grew into a youth, they sprang up and mocked him, most often while he was in the dark.

But this dark was worse than any other because of the fear it carried. Even as he walked through the tunnels, he could hear the dirt around him shifting. What if it came down again and he became one of the trapped, one of the dead?

Around one of the corners he saw another heap of dirt—with another hand sticking out of it. But this time the fingers were waving.

Ben shouted for help and began moving the rubble, yelling to the man inside that help was on its way. It only took a moment for three workers to uncover the man. They dragged him out and laid him on the ground to check him over for injuries. A Davy lamp was brought, and as soon as its light landed on their survivor, Ben could see that his legs were completely crushed.

"Ben, you stay here," his father directed. "I'm going to get a wheelbarrow."

Ben crouched down and touched the man's forehead. "What's your name?"

"Andrew Morgan," he gasped.

"You'll be all right, Andrew," Ben said. He felt completely useless. He didn't know what to say to a man who was at least crippled for life, and might die even yet. Andrew bled heavily, and Ben didn't know if he could stand to lose that much blood.

"It's bad, isn't it?" Andrew asked. "I can't feel my legs."

Ben couldn't lie to him. "It doesn't look good."

Andrew put his hand over his eyes. "I can't die. I can't. My wife needs me. I have children." He started to moan, shaking his head back and forth as his voice rose in pitch. "You can't let me die!"

Ben grasped Andrew's shoulder, trying to give comfort, but he had no words. He heard his father wheel the cart up behind him, and they worked together to lift Andrew up and over the side.

"I can't meet God this way," Andrew wailed as they pushed the barrow up into the fresh air. Ben pressed his lips together to keep them from trembling. They placed the cart a distance from the mine and went back inside, leaving Andrew alone.

Ben felt bad for abandoning him, but who knew how many others might still be inside, alive and waiting for help.

Hours later, the rescuers felt they had done all they could. So few survivors had been found in comparison to the hundreds of bodies they had retrieved. Ben felt tired to the core as he and his father climbed into the wagon that would take them back to the mine in Treboeth.

"What will happen to them? To the bodies?" Ben asked his father as Blongloha faded in the distance behind them.

"The families will be notified. They can come to collect their dead," William replied.

"What about Andrew?"

"He died." William's voice was curt. "They sent for the doctor, but he could do nothing. He's a man of medicine, not a magician."

Ben leaned back. Andrew wasn't ready to die—he'd said so himself. He had children. Tears began to course down Ben's cheeks. He pulled his knees up to his chin and hunkered down against the side of the wagon.

"I shouldn't have brought you here," William said. "You're a good worker, and we needed your help, but you're still a child, Ben. I should have protected you from this."

Ben couldn't reply. In his mind he still saw bodies with open eyes, arms and legs broken and sticking out at odd angles.

"I pray these men will find peace on the other side." William's words were almost a whisper against the noise of the wheels on the road.

Ben's parents, William and Jane Perkins, believed in the restored gospel with a fervency that sometimes intimidated him. They looked at life with faith and focus. Ben felt more skeptical. He had put off his own baptism, doubtful if he wanted to tie himself to any religious group—let alone the Mormons, the victims of so much taunting. Andrew's words kept ringing in his ears. *I can't meet God this way.* Several hundred men had died right along with him. Were any of them ready to meet their Maker? Was Ben?

He remembered the persecution his family had endured when his parents joined the Church so many years ago, and he didn't know if he could go through that again—especially with himself as the target. But as he thought about the men caught in the explosion, buried under thousands of pounds of coal and dirt, he realized his life needed to have purpose. He counted on God every day to keep him safe in the mines, to shelter him from the oppressive layers of earth that could, at any moment, collapse and crush him beneath the staggering weight.

He glanced over at his father. William sat looking straight ahead, his face lined with dirt and sorrow.

"Do you believe it, Father? Do you believe Christ is there to meet those men on the other side?"

William turned and gave his son his full attention. "Yes, Ben, I do. And He's not just there for the men who die, He's there for those of us who still live."

Ben settled back. His heart still ached so much, it was a wonder it still functioned. But underneath that pain came peace from his father's firm conviction—a peace he hoped he would someday have for himself.

PART ONE

❧ ✦ ❧

THE COAL MINERS

CHAPTER ONE

Treboeth, Wales
February, 1867

Ben Perkins sat back on his heels, surveying the wall in front of him. In the dim lamplight he could make out gouges in the surface, cut with his own chisel and hammer. He had been working for hours, yet his progress seemed slight.

He had been trying unsuccessfully to chase the memories of the Blongloha accident out of his mind. It seemed an impossible task. He forced himself to think, not of the beginning of that day seven years ago, but of the end. After arriving home that night, he and his father had walked down to the river Tawe, where William raised his hand in the sacred gesture and pronounced a blessing, then lowered him into the water.

Ben had never regretted his decision and planned to join the Saints in Zion as soon as he had saved the money for passage.

He wiped his forehead with his arm and mentally scolded himself for the time he had wasted with memories. He had another five pounds of blasting powder to set off before the whistle blew. He twisted wicks and set them in the holes he had created, then poured a thin line of powder along the edge of each hole. He struck the match, which came to life in a flame of blue and gold, and then he went from wick to wick, touching each with the tip of the match.

Gathering his supplies and standing in one motion, Ben sprinted down the corridor as fast as he could before the wicks burned their full length. He ducked and covered his head as the blasts sounded, then lowered his arms to peer through the dust. All had gone as planned—several pounds of coal lay exposed, ready to be extracted.

Ben smiled. Mary Ann Williams should be at the town dance that night, and he wanted to get there early.

* * *

It had taken a bit longer than usual for Ben to scrub the layers of coal dust from his hair, which was dark enough on its own that he sometimes had difficulty telling if he had washed it thoroughly. He resented the time spent getting ready, but he finally made it to the party an hour after it began. The music was lively, and his feet joined the stamping that filled the room. Skirts swirled in time to the beat, and laughter bounced off the walls.

He didn't have a partner, but stood in a corner, clapping his hands and enjoying himself. He loved music more than just about anything, and the fiddler tonight was especially good. His eyes roved around the room, hoping to catch a glimpse of . . . ah. He smiled. A certain girl in a blue dress twirled into view—the reason he had come tonight.

Mary Ann Williams. She was in the community choir and glee club, as was he, and he'd often seen her at church. But he'd never gathered up enough courage to talk to her. She was a beautiful girl, with dark hair that he could only imagine was soft to the touch. He had been attracted to her at first by the power of her singing voice, a sound that reminded him of the birds in the hills he climbed at every opportunity. He had taken to watching her out of the corner of his eye as they sang. Maybe tonight he would get the chance to speak with her.

As if in answer to his silent hopes, she passed by him a moment or two later on her way to the refreshment table. He straightened his shoulders and swallowed, trying to chase the nervousness out of his voice. He would not let the moment pass by without taking advantage of it.

"Miss Williams?" He took a step toward her, and she paused, a smile on her face. "I should have introduced myself long ago. I'm Benjamin Perkins."

"Yes, I know."

Her speaking voice was just as musical as her singing voice, and he got caught up in it before he knew it.

"You know my name?" he asked, unable to think of anything else to say.

"Of course, from choir and glee club."

"Yes, yes, of course." He nodded, wishing he had thought of some intelligent reply.

"It's a lovely dance, isn't it?" She gestured toward the couples that swayed in the center of the room.

"It would be even lovelier if I could dance with you."

For a moment he was surprised at his own boldness, but she rewarded him with a smile. "I would like that."

He took her by the elbow, and they found their place amidst the dancers. The music had mellowed into something soft, matching his mood as he held her in his arms, a feeling more sweet than he had imagined.

His life had always been pragmatic. Go to the mine, work his shift, come home and scrub all the dirt and grime from his skin, and maybe go out with friends for an hour or two before collapsing in bed, only to start anew the next morning.

As he danced with Mary Ann, he began to catch a glimpse of all he had been missing.

The dance ended two hours later with one last rollicking tune, and Ben offered to see Mary Ann home. She accepted, and they stepped into the night. The cobbled roads and stone walls that paved their path glowed white in the moonlight, and it was easy for them to find their way.

"Tell me, Mr. Perkins," Mary Ann said after a few silent moments. "Why have I never seen you at school? Your family has lived here as long as mine, have they not?"

"I've been working in the mines since I was six. I've never had the chance to go to school." Ben hoped his voice sounded casual. His lack of education made him feel vulnerable. "I can't read or write."

"I've heard tell that you are quite skilled at math."

Ben smiled into the darkness. So she'd been listening to what others had to say about him, had she? "I can do math. I just can't write it down."

"You can do math without a slate?"

"I wouldn't know how to do it with a slate."

"That's amazing!" Mary Ann turned and looked at him. "You hold all the numbers in your head?"

He nodded, wondering at the look of astonishment on her face.

"I have a difficult time with math, even with all the slates in the world in front of me," she said. "You have a gift. You truly do."

Ben considered that for a moment as they resumed walking. He had never thought of himself as possessing a gift. He had always felt hampered by his inability to read a book or write a letter. He straightened his shoulders a bit. Mary Ann Williams thought he had a gift. That was something worth considering.

* * *

Mary Ann couldn't stop smiling as she brushed out her hair. Ben Perkins had spoken to her at last. She had been watching him out of the corner of her eye for months, and knew he had been doing the same. It was only a matter of time, she had reasoned with herself. But she had almost given up hope—until he approached her at the dance the night before.

He was a wonderful dancer, leading her around the room with precise and well-measured steps, but gracefully, as though it was the most natural thing in the world.

Ben wasn't very tall—only slightly taller than herself—but she found it didn't matter as she followed his lead on the dance floor. They were perfectly suited.

She pulled her shoes on and gave herself one last look in the mirror. She had been told she was pretty, and she certainly had enough male attention to prove it, but she wasn't sure what she thought of her own looks. At times, she thought she looked very well indeed. But most of the time she saw herself as ordinary.

This morning, however, her eyes were bright, and she gave herself a nod of satisfaction. The small pin she had placed on the collar of her dress added just the right touch.

Choir practice that evening went much as usual, the altos and sopranos chatting together in the corner and trying to catch the eyes of the tenors and occasionally a bass. It was every bit as much a social event as the dance had been, only here the flirting was set to harmony.

Ben was late. Mary Ann glanced around the room several times, wondering where he could be. She hoped something hadn't gone wrong at the mine. Her father was an inspector there, moving through the tunnels to check the positions and the strength of the beams. He had told many stories of cave-ins and other disasters. She knew she was letting her imagination run away with her, but couldn't breathe a sigh of relief until she saw Ben walk in a few minutes later, stepping into place and joining in as though he had been there the whole time. He looked over her way and nodded, smiling.

She turned her head back to the conductor, suddenly feeling warm. She knew she was blushing, and didn't want Ben to see. She made the decision not to look at him anymore. It wasn't proper. But two minutes later she glanced over again to meet his eyes—eyes that were merry tonight.

After the rehearsal, she moved to gather up her things. She hoped he would come over and talk to her, but she wouldn't wait around to see if he would. She would pretend not to care. She would be collected and aloof.

"Miss Williams?"

She knew who it was without even turning around. She took a deep breath, trying to appear as calm and confident as she was pretending to be, despite the wild thumping of her heart.

"Hello, Mr. Perkins."

"May I see you home?" He held out his arm.

"I would be delighted."

They didn't say much until they were nearly halfway home. Mary Ann couldn't think of anything to say, and didn't trust herself to make suitable small talk. Ben eventually broke the silence, and she felt very relieved when he did.

"I had a bit of trouble at the mine today."

Her hand tightened on his arm. "What happened?"

"I couldn't concentrate on my work. I kept thinking about the dance instead."

She smiled, glad he couldn't see the way her heart leapt. "It was a very good dance, wasn't it?"

"Very."

"I confess, I've thought about it as well." She let go of his arm, suddenly shy.

Ben nodded. "I don't expect either of us will be able to get our work done tomorrow, either. Choir practice has also been having a strange affect on me lately."

"Has it now?" Mary Ann compressed her mouth together to keep from smiling too broadly.

"Miss Williams, I won't pretend that I don't find you the most appealing dance partner I've had for a long time. I'd like to repeat that pleasure again soon."

"I'm sure we can arrange that."

"Well, since that has been settled, let's stop being so formal with each other. I would like to call you Mary Ann, unless you object."

"No, I have no objections."

"Good, then we're agreed." They walked along another moment or two in silence, then he started to hum the song they had rehearsed that night, "Guide Us, O Thou Great Jehovah." Mary Ann joined him, singing softly, and soon their voices rose together in a comfortable duet.

Mary Ann's eyes were moist at the beauty of the song, and she was glad that Ben didn't glance over at her as he reached out for her hand. She didn't want him to see her crying, and yet, she felt he would understand.

* * *

That evening marked the first of many that Ben and Mary Ann spent together. After choir practice they would take walks through the village, picking their way along the stony paths between the houses. One night he had the opportunity to help her on with her cloak, and his hand brushed against her hair. It was just as soft as he had always imagined.

Almost without his realizing it, Mary Ann had taken a spot in his heart. When something good happened to him, he wanted her to be the first to know. If something bad were to take place, he could feel no comfort until he heard what she had to say. He was drawn to her by a compelling magnetism, and it surprised him when he came to understand just what it was that had happened to him. He had fallen in love.

This created a complication, however.

"Mary Ann," he said to her one Sunday afternoon as they strolled through a green field of grass, "I need to tell you something."

She stooped down and plucked up a flower that grew in her path. "What is it?"

"I've been planning for some time now to emigrate to America. The Church has been organizing shiploads of Saints to go across to New York and from there, Utah."

"I see."

He couldn't tell from her expression what she thought about that. He had hoped to see some glimmer of her true feelings for him, but she remained impassive. Perhaps he had read more into their relationship than she had.

"That sounds exciting," she said after a moment. "When do you plan to sail?"

"In a month's time."

"Oh!" She glanced off into the distance. "That's . . . very soon."

"It is soon, but it still seems so far away. I've been planning this for months and despaired at how long it was taking, but now . . ." He reached out and caught her hand. "Now I wish I had just a little more time."

She smiled and looked down at their two hands intertwined. "Aren't you afraid to go? I would be. It's so different there, and you don't speak a word of English."

"I didn't speak a word of Welsh until I was nearly two years old. I'll manage."

She laughed and gave his hand a little squeeze. "You'll do very well, Ben Perkins. I'm sure of it."

* * *

Mary Ann was proud of herself. She had managed to keep her emotions in check until she was in her room, but she had been crying ever since. She couldn't believe Ben was leaving. She had imagined that he cared for her as much as she did for him, but apparently she had mistaken a friendship for romance, and it stung.

"Mary Ann! Mother wants you!"

Mary Ann sat up and smoothed her hair into place. She knew her eyes were red and puffy—they always turned red when she cried. She felt in her pocket for her handkerchief and wiped her nose.

Her younger sister Sarah came in the room a moment later.

"Mother wants you to help with dinner. I've already set the table."

"Very good, Sarah. You're turning into quite a helper," Mary Ann said approvingly. Sarah was so eager to please, it was easy to praise her.

"Mother says that when I'm eight, she'll teach me how to make bread."

"That's a big job. Do you think you can do it?"

Sarah's dark eyes were serious. "I think so." She took a step closer. "Have you been crying?"

"Just a little."

"Why?"

Mary Ann smiled at the concern she saw on her sister's face.

"A friend is leaving, and I'm going to miss him. That's all."

"I'm sorry you're sad." Sarah wrapped her arms around Mary Ann's neck. "You can have my dessert at dinner."

Mary Ann laughed. "Thank you, Sarah. But you can keep it."

* * *

Late June, 1867

Ben pulled his wallet out of his top drawer and counted the money inside, already sure of the amount, but liking the way the numbers rolled off his tongue—evidence of all his hard work and saving. He put his week's wages in with the total and was immensely pleased to see that he finally had enough to pay his passage to America.

America! What a beautiful word! He had heard tales of America—wild tales of gold lying in the streets and men not having to work at all but lying back and enjoying themselves. He didn't believe the stories for a minute, but it was delightful to imagine that somewhere in the world there was a place so magical that anything could happen. He would be joining with the Saints in Utah—magic in and of itself.

The hardest part would be leaving his family. His brother Joe was coming with him, along with Mary and Naomi, his two sisters, and his brother-in-law John Evans. But there still remained at home his mother and father, not to mention his siblings Hyrum, Elizabeth, Ruth, Martha, and Daniel. There was simply no way to afford the passage for such a large group all at once. Ben would work hard once he reached America and send for his family, adding his earnings to whatever they were able to scrape together in the meantime. Hopefully it wouldn't be too much longer before they could all be together again.

His thoughts went to Mary Ann—dear, sweet Mary Ann. She had created a complication in his plans. He had never meant to form an attachment. He felt a strong calling to go to Zion, but how could he leave her behind? On the other hand, how could he ask her to come with him? She'd said it herself. America was completely different from Wales, and she would be afraid to go. They had been seeing each other for such a short time. He couldn't expect her to make that kind of commitment.

June twenty-first arrived—the day of his departure. All his friends and family, including many Church members, gathered at the depot to see him off. The weather was cold and gloomy, touched by a streak of fog that made everything look smudged like a watercolor painting. An inn stood near the tracks, and the group went into the lobby, blowing on their fingers and laughing a little louder, as though the sound would keep them warmer.

Ben wandered around the room, taking in the sight of those beloved people one last time. Mary Ann sat on a bench in the corner, participating in the party but still apart from it. Her eyes looked sad, though her lips smiled. He stepped across the room and sat by her side.

"I've been looking for you," he said loudly enough to be heard above the din, and yet quietly enough that no one else could hear him. "I meant to come by yesterday, but couldn't get away."

"That's all right," she said, glancing around the room. "You're certainly well liked in Treboeth."

"It's quite the going-away party, isn't it?" Ben took her by the elbow. "Come for a short walk with me. We'll stay in sight of the station so we won't miss the train."

The fog had only grown thicker, and Ben grasped her fingers as they made their way out to the lane. "I don't want to lose you in the fog," he joked.

"No chance of that," she replied. "I know this area well."

Something about the tone of her voice made him forget his previous decision to leave without her. He didn't know what she would say, but he had to take the chance.

He stopped walking, and then turned to face her. "I mean what I say, Mary Ann Williams. I don't want to lose you."

She studied his eyes, and he gazed into hers, the clear depths that often gave her emotions away when she tried so hard to hide them, yet at other times were unreadable.

"There's no chance of that."

"As soon as I have enough money saved, I'll be sending for my parents and younger brothers and sisters. Will you come with them?" He didn't take his eyes off hers—he couldn't, held there as he was, as if under a spell.

She looked away, first to the side then down to the ground. He couldn't see her face, and he wondered if he had made a mistake by speaking up. It was all too sudden. Perhaps he should have given her more time. He should have written from America. He opened his mouth to apologize, but she brought her eyes back to meet his.

"Yes, Ben, I'll come with them."

He felt lightheaded with relief. "I'll send enough money for your passage as well."

As if determined to break the moment, the train arrived with a long howling sound.

"Will you find a way to write to me?" she asked, reaching out to catch his coat.

"I will. I'll find a scribe and write every chance I get." He wrapped his fingers around hers where they clutched his lapel. They were being torn apart too quickly. He wished that he had proposed sooner instead of leaving it for the last minute.

"Ben!" his father called. "Hurry up!"

Ben turned back to Mary Ann, took her face in his hands, and kissed her. It was a quick and simple kiss, over far too soon, but it tingled on his lips as he climbed aboard the train and turned to wave goodbye.

Mary Ann waved along with all the others, her hand nearly lost in the sea of fluttering fingers.

But Ben focused his eyes on her alone and remembered the touch of those gentle lips. It was even more difficult to leave than he thought it would be, but he would work all the harder to bring his family to Utah—his family, plus one.

CHAPTER TWO

The Ocean Voyage
Late June, 1867

The *Manhattan* stood docked at Liverpool, waiting to take Ben, his brother Joe, and his sisters Naomi and Mary, along with Mary's husband, John Evans, to America. The train from Swansea had brought them into England, and all that remained for them was to board the ship and sail on. They were told that four hundred and eighty other Saints were to sail as well.

The ship left port and made its way out to sea to the cheers of those gathered on the dock to watch. Even those who weren't Mormon felt the excitement of going to America. After all, it was the land of opportunity, regardless of religion. A man could be anything he wanted there.

Archibald Hill—leader of this particular group of Saints— had his hands full for the first few hours getting the sleeping assignments all sorted out. Once he had everyone situated, he went about the remainder of his business, leaving the passengers to arrange their belongings as best as they could in the small quarters.

Ben didn't have much with him, so his unpacking consisted mostly of dumping everything on the bunk assigned him in the single men's section, then putting everything back in his sack, since he didn't need it right then. He was up on deck shortly, exploring the ship and making himself familiar with it.

The ride was smooth and comfortable for the first day, but Ben awoke the next morning to a foul smell coming from the corner of his below-decks quarters. Someone was groaning in their bunk—perhaps a great many someones.

"Who's sick?" he mumbled, sliding out of his shelf-like bunk and feeling for his shoes.

"I am," moaned a man down the aisle.

"So am I," came the voices of six or seven others.

The swaying motion of the ship hadn't registered on Ben's mind until that moment, but suddenly he noticed that the room was moving from side to side in a rhythmic dance. He reached out and caught the edge of the bunk.

"Joe?" He shook his brother's shoulder. "Joe, I need your help."

A moment later Joe slid out of his bed and looked around, wrinkling his nose. "What happened here?"

"I don't think we want to dwell on that."

Ben made his way to the quarters where the families were berthed. The stench there was nearly as bad as where he had come from. He moved around quickly, at last locating the bunk where his sister Mary and her husband John slept.

"John, are you awake?" he asked, touching the sleeping man's shoulder.

"Mmmmm?" John opened his eyes. "It can't be morning already."

"It is. Are you sick?"

John shook his head. "No, just sleepy."

"Then get up and help me."

The three men worked together to clear out the pail in the corner of the single men's quarters, then they fetched water for the sick men who couldn't leave their bunks. The rolling motion of the ship made it difficult to keep their footing as they moved around.

"I'm glad that's taken care of," Joe said, throwing a bucket of mop water over the side of the boat. "Now if we could just make sure that everyone actually made it to the bucket—"

"Don't remind me," Ben said, taking a deep breath of the salty air. "I'm in no hurry to return to the hold."

His sister Naomi came to the rail, holding on with white knuckles once she reached it. Her face was green, and wisps of her hair stuck out in all directions.

"I don't feel well," she said, pressing a hand against her face. "All the women are flat down in their bunks. I seem to be the best off out of the bunch, so they asked me to come up and fetch help."

"Many of the men are down, too," Joe replied. "I wonder how long these rough seas will last."

Ben, John, and Joe followed Naomi down to the single women's section of the hold. Ben paused a moment before entering.

"Please, Ben, just come in. They need your help," Naomi entreated.

Ben knocked on the doorframe. "Ladies, we've come to help you. Are you decent?"

A chorus of moans rose from within the room. Ben could only guess they meant to say yes, so he entered, glancing around cautiously at first, and then more bravely as he realized that all the women were clothed. In fact, most of them looked like they had fallen into their bunks and not moved in a full day. The smell of vomit was overwhelming.

About twenty-five older women and several younger girls comprised the cabin. The married women were in the family quarters, and from what Ben had been able to tell during his quick journey inside, they were getting enough care. But these ladies had no one, and he soon learned that he, John, and Joe were their only hope, being among the few who had not fallen sick.

The men spent the day helping the sick clean themselves up and swabbing the floors. Ben carried bucket after bucket of putrid water up to the top deck and dumped them into the sea. He felt sorry for the fish.

By the next day, several of the men felt well enough to help, and those in the family quarters had found enough healthy people amongst them to meet their needs. But Ben and his two helpers were still on duty in the single women's cabin.

Naomi was there and did the best she could, but she was just as sick as the other ladies and couldn't help for more than a few minutes at a time.

Every few hours, Ben would take a break and go up onto the deck, watching the fish jump out of the water, cresting the tops of the waves and flashing their silvery scales in the light. It was a glorious sight. They almost seemed to be playing a game—which could jump the highest out of the water, which could dive the farthest upon their return to the briny deep.

That night, after making sure that all his charges were cared for, Ben went up on deck and rested his elbows on the rail. The moon illuminated the water, and from time to time he fancied he could see a glimmer of fish in the darkness. The fresh air was invigorating. He filled his lungs again and again. He hadn't spent so much time out of doors in ages.

After his family had been released from the poor house when he was three, his father and brothers went back to work in the mines. He went there himself when he was six, carrying water back and forth to the thirsty miners. His fear of the dark was immense, but he had it impressed upon him that he had a job to do. With a Davy lamp in one hand and a pail of water in the other, he made his way up and down the dark corridors until his bucket was empty, then he would go back and refill it.

Later, as he grew older, he was put in charge of opening and closing the doors along the mineshaft. He sat in the dark for hours, waiting for a full load of coal to be pushed up the track. When he heard the approach, he was to open the doors as quickly as possible and let the cart through. Then he had to close it again, just as quickly. If he was late, he ran the risk of getting crushed. Many small boys were killed that way.

It was cold and scary, sitting in the tunnels for all those hours. Light from the miners' lamps cast shadows on the walls that flickered then disappeared as the workers passed by him, and his mind filled with images of prowling monsters lurking just beyond the corner.

Other times he would be so tired that he would long to go to sleep. But he was terrified of missing a cart, so he sat ramrod straight, waiting for the rumbling of wheels on tracks that told him it was time to do his job.

One day, he hadn't been so careful. A cart came through, and he wasn't out of the way. He was carried out of the mine with a broken arm, grateful that was all that had happened to him, but in pain nonetheless. He was allowed a respite from the mine while his arm healed, but his family needed his income. As soon as he was feeling better, it was right back into the soot-covered darkness beneath the ground.

Sea life was so different. Even with the two days he had spent cleaning up after sick passengers and trying to spoon broth down them, he had the opportunity to be up in the air and enjoy the moon and stars. He could look up to the sky instead of down to the earth. He felt free to choose his future and a path that did not involve squirming his way through the dirt like a mole. He hadn't realized how badly he hated being a collier until he was no longer one. He said a silent prayer, thanking God for guiding him on his journey and bringing him out of the darkness and into the sun.

CHAPTER THREE

New York City, New York
July 12, 1867

Naomi started to sway, and Ben reached out to catch her arm. She had made it off the boat without help, but as they walked down the pier, her strength was giving out.

"Thank you, Ben," she said as he led her over to a packing crate and helped her sit down, her back against the wall of a building. "I don't know when I've felt so weak."

"You've been very ill. It may take a while before you feel better."

She closed her eyes. "It's so good to be back on solid ground."

John Evans came up behind them, carrying a trunk. He set it down with a thump, and Naomi's hand flew to her forehead. "Please, John, not so loud."

John smiled. "I'll try."

Joe came along a few minutes later. "I've been talking to a man at the train station. The next train west isn't for a couple of days."

"That will give us a chance to rest," Mary said. She placed her hand on Naomi's shoulder. "And give this poor thing time to feel better."

Ben arranged sleeping quarters for all of them in a building near the train station called Castle Gardens, and they settled in quickly. Naomi didn't feel well enough to go sightseeing, so Mary stayed with her while the men toured the city. They came back with stories of tall buildings and shops on nearly every street.

After three days' rest, Naomi was well enough to board the train. They found seats near some of their Welsh shipmates and settled in for the journey.

The train pulled out of the station a few minutes late. At first, Ben thought it was exciting to look out the window and see the land go flashing by beneath him. Every glimpse he caught thrilled him. It was America! They had finally arrived. But before long, he found himself nodding off, the excitement of the last several days taking their toll.

He came awake with a jolt as the screeching of train brakes filled his ears. He leaned forward and caught hold of the seat in front of him to maintain his balance.

"Where are we?" he asked around a tongue that felt like cotton.

"I think we're taking a water break," Joe said, looking around.

Ben got off the train for a moment and stretched. The sunlight was warm on his back, and he took a deep breath, filling his lungs with as much fresh air as they would take. Matthew, one of the other Welshmen, soon joined him.

"It's a glorious day," he remarked.

"Yes, it is," Ben replied.

The man who was working the train station came wandering over and asked Ben a question. Ben couldn't understand what he was saying, but Matthew spoke some English and interpreted.

"He wants to know where you're headed."

Ben nodded and reached out to shake the man's hand. "I'm going to the Utah territory."

Matthew passed along the information, and the man's eyes grew big as he replied to Matthew.

"He says you shouldn't go out there. The Mormons are a bad lot," Matthew said.

Ben smiled. "Tell him I'd like to see for myself."

The man obviously thought Ben was making a foolish mistake, and waved his hand in a gesture of good riddance. Ben nodded in return, and climbed back aboard the train just as the whistle blew.

"Why are you going to Utah?" Matthew asked as the train pulled out of the station.

"We are some of those Mormons that man was talking about."

Matthew looked at Ben, astonishment on his face. "But he said the Mormons are bad."

Ben grinned. "Do I look bad to you?"

Matthew shook his head.

"Then the man was wrong, wasn't he?"

Matthew returned Ben's smile and settled back in his seat across the aisle.

The next day was monotonous. The view out the window changed from time to time as they passed through green pastures and wooded landscapes, but there wasn't enough variety to keep Ben's interest.

He crossed the aisle and sat in the empty seat next to Matthew. "I'd best learn some English," he said to the Welshman. "Can you teach me?"

"I don't know much, but I'm glad to teach you a little," Matthew replied.

At each stop, Ben took the opportunity to try out his new words on the people at the stations. Invariably, they would ask where he was going. And also invariably, they would try to talk him out of his destination. Mary and Naomi were starting to worry. It seemed that everyone along the way thought the Mormons were dangerous, that they would steal everything that the immigrants had, and take their women as well. Ben just laughed. He didn't know how the Mormons had managed to get themselves a reputation for thievery, but he knew it couldn't be true. The testimony he carried that gave him such peace and warmth in his heart was strong enough to contradict any rumors.

The train continued on its way, the wheels clacking against the tracks as they rolled through the prairie. Ben's English lessons continued for a good stretch before they finally pulled in to North Platte, Nebraska.

When Ben stepped off the train, the humidity hit him like a wet blanket. It was nothing unfamiliar to him, and made him think of misty mornings at home.

For a brief moment, homesickness settled over him, and he missed all that he had left behind. Who knew how long it would be before he could send for his family? He stepped aside and let the others stream past him. Would Mary Ann still want to come? Maybe she would have found someone else by then.

The conductor pointed the passengers to a long line of wagons that had come to a stop several hundred yards away from the train station.

"Those are the immigration teams," he told them. "They will take you the rest of the way."

Just as dusk was falling, Ben, John, and Joe carried the luggage across the dry grass and got their wagon assignments. All around them, the voices were harsh, and Ben heard several unfamiliar words.

"What are they saying?" he asked Matthew.

Matthew interpreted, a smile in his eye. "Those are some of the favorite American cuss words, from what I understand."

"We may want to keep a close eye on my sisters," Ben said. "I don't think they want to learn that kind of English."

The teamsters held a dance that night, and Ben was careful to keep the ladies far away from it. They fell asleep quickly in the tent provided, so tired they barely noticed the loud music that filled the camp until well into the night.

* * *

On the Trail from North Platte, Nebraska
August 1, 1867

The wagons moved out with a lurch, and Naomi's hand flew to her stomach.

"Are you all right?" Ben asked.

"I may never be all right again," she answered. "That ocean crossing ruined me forever."

The wagons moved slowly and deliberately, pulled by oxen rather than horses. The road was rough and bumpy, and Naomi's face was soon ghastly white.

"Perhaps you'll get used to it," Mary said.

"I know you're trying to comfort me, but it's not working," Naomi replied.

Their progress was slow the first three days. Many in the company were already ill, and they weren't holding up as well as they would have liked. The teamsters were starting to become impatient with the delays. They had made the trip several times before and knew what they were doing. They had a schedule to keep, and they didn't mind reminding Ben in very colorful language.

Mid-afternoon on the fourth day, Ben saw a wagon train similar to their own approaching from the other direction. As they grew near, the leader called out, and the teamster in charge of Ben's group, Captain Rice, returned the hail. They were too far away for Ben to make out the conversation, but his curiosity was soon put to rest as Captain Rice called for the men to gather around.

He waited until the last of the stragglers had joined them, then raised his voice to address everyone.

"Six men drowned in the Green River the other day when a boat broke loose. This captain needs six men to go back to North Platte with him and bring over another load of immigrants. He's far behind schedule, and he's willing to pay well. Any of you men want to go?"

Ben looked around. Only a few hands were raised. If he took the job, he could get a head start on earning money for Mary Ann's passage. John and Joe could escort the girls to Salt Lake City. It would mean a period of separation in a strange land. But still, the opportunity was being presented very attractively. Slowly he lifted his hand into the air.

"Ben! What are you doing?" Naomi hissed.

"You'll be all right with the others," he told her. "I'll only be a little way behind you."

"But—"

"John and Joe will keep you safe. And Matthew's going on, as well. He doesn't leave the wagon train until California." He touched his sister's arm. "It will work out."

He spoke to Matthew, John, and Joe, telling them his plans. They agreed to see the women safely to Salt Lake City. He then grabbed his bag from the back of their assigned wagon.

Naomi and Mary didn't let him take two steps before they wrapped their arms around him fiercely. He returned the hugs and laughed when his sisters wouldn't let go.

"I'll be all right," he told them. "I'll be joining you before you know it."

Finally they let go of him, and he walked off toward the other train. The captain, a man named Forbes, greeted him with a handshake and showed him which wagon he would be driving. It was pulled by six oxen.

Ben looked at the animals, and they looked at him. Neither were impressed.

"Can you drive them?" the captain asked.

"Yes," Ben said, trying to appear confident. He had never driven a team of oxen before, but the thought of his pay packet was encouragement enough, and it didn't look too difficult.

The captain nodded and walked back to his own outfit. Ben waved at his family and urged his animals forward, trying to swallow the lump that had formed in his throat. Perhaps he was making a big mistake, but there was only one way to find out.

* * *

On the Trail
August 6, 1367

Dawn came far sooner than Ben would have liked the next morning. He opened his eyes and saw a wagon cover stretched over his head, and it took a moment for him to realize where he was. He pulled on his shoes quickly, determined that his would be the first wagon ready to roll out that morning. He had picked up enough from the facial expressions of the men around him to know that the other teamsters didn't think he could do the job.

The wagons had been pulled into a circle around the oxen, and the animals hadn't moved much during the night. Ben went into the herd and grabbed the neck ropes on two oxen, then led them to his wagon. A yoke was supposed to go over their necks—a heavy piece of wood—and after much struggling, he managed to get it up on their backs.

Then one of the oxen stepped away.

"Come back here," he cajoled, but the ox looked at him with an expression of boredom.

Ben set the yoke down and reached out to grab the rope again. The ox didn't protest and stepped back into place. But then the other ox decided to take a stroll.

"The two of you have this all planned out, don't you?" Ben muttered. Around him, the rest of the camp was coming to life, and he could hear the lowing sounds of the oxen as they were led into place. He'd better get a move on or he wouldn't reach his goal of being first.

He grabbed both neck ropes in one hand and tried to lift the yoke with the other. It was an unwieldy piece of wood, smooth from sanding and use, and it slid out of his grasp and onto the ground. Ben was tempted to use some of those choice words he heard coming from the teamsters' mouths.

Finally, after several more attempts, he had his oxen in their yoke. He untied the neck ropes and threw them in the back of the wagon. He turned to the sound of yelling.

"Where's my ox? Somebody stole my ox!"

Several of the other teamsters ran over, looking around them. Ben came too, wondering who could be so thoughtless as to steal that poor man's animal.

"There it is!" one of the men yelled, pointing at Ben's wagon.

"Ben! Why did you take my ox?" The teamster, a man named Clint, yelled in his face.

"They look the same," Ben said. He didn't know that ox wasn't his. An ox was an ox, right? They were all big and ugly.

Clint looked at him, a mixture of disgust and amusement on his face. He took Ben by the shoulders and marched him over to the wagon.

"This is my ox," he said, pointing at the animal on the left. "That is your ox." He pointed out to the center of the wagon ring, where another animal grazed. They looked exactly alike to Ben.

Clint unhitched his ox from Ben's wagon and brought the other animal over. "And, this is the off ox. This is the near ox."

Ben looked at him, sure the confusion he felt was written all over his face.

"This ox goes on this side. That ox goes on the other side." He helped Ben yoke them up properly. By then, the sun was creeping high in the sky.

Clint helped Ben yoke the other four oxen, but even with the help, Ben's wagon was still the last one ready.

"Thank you," Ben said, passing a hand over his face.

"You're welcome. I hope you learned a lesson today." Clint strode off, pulling his hat more firmly down on his head.

Ben urged the animals forward, feeling guilty. Because of his lack of knowledge, both he and Clint had missed breakfast.

* * *

The day had been long and hard. Because of the accident which took the lives of the six men, the wagon train was off schedule, and they had to hurry to meet the next batch of immigrants. Ben had no idea how to make oxen hurry. It seemed impossible.

After bringing his wagon to a stop at camp that night, Ben caught himself before he stumbled. They had traveled all day without stopping for more than ten or fifteen minutes at a time, and the men and animals both were worn out. He unyoked the oxen and let them to the center of the wagon circle.

"Ben, fetch some water," the captain called out. They were camped near a river, and the grass was green around the banks. Ben grabbed two buckets and headed out, then hauled the water back to camp.

"Ben, we need firewood," one of the other men yelled as soon as he returned.

Ben walked a short distance from the camp, gathering up whatever firewood he could find. There were some dead trees that had branches broken off, and he managed to gather a good armload.

The teamsters kept him busy the rest of the evening, giving him one task or another until bedtime. He was exhausted. He didn't enjoy the extra work, but he didn't know how to handle the situation. He was doing them a favor by coming along, but they were doing him a favor by paying him well. He would endure it, he decided. They would soon get tired of ordering him around.

* * *

On the Trail
August 7, 1867

Early the next morning, Ben pulled the oxen a bit closer together and placed the yoke over their backs. He put the pins in place and stepped back to admire his work. There, six oxen, yoked and ready to go.

"Where is that idiotic Welshman?" Ben turned to see Nathan, one of the other drivers, storming up to him. "You took two of my oxen!"

Ben examined his team. They looked the same to him as they had yesterday. When was he ever going to learn to tell the difference?

"Stay away from my animals," Nathan snarled, yanking the pins out and leading the oxen away.

Ben retrieved the correct oxen and yoked them. Surely there had to be a way to solve the problem. He stared each of them in the eye, trying to establish some sort of connection with them, but none of them were interested in forming a lasting relationship. With a sigh, he picked up his prod and began another day.

* * *

On the Trail
Mid-August, 1867

"Ben, fetch some water," David ordered.

Ben had taken all he could take. For a whole week the taunting had continued—the men harassing him about the oxen in the morning and sending him on a dozen little errands at night. He wasn't their slave. He opened his mouth and in his plainest English told the other man what he thought, using some of the language he had learned on the trail.

David ripped off his coat. "What did you say?"

Ben ripped off his. "You heard what I said."

David charged at Ben, who neatly stepped to the side and watched David tumble to the ground. He stood slowly, shaking his head.

"Now you'll get it, Welsh boy."

David came running again, but this time Ben was not so quick. David's head caught him right in his stomach, and Ben went flying backwards.

"That's enough!" Captain Forbes strode up to them. "Enough, I tell you!"

Ben reluctantly let go of the good grip he had on David's hair.

"Ben! David! I said that's enough!"

The two combatants came to their feet, wiping sweat from their faces.

"I will have no more fighting on this trip." The captain looked them both in the eyes. "Do you understand?"

"Yes," they both muttered.

"Very well." The captain took a step or two, then turned. "Ben, get some water."

* * *

On the Trail
Mid-August, 1867

"Captain?"

Captain Forbes looked up from his paperwork. "Yes?"

Ben wrinkled his forehead, trying to figure out how to phrase what he had come to say. His English was improving daily, but it mostly consisted of the cuss words he heard the teamsters use, and his vocabulary of useful English was still rather small.

"I would like to leave."

Captain Forbes sat back. "Why?"

"The men don't like me." That wasn't quite how Ben meant to put it. How could he explain that he had been under constant harassment ever since joining the outfit? He wasn't trying to duck out of a job—he had worked hard his whole life and wasn't afraid of it. But the other men were making his life miserable, and he couldn't see how he could work with them.

"Just stay with us until Echo Canyon," the captain said.

Ben tried his best to explain that his family was waiting for him in Salt Lake City, and that he was earning money to bring the rest of his family over. He hesitated for a moment, then mentioned that Mary Ann would be coming as well.

The captain's eyes twinkled. He reached into his wallet and pulled out forty dollars.

"God bless you. Take this," he said, handing the money to Ben. "Work for me until we get to Echo Canyon, and I'll pay you the rest of what I owe you, plus a little bit more to bring that girl of yours over here."

Ben shook the captain's hand and agreed to stay a short time longer. He was disappointed that the captain hadn't agreed to an immediate release, but the extra money was good incentive.

After he left the captain, it was only a matter of minutes before the heckling began again, but he didn't mind it so much. He hauled four buckets of water, all the time thinking of the money in his pocket and how much closer he was to sending for Mary Ann. He grimaced as the next order came for wood.

Mary Ann had better not change her mind.

CHAPTER FOUR

Treboeth, Wales
April, 1869

Mary Ann pulled the handkerchief from her head and shoved it in her pocket as she entered the front gate of her parents' home. Her hands were blistered from scrubbing the floor for her employer.

"Mary Ann!" Sarah ran up, holding an envelope. "You got a letter!"

Mary Ann quickly pulled off her coat and took the letter from her sister. She turned it over in her hands, noting the return address. It had to be from Ben—she knew no one else who would be writing to her from America.

"Thank you, Sarah," she said. "Please tell Mam I'm home and that I'm in my room."

She went upstairs quickly and closed the door behind her. Ben had sent one letter shortly after arriving in America, written for him by someone named Matthew. She hadn't heard from him since, and it had been nearly nine months.

Dear Mary Ann,

> *By now you'll think I've forgotten you. Nothing is further from the truth. I've thought about you a great deal. I've taken a job working at Echo Canyon, a Mormon camp on*

the railroad. For a time I worked as a teamster, but when I came to this place they offered a job and I took it. I've heard from John and Joe, and between the three of us, it won't be long until we have enough passage money for the whole lot of you to come over. I hope to see you soon and that you are well.

Ben

Mary Ann folded up her letter and placed it in her pocket, unable to keep from laughing with delight. It was so good to hear from Ben, even if his words were written by someone else. It wouldn't be much longer until they were together again.

She looked down at her hands, rough from so much work. She remembered a time when they were white and dainty, but that seemed far in the past. She knew she looked tired, and her forehead seemed creased a million times over from worry. Would Ben still find her pretty when he saw her again?

* * *

Treboeth, Wales
May, 1869

"It's a terrible journey, Mary Ann," her father said, trying to take a firm stance with his beloved eldest daughter. "The smells, the crowded conditions of the boat, the seasickness—you'd wish you'd never gone."

Mary Ann turned away. How could she explain all the feelings in her heart? She knew he loved her, but Ben loved her too. She was torn between those two good men, and sometimes her chest ached from holding in so much emotion. No matter which path she chose, she'd be hurting someone she loved. How could she choose whose heart to break?

"I must do this, Father," she said at length. "He sent enough passage for me to go with his family. I promised I'd come."

"So you love this man?"

"I do, Father. I truly do."

Evan Williams shook his head. "I think it's foolishness. There are plenty of young men right here, and I happen to know they've been gathering around outside like foxes to a henhouse, just waiting for you to forget Ben Perkins and take up with one of them."

Mary Ann held up her hands. "I'm not going to forget Ben Perkins, Father! It's been two years. If I were to forget him, surely I would have done it by now."

"Can't I change your mind, daughter?"

She raised her chin a bit and looked him in the eye. "My mind will not be changed. If I must wait until I'm of age, that's what I'll do—but I'll be eighteen in two months. Either way, Father, I'm going, and I'd like your blessing." Her voice sank into tears. She had determined not to cry in front of her father, but she couldn't help it. Every bit of her soul wanted to be on that boat to America, but she knew she'd regret it if she left without her father's blessing.

Evan exhaled slowly. After a long silence, he said, "Very well. I can see there's nothing I can do to talk you out of it."

Mary Ann closed her eyes as relief washed over her, and she only smiled at her father's next words.

"But I still think it's foolish to travel halfway around the world for a young man."

"Mother would have done the same for you," Mary Ann replied, opening her eyes and smiling at the big bear of a man who sat in front of her.

"She would, eh?" Evan thought about that for a moment. "I suppose she might."

"As much as I love Ben, he's not the only reason I'm going. It's Zion! I'm not only going to be with the man I love, but I'll be surrounded by the Saints, and close to the prophet." Her eyes alight, she reached out a hand to her father. "It will be Heaven. Ben *and* Zion. How could I want for anything more?"

Evan pursed his lips. "I can't say that I'm happy about this, Mary Ann, but go. My blessings will be with you."

Mary Ann's departure party was not as merry as Ben's had been two years before. The crowd that gathered was tearful, afraid they would never see Mary Ann again. She herself was in high spirits, full of excitement, until she caught a glimpse of the sorrow on her mother's face.

"I shall be all right, Mother," she reassured her. "Father's coming as far as the ship. The trip will go smoothly, and I'll be greeted by the man I love when I come to the end of it. And I'm traveling with the Perkins' all the way—I won't be alone."

Mary nodded, wiping the tears from her eyes. "I know. You shall travel in God's hands. But what if we never see you again?"

"As you say, it's in God's hands. I can't help but feel we will be brought together again."

The whistle sounded, and the train pulled into view. Mary Ann smiled to think of that last moment she had with Ben, his kiss on her lips. She relived that moment often, usually while she was supposed to be thinking about something else.

Goodbyes were said all around. Then Mary Ann turned to her younger sister Sarah. "You listen," she said to the serious nine-year-old. "You are Mother's special helper now. You do what she says, and be a good girl."

"I will," Sarah answered. She wiped away a tear that ran down her cheek and gave Mary Ann a hug. She hugged the little girl tightly, struggling against the sob that threatened to break out of her own chest. She took her seat as soon as she was able, knowing that if she stayed any longer, she might be tempted to stay behind after all.

The train slowly pulled out of the station, and Mary Ann could feel the rhythm of the wheels as they clacked along beneath her seat. She wished she didn't have to travel so far on the train, but the ships that went to America left from Liverpool. Every second that passed took her farther away from her family, and her chest continued to ache. She had never dreamed she would leave Wales until accepting Ben's proposal. It was her home. She loved the lush green hills and the stony walkways. She loved the sound of singing that would often rise up from those hills and echo around the village to be joined by the voices of all who heard it.

Sometimes it seemed as if the whole country was singing—and that was just the way she liked it.

She didn't know what America looked like or what it would hold for her. She hoped there would be singing. She only knew that Ben was there, and that was enough.

* * *

Liverpool, England
May, 1869

Evan Williams stood on deck, watching the stevedores load the hold. He turned at the sound of a greeting.

"Brother Williams! A pleasure to meet you. I'm Elias Morris."

Evan reached out and shook the hand that was offered. "Brother Morris."

"I'm in charge of this group of Saints heading across this time around. I understand your daughter is coming with us."

"She is. Her name is Mary Ann, and she's traveling with the Perkins family. I trust you'll take good care of her."

"I will, I promise you that."

Evan milled around on the deck of the ship for a short time, taking in the atmosphere of the place that for the next few weeks would be his daughter's home. He hadn't fully reconciled himself to the fact that she was leaving. But she was a determined soul, and no ocean was going to stand in her way. He chuckled. She was so much like him.

The *Minnesota* would soon be leaving the dock, and Evan gave his daughter a final hug and kiss on the cheek. She was in tears and clung to his coat a moment.

"I'll write often, I promise," she said with a sniff.

"We'd better hear from you at least once a month."

"You will."

He placed his hands on his daughter's shoulders and searched her eyes with his own. "Are you sure you want to do this?" He hoped she would change her mind, that she would ask him to fetch her luggage and take her back to the house.

But her face was resolute. "More than anything, Father."

He nodded slowly. "I wish you Godspeed, then." He gave her shoulders a squeeze, then let his hands fall slowly to his sides.

He walked over to the rail, where William Perkins stood. "I'm entrusting my child to you, and then to your son," he said. "She is a precious girl. I hope I can have faith that you will protect her."

"I will not let a thing befall her, Evan." William reached out and clasped Evan's hand in a firm shake. "I give you my word on that, and so does Benjamin. He loves her more than his own life."

Evan walked slowly down the length of the dock, not wanting to see the ship pull away. But as he heard the crowd behind him go up in a cheering hurrah, he couldn't resist the urge to turn. Mary Ann stood by the rail, waving her handkerchief in his direction for all she was worth. He raised his hand one time in greeting, then continued toward the train station and his home—a world that would seem so empty without Mary Ann.

* * *

The Voyage
May - June, 1869

It was a three-week trip across the ocean, with very little happening. Mary Ann had brought along a journal, but didn't find much to write about, aside from describing the color of the sea and the names and peculiarities of the passengers. She spent time getting to know the Perkins family better—those strangers who were soon to be her family. She found them delightful and full of humor. She especially bonded with Jane Perkins, who would be her mother-in-law. Mother Perkins soon filled part of the void left by the separation from her mother, although the deepest part of the ache still remained.

Mary Ann had feared the crossing. She'd received a letter from Ben shortly after his arrival in America, written by a scribe, in which he told her of his adventures while at sea. He delicately described the sickness of the passengers, but even through his careful wording, she could tell that the journey had been hard and miserable.

The seas were calm, however, and after the first day of getting accustomed to the rolling motion of the ship, she felt all right and was up and about, enjoying the trip very much.

The *Minnesota* docked in New York to great cheering from the passengers. They were all grateful for the safe journey and could not wait to get off the ship. Captain Morris had warned Mary Ann that it would be difficult for her to keep her balance when she first stepped onto solid ground, but she didn't quite believe him. She had been walking on solid ground her entire life and had never found it a problem. As her feet left the gangplank and carried her the first few steps onto the dock, she thought she had the situation well in hand. But then vertigo overtook her, and she swayed. William Perkins was right behind her and caught her elbow.

"Thank you, Brother Perkins," she gasped. "My knees are a bit wobbly."

"They're bound to be, for the first little bit," he told her. "We've got to get our land legs back."

There was quite a bit of commotion at the train station when they went to buy their tickets. Newspaper reporters were everywhere, notebooks and pencils in hand. Mary Ann couldn't imagine what was causing all the fuss. William disappeared into the crowd, searching for answers.

"It turns out that we're news makers," William reported to the family. "A great railroad, from here to the other side of America, has just been completed, and we're to ride on the first train."

"The very first one?" Daniel Perkins, twelve years old, asked.

"The very first. Aren't we the lucky ones? The man over there tells me that when they laid the track, they began in the west and another group started laying track in the east. The place where the two tracks met was joined together by a spike made of solid gold." Daniel's eyes were as big as dinner plates. "And," William continued, "the spike is in Utah. Perhaps we'll go and see it someday."

As they traveled, there was much talk about the new Transcontinental Railroad. It was said to be the longest railroad line ever built, stretching all the way across the United States. Mary Ann had heard many tales of the covered wagons which previously had taken the Saints across the plains. A train seemed like sheer luxury, and she almost felt spoiled that so many had gone before her and suffered day after day on a wagon seat.

But after the first few hours, she was instead grateful for progress. She didn't think she could have handled a trip that long by wagon.

* * *

Ogden, Utah
June 23, 1869

The train let out a hiss of steam as it pulled into the station in Ogden, sounding for all the world like it was worn out and relieved to finally reach the end of the journey.

Mary Ann smoothed her hair with hands that trembled as violently as her knees. It had been so long since she had seen Ben, and now he should be waiting just outside the train, somewhere in the swarming crowd. Evan had sent him a letter, telling him when they expected to arrive. Would Ben take one look at her and change his mind? She pinched her cheeks and straightened the pin at her throat.

Jane caught sight of the last minute primping and laughed. "You look beautiful, Mary Ann. There's no need to fret."

"It's just been so long, Mother Perkins. What if—"

"What if nothing, child." She rested a gentle hand on Mary Ann's shoulder. "My son loves you. I tell you that truly."

The passengers lined up to disembark. Mary Ann gathered some of the children's things to carry off the train, but Jane took them from her. "You'll have better things to do with your arms, I should imagine. Go ahead, you get off first."

Mary Ann mumbled her thanks, embarrassed that Mother Perkins was so anxious to get her off the train and into Ben's arms—although that wasn't such a bad idea. She edged her way around the family to join the throng that pushed to get off. It took a long time to clear the car of all the passengers, and her heart beat more wildly by the second. If only she could get off the crowded train and into the fresh air!

Then it was her turn, and for a moment, she changed her mind and wanted to stay on the train forever. Perhaps it had been a mistake. She was so far from home—far away from anything that was familiar.

But the Perkins family was right behind her, and their momentum pushed her forward.

She was blinded for a moment by the contrast between the dimly lit car and the bright sunlight outside. She blinked and held a hand up to her eyes as she came down the steps. The crowd had thinned somewhat—most of the onlookers had already found who they came to collect and were on their way. She didn't see Ben anywhere. Her heart sank. Perhaps he wasn't here after all.

A moment later she saw a young man pushing his way down the line, threading between the people who remained. He stopped when he saw her, then took the next several steps in a run and caught her up in his arms. He twirled around with her several times, nearly knocking all the breath out of her, while the rest of his family streamed out of the train, laughing to see their son and brother acting that way.

After a moment, he came to his senses and set her down, resting his hands on her shoulders and staring into her eyes.

"Mary Ann," he said breathlessly. "You've come at last."

"Hello, Ben," she said, grateful for his hands on her shoulders. She was dizzy from his enthusiastic greeting and would have fallen down without support.

"Mother! Father! Hyrum!" Ben greeted each member of his family by name, grasping Mary Ann around the waist and reaching out to the others with his other arm. She could sense his happiness as it radiated from him. "It's so good to see you."

Mother Perkins gave her son a hearty kiss on the cheek. "You look wonderful," she told him. "The air in Utah must agree with you."

"I imagine there are several reasons for my good health," he replied. "Seeing all of you is certainly reason enough." He gave Mary Ann a slight squeeze, firm enough for her to feel, but not obvious to the others.

After greeting everyone all around, Ben loaded the group into the wagon he had brought with him. "Where to first?" he asked.

"Captain Morris promised me room and board at his home," Mary Ann said. "He lives in Salt Lake City."

"What about you, Mother, Father? I'd take you home with me, but I don't have one at the moment."

"We don't have arrangements yet, but I imagine we could find some near Mary Ann," William replied.

"Then on to Salt Lake City it is." Ben shook the reins, and the horses began to plod forward, one foot after the other as though they were already weary. Ben did give the horses a small break at a hotel, where the travelers went inside to eat some lunch and freshen up a bit, but the plodding didn't increase in pace as the horses resumed their journey.

Ben's parents asked him questions, wanting to know how he'd been. He told them about the experiences he'd had as a teamster, making them all laugh with the tale of the fight with David and how he'd finally ended up smearing mud on his oxen every night so he could tell them apart from the others in the morning.

After a couple of hours, Ben pulled on the reins and brought the horses to a stop by the side of the road. "I think we need to stretch our legs for a bit. We've still got a ways to go before we reach Salt Lake City."

Ben came around the wagon and helped Mary Ann down, then tucked her hand through his arm and led her a short distance from the wagon. She glanced back and saw that the rest of the group purposely ignored them. She nearly laughed out loud at their obvious attempt to give her and Ben some privacy out here in the middle of nowhere.

"Tell me truly, Mary Ann. Are you glad you came?"

She looked up into his dark eyes and smiled. "I'm very glad, Ben. I was a little nervous on the train, wondering if I'd made the right decision, and if you'd still want me once I got here. But then when I saw you, I knew I had done the right thing."

He picked her up and swung her around again, much as he had done at the train station. "You don't know what it means to hear you say that. I've had dreams of this day. And I've had nightmares too, where I feared you'd come, take one look around, and demand to be shipped back to Wales."

"You're not in Wales, Ben," she said, glancing back at the wagon to make sure they were still being ignored. "You're in Utah, so that's where I am too."

He lowered his head to hers, slipping his arms around her waist, and whispered in her ear, "Welcome home." Then he kissed her—a kiss that lasted a good deal longer than the one they had shared two years ago at the train station in Wales. Mary Ann was breathless when he finally released her. She took a slight step back, feeling her face go red, but the expression in Ben's eyes drove her into his arms again, and her embarrassment left.

They reached Salt Lake City as night fell. They had no trouble finding Elias Morris' house, and Mary Ann was more than grateful to get down from the wagon seat. Even though they had stopped several times, she was stiff and sore all over and couldn't wait to crawl into bed.

The Morris family put the Perkins' up for the night, making beds out of quilts all over the house. They had arranged a special room for Mary Ann—a space behind the kitchen with a bed and small washstand—to be hers until her marriage.

"I told your father I'd look after you," Brother Morris said when she protested that they had done too much. "I'd want someone to do the same for a daughter of mine."

"Thank you," she said, a small catch in her voice. Even though her father was across the ocean, she still felt his watchful eye over her in the form of Elias Morris.

She took small Martha Perkins with her and made a nest for her at the foot of her bed. The room was near the stove, and they were comfortable all night, although it did take her a while to fall asleep. She could still feel Ben's arms around her waist and his mouth on hers. She'd never felt so beautiful, so alive.

Early the next morning, Brother Morris greeted them with the happy news that he had been out to visit a few of the homes in the neighborhood and found a family with extra space that would willingly take the Perkins family in for a time.

That set Mary Ann's mind to rest. She had been worried about them. It was an entirely different thing to find lodging for one girl than to find it for an entire family—and a large family at that.

Sister Morris fixed a nice breakfast, and then the Perkins' went to meet the family they would stay with.

"And I have other news," Brother Morris said. "It would seem we made the paper." He held up that day's edition of the *Deseret News*.

"What does it say?" William Perkins asked.

Brother Morris read, translating into Welsh.

The first fruits of this year's immigration from Europe reached Ogden last evening at five o'clock. They left Liverpool on the steamship Minnesota on the second instant, under the charge of Elder Elias Morris, late president of the Welsh district, the greater part of the company being from the Welsh principality. A little more than three weeks has brought them the whole distance of the weary way that once took the best part of the year to travel. This being the first company which has come all the way across the continent from the Atlantic to Utah on the Great Highway, their journey will long be remembered as inaugurating an epoch in our history. Early this morning the greater portion of the immigrants had found homes, numbers leaving to settle in the northern counties of the Territory.

"They mentioned you by name," Sister Morris said.

Her husband was clearly embarrassed. "No need to make a fuss," he replied.

* * *

Salt Lake City, Utah
October, 1869

October came before they knew it, and thus arrived the day that Ben and Mary Ann had chosen to get married at the Endowment House. Ben had frequently been at the Morris home to see Mary Ann, staying with his family the rest of the time. At last they would begin their lives together as man and wife.

Bright and early on the morning of the fourth, Ben arrived to collect his bride. William and Jane came with them, and they traveled together into the heart of Salt Lake City where the Endowment House stood. Ben took Mary Ann's elbow, and they knelt at the altar to hear the words that would bind them together for eternity.

Mary Ann's heart was filled with so much love for such a good and handsome young man, she could scarcely believe she was the one chosen to be his wife.

Then she and Ben watched as William and Jane were also sealed.

It was a wonderful, glorious day that Mary Ann stored in her memory to bring out to treasure during quiet moments. She felt so blessed. Only one thing remained on her list of wishes—to see her own parents sealed, as William and Jane were, and to know that her whole family was knit together with those eternal bonds that would not break.

CHAPTER FIVE

Treboeth, Wales
October, 1870

Sarah, ten years old, looked back and forth between her brother Thomas and her father. She sat across from them at the dinner table, but no one ate, their food growing cold in front of them. The chair where Mary Ann used to sit was still pulled up to the table, but the family had learned in the last year to stop setting a place for her as they had the first month after she left—setting it and then remembering and returning the plate to the cupboard.

"Father, I don't want to be a collier." Thomas brought his hand down on the table.

"Don't upset your mother's china," Evan said.

"All right, I won't upset her china." Thomas pushed his plate to the side. "But we have to discuss this sooner or later. I want to go to Australia and work with Uncle Davies in his shipping business."

"No son of mine is going to leave this family and take off for Australia."

"Mary Ann went to America. Or doesn't she count, because she's not your son?"

"You will not take that tone with me, Thomas. Mary Ann would have gone, with or without my permission. Besides which, she was of age. You aren't yet seventeen."

"I can go without your permission. And I'll be eighteen soon enough."

Evan sat back and looked at his son. Sarah could see that her father's eyes were angry, yet contemplative. "I know you'll soon be of age, Thomas. Your life is yours to choose. But know this. If you leave this family and go to Australia, it would devastate your mother. You know our wishes." He picked up his fork and resumed eating.

The little children around the table looked frightened. They had never seen such an argument at the dinner table. Neither had Sarah. She remembered loud voices when Mary Ann had asked for her father's blessing to go to America, but Evan wasn't the kind to shout when angry.

Thomas only stayed at the table a few more minutes, then he asked to be excused, and Evan gave permission as though nothing had happened. Sarah's mother Mary went upstairs to put the little ones to bed while Kate swept the floor and Sarah cleared the table.

She was washing the first of the cups when she heard her mother and father's voices coming from the other room. She knew it was bad manners to eavesdrop, but she worried too much about her brother to care about manners at that moment. She kept her hands still so she could concentrate on listening, but didn't put the cup down in case her mother discovered her—she could say she'd been washing the whole time.

"I fear for the boy," Evan said. His voice sounded sad, not at all like he had when talking to Thomas.

"I know you do, Evan, and I think he knows it too. You're a good father, and you only want what's best for your children," Mary's voice soothed.

"Then why do they want to leave? They act as though I'm chasing them away. First Mary Ann, now Thomas."

"They want other things, that's all. Mary Ann fell in love, Thomas wants adventure. You've given them a good life, but they want to try something new."

"There's nothing wrong with being a collier. I've been in the mines since I was a child."

"Thomas isn't saying that being a collier is wrong. He's just saying it's not what he wants for himself."

Sarah wished she could see into the other room. Her father hadn't replied, and she didn't know if he agreed or disagreed with her mother. She rinsed the cup and picked up a plate.

"I also don't understand this desire to go to Zion." She could hear her father's footsteps as he began to pace the floor, and Sarah moved very slowly so she wouldn't miss a word. "But then you know me. I've never been much for organized religion."

"You know the gospel is true, Evan. I've seen your face aglow when you listened to the apostles and the missionaries."

"I wouldn't have been baptized otherwise. But all this sitting in meetings, wearing high collars and shoes that pinch—give me a midnight meeting in the woods any day."

Mary laughed. "You know that old Druid society was nothing but foolishness. I never should have let you take Sarah to those meetings."

"It may have been foolish, but it was more fun to be a Druid than to be a Mormon."

"Evan!" Mary sounded shocked.

"Well, it's true. There's no law that says you have to think a religion is fun to believe it, is there?"

"No, I don't suppose so." Mary didn't sound sure.

"I enjoyed meeting under the stars. They should start having Mormon meetings that way. Attendance would be better."

"Would you come back if they held meetings under the stars in the middle of the night?"

"I might."

Sarah knew her parents were teasing each other, and that the serious part of their conversation had ended. She hastened to finish up the dishes.

Sarah had enjoyed those Druid meetings. It wasn't because of the doctrine they preached or the way they lived, but like her father, she enjoyed the free spirit of the meetings, how unstructured they were. Most of the time she sat and looked around instead of listening. Her father hadn't taken her to a midnight meeting in some time.

Maybe being a Druid was more fun than being a Mormon, but she didn't know. She didn't belong to either group.

Her parents and older siblings had been baptized into the Mormon religion, but she wanted time to make up her mind. No point in tying herself down unless she was sure, she thought. She listened carefully to the Mormon preachers and thought about what they said, but nothing about them seemed particularly special, so she hadn't followed her parents to baptism. She found herself leaning more toward the Methodists, when she leaned at all.

"Dear me, Sarah, haven't you finished yet?" Mary asked as she came into the kitchen.

"I'm sorry, Mother. Some of the plates were sticky."

"I know. The sauce caramelized a bit. Very well, off to bed."

Sarah went as directed, pulling on her nightgown and sliding under the covers. She stayed awake a bit longer, gazing off into the darkness. She heard Thomas come in late, tiptoeing, but her father heard him nonetheless and met him in the hall. They talked for a moment, but their voices were soft, even kind, and Thomas moved off to his room. They weren't fighting any more.

Sarah rolled over and pulled her quilt up over her shoulder, comforted. What remained of her family was still intact.

* * *

Treboeth, Wales
Late October, 1870

Evan lowered himself into his chair, then looked down the length of the table. "Where's Thomas?"

"I don't know, Evan. I haven't seen him all day," Mary replied.

Evan shook his head, disgust on his face. All the children were expected to be home at dinnertime, and it was the height of disrespect to miss the meal.

He slid back his chair and stood, which he only did when he had something very important to say. Sarah laid her fork down and turned her full attention to him.

Evan waited until everyone stopped eating, then spoke, his full dark beard bobbing with each word.

"I've been given quite an honor. The English government wants to send some miners to Russia to help with a project, and I've been selected to be in charge."

Mary gasped, but didn't move. The children looked around the table at each other.

Russia? Sarah thought. The place where people wore tall furry hats?

"I realize this comes as a surprise. But the owners of the mine have placed a lot of confidence in me, and I should take this position."

"When do you leave?" Mary asked in a tremulous voice.

"Three weeks."

"How long will you be gone, Father?" Richard wanted to know.

"I don't know."

"A week?" Richard asked, and Evan laughed.

"It will be much longer than a week, I'm afraid."

Dinner eventually came to an end, having been a long, silent meal. Sarah fetched a rag to wipe up Jane's hands and face, then sent her off to play. She couldn't imagine going about everyday life without Father there. What would they do without him?

The door burst open just then, and Thomas came through, closing it with a slam. He turned and held the doorknob, but a second later, loud voices came from outside, and a smattering of fists beat on the door.

"We know you're in there!" a man shouted angrily.

Evan walked over to the door and moved his son to the side. He turned the knob, and the man on the outside fell into the room, obviously not expecting the door to open so quickly.

"I'll have your hide!" he shouted, lunging toward Thomas. Evan stepped forward and caught the man's collar—an easy motion as he had at least a foot on him. Mary worked quickly to usher the little ones out of the room.

"Tell me why you're after my son."

The stranger looked up at Evan, the tall, towering hulk of his frame and the expression in his eyes. "Beg pardon, sir, but your son tried to stow away on my ship."

Evan pressed his lips together. "He's not on your ship now, is he?"

"No, of course not."

"I see no point in chasing the lad through the streets and yelling at him in his mother's home. You and I can discuss this calmly, or, since you've done your job in removing him from your ship, you can go on your way."

The man looked Evan over again, clearly intimidated by the calm manner in which he spoke. Sarah stood rooted to the spot, unable to leave the room as she knew she should.

"I'll take my leave, then," came the answer.

"I'm sorry for your trouble, and I'll guarantee you that my son will not go near your boat again." Evan released his tight grip and showed their surprised visitor to the door. He closed it slowly, then turned to face Thomas.

"What was all that about?" His voice still sounded calm.

"I'm going to Australia." Thomas hunched his shoulders and looked down at the floor. A lock of his dark hair fell forward into his face, and Sarah couldn't see his eyes.

"Against my wishes?"

Thomas shrugged.

"By stowing away?"

"Yessir."

"You know that's dishonest. Plenty of folk work hard to pay for their tickets. You can't climb aboard for free and expect to be treated the same."

"I know." Thomas still wouldn't meet his father's eyes, and the silence hung heavy in the room.

"Have you nothing else to say?" Evan asked after several seconds, his voice rising.

"No, Father."

"I think you'll have plenty to say in the morning. Straight off to bed with you. And, Thomas," he added, "you'll not miss dinner again."

Evan watched as his son went up the stairs, then turned and saw Sarah. "What are you doing there? Haven't you got dishes to wash?"

"Yes, Father." Sarah was finally able to move her feet and go into the kitchen. She didn't know exactly what punishment Thomas would get in the morning, but it would probably have something to do with a belt.

* * *

Treboeth, Wales
November, 1870

Sarah's father had been gone for two weeks. During the day, the family routines carried on the same as they always had—they were used to Evan's absence from sunup to sundown. But as the dusk came and the lamps were lit, there was a hole where their father used to be. It was too quiet at night. Even baby Evan Edward sensed the change and was fussier in the evenings.

Thomas had been grumpier since Evan left. Sarah often heard him muttering under his breath, and more than once Mary went out looking for him late at night. Sarah knew her brother was deeply unhappy, but she didn't understand why he wanted to go to Australia. He could work on a farm or in millinery. He didn't have to be a collier if he didn't want. She suggested as much to him one day, and he only grunted. The suggestion was not what he wanted to hear.

One morning, Thomas didn't come down to breakfast. Mary went to roust him out of bed, but he wasn't there. Sarah set his place for dinner that night, but he didn't come home. Mary told Sarah to mind the younger children, and she went out, covering her head with a shawl.

Sarah bathed the two youngest and put them to bed, then read Richard a story. The clock on the mantle seemed louder the later it got. She put Richard to bed and started some bread.

She was in the kitchen measuring flour when she heard her mother come into the house at last.

"He's gone," Mary said. She draped her shawl over the back of the tall kitchen chair and sat down, looking tired and drawn. "I asked everyone I met, all the way to the docks. No one had seen him, no one knew anything. When I made it down to the shipyard, I met a toothless old man who smelled of whiskey. He told me I would find my son on the way to Australia by now. I didn't believe him at first, but then he gave me this." She held up a scrap of paper. "He said he'd been watching for me. Thomas gave him this note in case I came looking for him."

"What does it say?" Sarah didn't stop kneading the bread—she had to keep her hands busy or they would tremble.

"I can hardly make it out. His handwriting never did improve, even with some schooling. It says that he went to Australia to find Uncle Davies, and that he's sorry."

Mary suddenly gasped, as if she had just realized her son was gone, and tears began to stream down her cheeks. "How could he do this? How could he leave against our wishes, especially now that your father is gone, and leave us here all alone?"

Sarah wiped her hands on a towel and wrapped her arms around her mother. She had never seen her so upset. "Everything will be all right, Mother," she said. "We'll manage. We'll get by."

Mary was still for a moment, and then nodded. "We will. We'll find a way. But I'm going to need lots of help." She wiped her eyes. "I'm in a family way again, Sarah."

Sarah tightened her hug as her mother's shoulders trembled. She didn't know what to say or do, so she was silent, and let her mother sob out her grief.

A short time later, a mask of resolve settled over Mary's face, and the tears left as quickly as they had come.

"Off to bed with you," she said brusquely. "Morning will be here before you know it."

Sarah went to bed as she was told, but as she drifted off to sleep she could hear her mother pacing back and forth on the rug.

* * *

Treboeth, Wales
September, 1871

Sarah looked at the calendar and marked off another day. Several months had passed since Thomas had run away from home. Mary had not given in to tears once since the night Thomas left, but had stoically marched forward, making decisions and plans for the good of her family.

For some reason Evan's wages weren't being sent from Russia, and although it broke her heart to do it, Mary sold their home and purchased a smaller and more affordable one—a row house that stood with many others just like it. She opened a bakery in the home and kept Sarah and Kate busy tending little ones and keeping house while she ran the business, trying to make ends meet. Eventually Sarah helped her mother with the baking, as well.

"I'm sorry I can't send you to school," Mary told Sarah one night after the younger children were in bed. "I would dearly love to see you finish your education."

"I know enough to get by. You need me here right now."

Mary reached out and touched her daughter's shoulder. "You're a good girl, Sarah."

Sarah didn't feel good or bad or in-between—she was too tired to feel much of anything.

The next morning, they received a letter with an odd-looking postmark.

"Why on earth would we be getting a letter from New Zealand?" Mary slit the envelope open with a butter knife and pulled out the page. She began to read, then grabbed a chair and sat down in it quickly.

"What's the matter?" Sarah asked. Mary didn't answer, but handed her the letter. Sarah read it aloud.

Dear Mother,

Sarah stopped. "It's from Thomas!" She held the page up a little higher.

> *I hope all is well with you and the family. My boat was shipwrecked off the coast of New Zealand. Most of the people on board were killed, save for a few of us.*
>
> *We floated in the ocean for a time, holding onto debris, then were rescued. We'll be taken to Queensland tomorrow, but I wanted to get this letter off to you right away.*
>
> *I'm all right, Mother. Don't worry about me. I'll find Uncle Davies, and we'll get along well.*

Your son, Thomas

"He could have been killed," Mary said. She took the letter back from Sarah and scanned it up and down again, her lips pressed together. "That foolish boy could have been killed."

"But he *is* alive," Sarah reminded her.

"Yes, he's alive. I know I should be grateful for it, but right now I'm too angry." She looked at the postmark. "This letter was mailed six months ago! Who knows what he's been doing in the meantime. Has he found Uncle Davies? Is he getting enough to eat?" Evan Edward began to cry, and the new baby, small Gwilym, joined in. Mary turned her head toward the sound. "Life goes on, whether we will or not. I'll feed Gwilym. Please take the bread out in ten minutes." Mary set the letter on the table and went to care for the baby.

Sarah turned the envelope over and over in her hands after her mother left the room. What kind of place was New Zealand? She had no idea. She could understand her mother's anger, but Sarah was too relieved that Thomas was alive to feel anything else at all.

CHAPTER SIX

Cedar City, Utah
February 5, 1873

Mary Ann held her baby son close to her heart while three-year-old Mary Jane climbed on the bed.

"This is your new brother," Ben said, sitting down on a chair nearby. "His name is William, like your Grandpa Williams back in Wales."

Mary Jane reached out a chubby finger and touched the baby's face. He screwed up his eyes and let out a bellow. Ben laughed and reached out to catch his daughter's hand before she tried again.

"He's sleeping," he explained. "You can talk to him later."

Mary Ann couldn't take her eyes off the baby. His head had a soft covering of brown fuzz—which she assumed would turn into hair at some point. His tiny fingers, his tiny toes—she had already counted all of them to make sure they were there. She wondered if every mother the world over did the same thing.

"Your mother's tired," Ben told Mary Jane a few minutes later, and led her out of the room. Mary Ann closed her eyes, enjoying the feel of the baby's breath on her neck as she drifted off into a well-deserved nap.

She woke an hour later, sensing that something was not right. Except for the embers in the fireplace, it was dark in the room, and that added to her feeling of uneasiness. She listened to the stillness around her. It was very quiet. Too quiet, in fact. She couldn't hear the baby breathing.

She placed her hand on his chest. She couldn't feel even the tiniest flutter

"Ben!"

Ben was on the other side of the room, rocking Mary Jane to sleep. He quickly laid the child in her bed and came running.

"The baby! The baby!" Mary Ann held him out to her husband, her arms shaking.

Ben took the infant and carried him over to the fireplace, where he turned him over and over in the faint light. "I can't see anything," he said. "I can't tell what's wrong."

Mary Ann dragged herself out of bed and over to the lamp. She could hardly light the wick—her hands fluttered like moths. Finally the lamp glowed to life, and Ben unwrapped the baby on the table.

He looked perfect, just as he had at birth. But his chest didn't rise, and his lips had turned blue.

Ben stooped over and listened to the tiny heart, placing his ear right on the baby's chest.

"Nothing." he muttered a moment later, stepping back and dropping into a chair.

"No! You're wrong!" Mary Ann rested her own ear on the baby, willing her child to wake up. With every passing moment she grew more and more afraid, her breath coming shallow and rapid. She picked up the baby and shook him gently, trying to get any response. There was none. She tickled his feet with no reaction. Ben took the child from her just as she fell to the floor with grief. Her baby was dead.

* * *

Cedar City, Utah
February 23, 1873

Mary Ann sat in her rocking chair by the fireplace, a shawl wrapped around her shoulders. She clutched the edge of it with her fingers, pulling it as tightly as she could around herself. No matter what she did, she couldn't stay warm enough. But the cold was not on the outside, where it could be melted away with blankets and coal. It was deep, down into her heart.

"Mam?" Mary Jane toddled up to her chair. "Mam, I'm hungry."

It took a moment for the child's voice to register on Mary Ann's mind. She slowly pulled herself up and cut Mary Jane a slice of bread, then sank back into her chair.

"Mam, where's the baby?"

Mary Ann closed her eyes. Mary Jane had asked that question repeatedly over the last two weeks, and Mary Ann had no answer. How could she explain to her daughter that little William had died? She couldn't understand it herself, and she didn't know how to make her child understand. Oh, how she wished her mother were here! Mary always knew how to comfort her.

Ben came home soon after and entertained Mary Jane with stories until she went to sleep. Then he pulled a chair over to the fireplace and took Mary Ann's hand. She tried to smile at him, but it was so hard to make even the smallest effort.

"Sister Thurston passed away yesterday," he told her gently. "She leaves behind her baby, only eleven days old."

"I'm sorry to hear it," Mary Ann said automatically.

"Brother Thurston is beside himself. He doesn't have any close family to take care of the baby." Mary Ann turned her eyes to her husband. He finished his thought in a rush. "I told him he could bring the baby here."

"You did?"

"Yes. He'll be here soon."

Mary Ann was furious. How could Ben believe that bringing a new baby into the house would replace the loss of William, that her grief could be mended so quickly? Didn't he care? Didn't he understand the wracking torment that lived in her body?

"It will be all right, Mary Ann. You'll see," Ben said, resting his hand on her shoulder before he turned away.

She didn't reply. She had no words.

Only a half hour later, Brother Thurston knocked on the door. Ben opened it wide, and the man came in, a bundle in his arms. He walked across the floor and greeted Mary Ann, placing the tiny baby in her arms. "Her name is Caroline Cordelia." He took a step back and cleared his throat. "Thank you for taking her, Sister Perkins."

Mary Ann took a deep breath before looking down. She steeled her heart, telling herself not to love, but as her eyes fell on the beautiful little girl with the delicate features and upturned nose, the ice in her soul began to melt. "It will be a pleasure," she told Brother Thurston, and to her surprise, she believed her own words.

She carried the bundle over to her chair and sat down, leaning back to start the slow rocking motion, which she was sure the baby would like. She knew the child would not remove all of her longing for William, but she had to admit, it felt wonderful to hold a baby again.

* * *

Treboeth, Wales
June, 1873

Evan Williams sat near the fire with a lap robe across his legs. He looked like a skeleton wearing a coat and trousers. Kate warmed his slippers on the hearth. Sarah tiptoed around him, afraid of making too much noise.

"Sarah." Her father's deep voice sounded like a bear rumbling in the spring.

"Yes, Father?"

"Come here, child."

She walked across the floor on the balls of her feet. Her mother had warned her not to be loud so her father could rest, and she didn't dare disobey.

"How old are you now?"

"Thirteen."

Evan shook his head. "It seems I was gone so long."

"Three years, Father."

"At least a lifetime," he responded. "Sit down here and talk to me for a while."

"Mother said I should let you rest."

"I don't want to rest. I'm tired of resting." He sounded like a petulant schoolboy. "Tell me what you did while I was gone."

She sat down on the rug near his feet. "I helped Mother with the baking in the mornings, and in the afternoons I did housework for the ladies in the neighborhood. I also tended the little ones. That's really about all, Father. Now tell me about you. You've had an adventure, I'm sure."

Evan grunted, shifting his legs under the lap robe. "I'd hardly call it an adventure."

"But Russia! Just the sound of the word makes me think of adventure. Tell me all about it." She leaned forward a bit, ready to hear a story.

"The days stretched long and hard, and the nights were worse. It was so cold that I didn't think I'd ever get warm again. But the worst was being away from all of you. They kept telling me that the job would soon be over, but I could see another six months, eight months, looming in the distance. I'm no fool to be dangled along with promises. When they finally said I could go, I almost didn't believe them. Three years of that, and look how much I've missed. You've gone from a little girl to a young woman. The little ones hardly know me."

"You're glad to be home?"

"More than I can even tell you." He reached out a hand and rested it on his daughter's head. "It is good to be home."

His eyes grew heavy, and soon his hand slid from Sarah's hair and fell onto his lap. Sarah fetched another blanket and placed it around his shoulders. He shivered all the time.

He had explained to her how very cold it was in Russia, that the wind could cut right through your coat and make you feel frozen alive where you stood. Sarah had a hard time imagining being so cold that even at home, surrounded by blankets and seated in front of a fire, you could still feel the chill clear down to your bones.

"Has there been any word from Thomas?" He spoke from a faraway place, somewhere near sleep.

"No, Father. There's just been the one letter."

Mary had written to Evan to tell him that Thomas had run away, and another letter about the shipwreck, but neither letter had reached Evan. He had returned home to discover that his son was gone and their home had been sold. The news took as much out of him as the cold Russian winters.

"I shouldn't have made him go and work in the mines," he said, rousing from his sleep and bringing a hand to his face. "I knew he hated it. All the children hate it. But I thought, as he grew older . . ." A cough took Evan's voice and seized his body for a moment. Mary heard the noise from the other room and came in with a glass of water to ease her husband's discomfort.

"The mines are no place for a child," he said when he regained his breath. "I should never have made him go."

"You did what you thought was best," Mary consoled him.

"But he rebelled against me and left us behind."

"Hush, Evan. We don't know why he did it. But he's still our own boy, wherever he is." Mary stroked his head.

"Yes, he's our boy." Evan grew silent for a moment. "I wish I knew where he was."

He coughed again, his shoulders hunched forward. He reached out a hand and pointed to little Gwilym who had been born during his absence. "I won't repeat my mistakes, Mary. This one, and his brothers, shall never work in the mines."

PART TWO

THE IMMIGRANTS

CHAPTER SEVEN

Treboeth, Wales
January, 1878

Sarah stood for a moment on the steps of the Methodist church and pulled her scarf over her head. The eastern breezes had brought fog from the ocean, and it hung thick and ghost-like over the town, wrapping itself around the tall steeples of the church. She loved days like that—days when the sun would peek through the clouds only occasionally, giving hints about what might be to come but not letting on too much.

The crowd that escaped the dimly lit cloister of the church soon dissipated, and still Sarah waited on the snow-dusted steps. She hadn't seen Tom Wilcox inside, but she hoped to catch a glimpse of him before she headed back home. She looked up and down the street, trying to appear disinterested, but her heart quickened when she saw his familiar form emerge from a side street and make his way toward her.

"I'm glad I caught you before you left," he said, sweeping his cap off his head. "It wouldn't be a proper Sunday without seeing you. Of course, it doesn't matter the day of the week. All days are better with you in them."

Sarah smiled and shook her head as she took the arm he offered. "Tom Wilcox, sometimes I don't know if you're speaking the truth or just trying to turn my head."

"Can't I do both at the same time?"

"You do both quite well."

They rounded the corner and headed up a cobbled street, away from the center of the village and toward the hills that they could only just make out through the mist up ahead.

"You were missed in church today."

Tom grinned. "Who missed me?"

"Several people wondered where you were."

"One person in particular?"

"You know I was looking for you, Tom." She tugged his arm slightly.

"I came, didn't I?"

"You did, but long after I expected you."

"I was visiting with Richard Jones." Tom paused, taking in a deep breath as well as the scenery. "You heard about the accident in the mine yesterday?"

"I heard there was an accident, but I don't know the details. What happened?" Her heart began to race. Underground, working under thousands of tons of earth and rubble, the mine workers were in danger every minute of every day. One slip of a chisel or one explosion gone wrong was the difference between life and death for the men and boys who worked there. She was glad her father hadn't worked in the mines in the five years since he had returned from Russia. "How badly is Richard hurt?"

"His coal cart had faulty brakes. He was coming up an incline, and the cart rolled back on him. He couldn't get out of the way on time and broke both his legs."

"Oh, no." Sarah knew that Richard Jones' family was destitute and depended on his income for every last scrap they had. If he was not able to work, they wouldn't have enough to eat. Several of the collier families were in the same position. It was a terrible life, tied to the mine to support your family and yet being in constant danger. "How is his wife?"

"She seems pretty stalwart. You know her, though. She wouldn't let on if there was a snake down her back."

Sarah smiled, although her thoughts were still with the predicament of the Jones family. "Did they tell you what the doctor said?"

"He thinks it'll be at least two months before Richard can get around on his own. He's not making any promises about when he can return to work, though."

Sarah felt tired as they continued their walk. As much as she loved her home, she hated that it was tied so closely to the mining community. Mary Ann wrote letters of her home in Utah, where many of the Saints were farmers, but there were also storekeepers and milliners, train engineers, and tradesmen of all kinds. They had those occupations in Wales, of course. But by and large, the money was made by coal mining, and the men didn't seem to have much choice as to what they did. In Utah, though, the opportunities seemed endless.

"So you see, I was a bit delayed coming to church," Tom continued, and Sarah realized that she hadn't been listening.

"I'm glad you came when you did," she said, turning her attention to him.

"Are you, now?" He flashed a smile of brilliant white teeth.

"Of course. You know I have more than one reason for coming to church."

He pressed his hand over hers where it rested on his arm, and they continued their walk, each silent with their own thoughts, but content to be together.

* * *

Evan Williams sat at the head of the family table, a bear of a man but weaker than he had ever been. He presided over the meal as usual, but Sarah could see that it took an effort for him to remain upright. She wished that he would forego his pride and go lie down.

"We're glad you could join us for Sunday dinner, Tom," Evan said. "You're a welcome guest in our home."

"Thank you, Mr. Williams. I can't think of another home I'd rather be in."

Mary set a steaming bowl of potatoes on the table, then took her seat. "I understand Richard Jones saw a bit of hardship yesterday."

"Yes, indeed he did. I was over there for a while this morning. It's a hard thing to bear, but his spirits are good," Tom said.

"I'll go pay the Jones a call myself this afternoon," Mary said.

The chatter around the table fell silent as the family began to eat. After glancing around at the group, Evan cleared his throat. "I have something to tell you, children, and now is as good a time as any."

"What is it, Father?" Jane asked.

"It's no secret that my health has been poor since I returned from Russia."

Sarah was surprised by such an admission. Although she and every other member of the family knew his health was failing, thitis was the first mention he had made of it. He had chosen to act as though nothing at all had changed, and that he was still invincible.

"I've been to the doctor several times over the last year, and he has suggested remedies and treatments for my asthma, all of which have failed. Tuesday I met with him again. He recommends that I do something rather unusual."

Evan paused and took a bite of his meal. Sarah sat still, her hands clasped in her lap. She knew it was not her father's way to speak quickly or abruptly, but she wished he would just have out with it rather than making them wait.

"It seems the climate in America is much different than here. Additionally, the sea air has been known to cure some patients of their ailments."

Again, he paused. Sarah couldn't believe what she was hearing. Was her father really suggesting . . . ?

"Your mother and I have been talking it over for the last few days, and we have made it a matter of prayer. We've decided that we should go to America."

"For how long, Father?" asked Gwilym, the baby in the family at seven years old. To Sarah, it seemed like just yesterday that Evan Edward had been the baby, but he was already a big boy of nine.

"We shall move there, Gwilym. It will be our new home."

"Will we live by Mary Ann?" Jane wanted to know. She could barely remember her oldest sister, but they had spoken of her frequently in the nine years since she left, and at times, it was as though she was still there, for the way her presence was felt.

"Yes. We will move to Utah and be near your sister."

Sarah could hardly contain herself. She had wanted to go to Utah ever since Mary Ann left. She missed her sister terribly, and was entranced with the letters that came every month, telling about the things Mary Ann had been doing. And Mary Ann was already a mother, with children Sarah had never seen. Could it be that they were really going? It seemed too good to be true. In fact, she wondered if it was.

"Father, this is a hard journey," she interjected. "Is the doctor sure it will be good for you?"

"He said it would either kill me or cure me. Rather even odds, don't you think?" Evan smiled with a twinkle in his eye.

"Kill you? Father, was he serious?"

"You're not to worry, Sarah. Your mother and I have prayed about it, and we feel this is the right thing to do."

Sarah wished she could have his confidence. She knew her mother was religious and truly believed the things she was taught at church. Although her father didn't hold with organized religion, he still communicated with God regularly, in his own fashion.

Sarah felt more cautious. How could they know that they were receiving promptings from God? Perhaps they just missed Mary Ann and used their own feelings as an excuse to go and see their daughter under the guise of religion. As excited as she was to go on the journey, she couldn't help but feel it would be her father's undoing. She wished that there was some guarantee that he would recover, that it wouldn't be left to chance.

Dinner continued with much talking and planning. All the children were excited to go, although they each said they would miss their friends. Evan's laughter boomed across the table frequently, and Sarah could see that merely talking about the trip made him feel better. His eyes were alight with the idea of the new frontier and all the possibilities that stretched before them. He spoke of building a new home and digging a garden for Mary. His shoulders were a little straighter, and he seemed less tired. Sarah inwardly shrugged. If just the thought of going to America was going to improve her father's health, perhaps it wasn't a foolish idea after all.

Shortly after the meal ended, Tom took Sarah's elbow and escorted her out into the yard behind the row of houses where they lived. He led her behind a large tree that grew a hundred yards away, and surprised her by wrapping his arms around her waist and pulling her close.

"Tom," she protested softly. "What if someone sees us?"

"What if they do?" he said. "They'll just think that we're two young lovers out flirting in the dark."

"But—"

"Isn't that what we are? Be honest with me now, Sarah. You know my feelings."

She looked up into his clear blue eyes. Yes, she knew how he felt. Standing here with him in the darkness, his arms around her and his cheek close to hers, it was hardly a mystery.

"Ah, you don't have to answer. I can see it on your face. I love you, Sarah Williams, and I know you love me. It's been coming on for a long time. Seems I must speak now, or run the risk of losing you. Don't go to America with your family, Sarah. Stay here and marry me."

Sarah would have taken a step back, but Tom pulled her closer and found her mouth with his. It was a sweet kiss—gentle and swift—but it set her mind whirling.

"What do you say?" he whispered.

"I do love you, Tom," she said. She reached up tentatively and touched the lock of sandy hair that fell across his forehead. "But I need some time to think." She was flattered, confused—she wasn't sure how she felt.

"I can give you that. But please make up your mind before it's time to get on that ship." The moon shone just enough to light up the humorous glint in his eyes. "I'd best be going now before we give this old tree more to tell."

He walked down the garden path and out to the road, whistling softly, his breath causing small clouds of white in the cold air. He cut a fine silhouette against the night sky in his flannel coat. His kiss had felt so right and familiar on her lips. He would make her a good husband, she knew that. It would be easy to be married to him, with his kindness and quick wit. He would be able to build her a small home of her own, and she wouldn't have to leave Wales.

But on the other hand, could she say goodbye to her family? It had been nine years since she had seen Mary Ann, and she might never have the chance again. If she saw her parents and siblings off on a boat, would she be saying goodbye to them forever, as well?

Sarah walked slowly back into the house. She needed time to think. The road that was her life had come to a fork, and she didn't know which way to go.

How she needed wisdom!

CHAPTER EIGHT

Cedar City, Utah
April, 1878

Mary Ann glanced up from changing the baby as Ben walked into the small house they shared with their three children. He brought with him a blast of spring sunshine from outside.

"There's a letter for you, Mary Ann," he said, tossing it on the table.

She greeted her husband with a smile. "From home?"

"It looks like your mother's handwriting."

Mary Ann finished, then laid the baby in her cradle and picked up the letter. She opened it and read it quickly. Her eyes widened.

"Ben!"

"What's the matter?"

"Mother and Father are bringing the family to Utah!" Her voice rose with excitement until it ended with a squeal.

Ben was at her side in an instant, looking over her shoulder, although he could not read the words on the page. "When?"

"The end of May," she said, her eyes shining. "That's only six weeks away." What a marvelous blessing! She had hoped they would someday make the move, and had mentioned it in her prayers frequently—but always with the knowledge that it would take a miracle to bring such a thing about.

"This is wonderful," Ben said, slipping his arms around his wife. "You've missed them so."

"I can't wait to see them. And there's so much to be done before they get here! We need to finish planting the garden. I must put up the new curtains. And—"

"They won't be here for weeks," Ben laughed, his dark eyes twinkling. "We have plenty of time."

"You're right. I'm just so excited. I need to make a list of everything that must be done." Her hands trembled as she hunted down paper and pen.

"I believe you'd be jumping up and down, if your ladylike upbringing wasn't keeping you from it."

She laughed. "You're right, Ben Perkins. In my heart, I'm skipping." She placed the paper on the table, prepared to write. "I wish there was time to send them a letter."

"It would never arrive before they left."

"I know." She nibbled the end of her pen. "I'll have to make do with making a list."

She wrote down everything she could think of right off, then put down her pen and looked around the room, trying to imagine what her parents would see when they came to her home for the first time. She and Ben didn't have a lot of pretty things, that was certain. But what they did have was clean and well-kept. She saw to that with a sense of duty and decorum taught by her mother.

Ben had taken various jobs since his arrival in Utah, learning skills he never had in Wales. He learned carpentry and helped build several houses around the area, including time in Manti building the temple.

Farming was his current occupation, working for some of the local men on their property. It didn't pay much, but was enough.

But Mary Ann wished that they had just a little more so she could set a finer table when her parents arrived. She wouldn't say as much to Ben, though—she wouldn't hurt his feelings for the world.

She wondered what her parents would think of Utah. It was as different a place from Wales as she could have imagined. Where Wales was green and lush, Utah was dry and brown. It rarely rained, and one could drive for miles without seeing a tuft of grass. Mary Ann remembered long walks taken on grass so verdant you could gather up a handful and almost squeeze the moisture out of it. What she wouldn't give for a garden full of grass! Of course, in America they would call it a yard. She sighed. There was still so much to learn.

* * *

Treboeth, Wales
April, 1878

Tom Wilcox took Sarah's hand as they walked through the trees of the forest on the outskirts of town.

"How is the packing going?" he asked.

Sarah sighed. "Mother is trying to think of a clever way to pack her grandmother's china so it will survive the journey. Father put the house up for sale. The children think they need to visit every old haunt one last time. And I'm rushing from one thing to the next, trying to help everyone, but not getting much done." She shook her head. "There's been so much chaos, I can hardly think."

"I hope you've had time to think about my offer," Tom said.

"It's been on my mind constantly." Sarah turned to look at him. He wore such a hopeful expression on his face. She knew he deeply wanted to marry her. So why was she having such a hard time deciding what to do?

He walked her back to the gate of her home and placed a small kiss on her forehead. "I'll be waiting," he said.

She waved her hand to him as he reached the head of the lane. He was a good man, but Sarah still didn't know what to say.

* * *

Treboeth, Wales
Mid-April, 1378

The hushed sounds of evening filled the small house—the crickets chirping outside, the sleepy breathing of her younger brothers and sisters in their beds, the fire crackling in the hearth. Sarah held a book in her hands, but was not reading. She couldn't concentrate on the words long enough to make them form a thought in her head.

Evan sat in his chair near the fire, his beard touching his chest as he slept. Mary moved quietly around the kitchen, preparing tomorrow's breakfast ahead of time. Sarah's heart swelled with love for her parents. They had given her so much.

Although she had done without most of the things she would have liked, she looked back on her youth as a happy time. Many of the little girls in her neighborhood had been sent to the mines, just like their brothers. They were put in charge of things like opening and closing the air doors rather than heavy labor, but they worked long hours and came home filthy—often sick.

For the families that did send their young children, the few additional cents meant the difference between starvation and living to see another day.

Sarah did not fault the parents who made the difficult choice to send their children into the colliery. She was ever grateful that her parents had done what they could to keep her from it.

Sarah closed her eyes and tried to imagine for a moment what it would be like to say goodbye to her parents and brothers and sisters, and stay here in Wales with Tom. She would be loved and well cared for. She wouldn't have to leave her beloved green hills or misty mornings—perfect for walking through the woods. She could continue to attend the *Eisteddfods* and other festivals she loved.

But she would be losing so much more. Her family meant everything to her. She missed Mary Ann more than she could say at times, and it had only been nine years. What if she never saw her family again—a whole lifetime of aching for those she loved?

She squeezed her eyes more tightly and tried to think from a new angle. What if she was to leave for America and say goodbye to Tom forever? She would have her parents by her side, as well as her brothers and sisters. She would be reunited with Mary Ann. And she would be seeing a whole new country, full of sights and smells and experiences that she had never known before.

Her mother and father went to bed after a bit, but Sarah stayed up and watched the fire burn down to orange embers.

Perhaps that was an answer, of sorts. If she went to America, she wouldn't have the high flames of her love for Tom, but she would have the warmth and comfort of her family to sustain her, and she would find that to be enough.

"God, please help me," she whispered.

She didn't want to make a choice and have it turn out to be a giant mistake. She wanted to be able to move ahead with confidence in her future, ready to tackle what lay in her path without the constant worry that she had done the wrong thing.

Mary Ann had left her family behind and gone around the world at Ben's summons. Sarah sighed. Mary Ann knew how she felt about Ben, beyond questioning. Tom asked the same kind of commitment from Sarah. Why did she feel so hesitant?

For the thousandth time, Sarah wished that Mary Ann lived close by, so she could ask her what to do. Mary Ann always seemed sure.

* * *

Treboeth, Wales
Mid-April, 1878

The miners had come home from work an hour or so before, swinging their lunch pails as they walked. Sarah knew Tom liked to walk around the village after his shift, so she stepped out onto the lane, wondering which direction she should go to find him. She didn't have to wonder long—he soon found her.

"I'm glad you came by," she told him, taking the arm he offered.

"And where else would I be on such a beautiful night?" he asked with a wink.

They walked along the path until they reached a quiet grove of trees, then she tugged his hand, and they sat on the grass.

"Tom, I need to talk to you."

His gaze dropped, but he still smiled. "I've never had a pleasant conversation that began that way."

She let go of his fingers. "I'm afraid this conversation won't be very pleasant for either of us."

Tom pulled off his cap. His hair was damp along his forehead. He raked his fingers through the mop and laid his cap on his knee. He looked so vulnerable. Seeing him that way, Sarah nearly changed her mind, but she knew she had made the right decision. She took a deep breath and tried to keep the sob out of her voice.

"I need to go to America with my family. I'm so sorry, Tom."

He didn't say anything for a moment, and just looked at her. The sorrow built in her heart until she almost couldn't stand it.

"Are you settled on this?" he asked, taking her hand and squeezing it. "Can't I say or do anything to change your mind?"

"I've been thinking about this for days now. I don't want to hurt you, but I truly feel that I need to be with my family."

"I could be your family, Sarah." His voice was pleading.

"You're sweet and wonderful, Tom, but my decision is made. My place is with my family, and they are going to America. I must be with them."

"Couldn't they get along just as well without you? They have other children, but I only have one sweetheart." He waggled his eyebrows at her.

"It's not a matter of them needing me. I need them," she answered truthfully. She simply was not ready for such a large step in her life. "And, to be honest, I've had questions my entire life. I tried to answer them by going to different churches, thinking that it had something to do with religion. Perhaps it does, I don't know. But I really feel that the answer for me lies in America. If I don't go, I'll never know whether that was the truth."

"You really feel you have to do this?"

"I do, Tom."

He sighed. "Then how can I argue with you? I love you too much for that, Sarah. If the things you need to be happy are in America, then you need to be in America too."

Her eyes filled with tears. "And that's part of why I love you. I knew you wouldn't try to hold me back. You've always wanted what was best for me."

"I wish *I* was what's best for you," he said. "I hope you find whatever it is you're looking for."

"I believe I will. And I believe you will, too."

He lifted her fingers and kissed them.

Word had spread quickly that the Williams family was leaving, and it took off like wildfire that Sarah was going with them. In their small village, everyone knew that she and Tom had been keeping company, and there had been much speculation that she would stay behind. She and Tom had said nothing of their romance or their plans, but they didn't have to. The wheels of gossip rolled along as they ever did, and soon the town knew more about their lives than they did themselves.

Sarah's Methodist minister was not immune from hearing the cackling of the hens, and he met her at the door of the chapel the Sunday before she was to leave.

"Sarah, I am gravely concerned for your welfare," he intoned. "Not only do I fear for your temporal well-being, but your eternal salvation, should you fall in with these Mormons."

"Reverend, my family is Mormon, and I've lived with them my entire life. No harm has come to me yet."

"Ah, but once you reach Utah, you will be in their lair. Take heed lest they pull you into their net of lies and deceit, and you become seduced by their fancy words."

Sarah pressed her lips together to keep from smiling. He was so serious about keeping her out of the Mormons' clutches, she couldn't offend him. But neither could she tell him that she had never been seduced by anything in her life, and was not about to be now. She studied everything out before entering into any kind of agreement, and was not easily swayed by banter and hyperbole.

"You have no need to fear, Reverend. I have attended some of the Mormon street meetings and was not overly impressed. I have no desire to join their church."

"Bless you, Sarah, for your pure heart. The Lord will surely protect you as you face this danger." He fished around in an oversized pocket and handed her two books. "I wish you to have these. They will keep you going straight."

Sarah accepted the gifts. They were beautifully bound volumes of the Bible and a book of hymns. She loved to sing hymns and would cherish those items, even if she did feel the preacher's concern was unjustified.

"I will use these daily. Thank you."

"Remember what I said, Sarah. Take care lest the Mormons weave a net of silken threads bit by bit and one day ensnare you."

Sarah gave the earnest man her word of honor and continued on her way home, chuckling as soon as she was out of earshot.

CHAPTER NINE

Liverpool, England
May, 1878

Sarah saw Tom's head above the crowd before he turned and made eye contact with her. Richard and Jane pulled her hands, urging her to hurry. She didn't think she could go any faster—her breath came in short gasps and her feet ached. But when Tom saw her approaching and smiled, she had a new surge of energy which carried her the remaining distance to the section of the dock that kissed up against the side of their ship.

"Tom! You came all this way to say goodbye?" She was glad to see him, but at the same time her heart sank, knowing that she would have to leave him behind . . . again.

He shrugged. "I couldn't help myself. The train ticket just appeared in my hand somehow." He took her elbow. "I've been waiting for you."

"We had a late start," she explained. "Mother had a hard time leaving the house."

"No matter. You don't sail for an hour."

"But they wanted us on board ahead of time." Sarah turned and looked behind her. "The children dragged me all the way here, but Mother and Father are still lagging."

"Let me go back and see if there's anything I can do to help them," Tom said.

"Thank you," she said, touched by his generous spirit. She had come to terms with leaving Wales, her church, and all her friends, but leaving Tom would be the most difficult.

Sarah kept Richard and Jane occupied by telling them to count how many people boarded the ship in the space of one minute, and then to add all the minutes together to get a grand total. She kept searching the dock with her eyes, and finally saw her parents weaving through the crowd with Tom leading the way. It had been nearly fifteen minutes since he went to look for them. What was taking so long?

"Sorry, Sarah," Tom said once he reached her. He spoke in a quiet voice meant for her ears only. "Your father had a bit of a dizzy spell as he was getting out of the wagon. He's all right now, but we need to get him aboard as soon as possible and into his bunk."

"Of course," she replied, feeling selfish for her impatience. She knew her father looked forward to starting their journey and would not have delayed it intentionally—she should have suspected something was wrong.

Tom helped the family find their quarters, then went up top to make his way off the ship. Sarah followed, wishing for a proper goodbye. It was all happening so fast. If only there was some way to slow time so she could spend a few more minutes with him and lessen the sting.

They walked together toward the gangplank. Tom glanced around and led her to the railing.

"I wish it wasn't ending this way, Sarah," he said, taking her hands in his.

"I know. I've thought about it time and again, and I just don't see a way around it." She squeezed his hands. "You've been very good to me."

He smiled. "Will you think of me every so often?"

"I certainly will."

His face wore an expression so unlike his usual cheerful self, she wished she could change her mind and stay here with him. But in her heart, she knew that was not the answer.

The call came for visitors to leave the ship. Tom reached out and touched Sarah's dark hair, then headed down the gangplank. She stood at the railing of the ship, watching him until the anchor raised and the vessel began its long journey. Soon Tom appeared to be only a speck in the distance, and Sarah went to find her family, feeling a mixture of sorrow and anticipation. America lay before them. She didn't want to think about what she left behind.

* * *

New York City, New York
May, 1878

The huge anchor dropped into the water, and the gangplank was lowered until it hit the pier with a crash. Sarah stood on deck, her arms wrapped around herself to ward off the chill that suddenly rose in the air. Below her lay American soil. In a few minutes she would walk off the ship and become an American. It was almost more than she could bear, and she rocked back and forth with the excitement of it.

A sharp gust of wind came up and blew her hat off her head. She made a wild attempt to get it, but it was carried away before she could manage to get hold of it.

"Sarah! It's time to get off the ship!" Jane came running up. "Did you hear me?"

"I heard you," Sarah replied, looking one last time in the direction of her runaway hat. "You said it's time to get off the ship."

"Yes! So why are you still standing there? Let's go and become Americans!"

Sarah smiled. "Yes, let's." She moved to join her family as they stood in line to exit the ship.

"Sarah, where's your hat?" Mary asked.

"It blew overboard a few minutes ago, Mother," she said.

"What a shame, to enter your new country with a bare head. Well, I suppose it can't be helped."

"But I can help it." Sarah reached into her pocket and pulled out a large handkerchief, tying it over her hair. "I may not be fashionable, but at least I'm decent."

"I can't wait to tell Mary Ann everything that happened on the ship. How we saw a whale and what we had for dinner and . . ."

Jane's chattering became background noise for the thoughts that were milling around in Sarah's head. Her feet were unsteady as she stepped onto the gangplank, and if it weren't for the rope that ran up the side, she might have fallen into the water.

At last the family stood on shore, waiting for their luggage. A shop stood near the quay, and Sarah decided to go inside. She took Richard along with her and stepped through the door.

"Excuse me," she said to the man behind the counter. "I would like to buy a hat." She smiled, hoping that would make up for her faltering English.

He looked at her and began to speak so rapidly she couldn't follow him. She raised her hand and tried to slow his torrent, but he continued at a brisk pace, and she wasn't able to make him understand that she didn't know what he said. She left the store feeling disappointed. She wanted to get a new hat before they began the next leg of their journey, but didn't know how to ask for one.

She and Richard walked back to the dock where the stevedores were unloading their luggage.

"We'll be taking all the trunks and boxes to that building," one of the Welsh sailors said to Evan. "It's called Castle Gardens. Your things will be safe there until it's time to go."

"Thank you," Evan said. "And where can we exchange our money?"

"Same place."

Evan bent down and picked up a small valise that carried the family's personal care items. Sarah was continuously amazed at the new health and strength her father had gained on the voyage. In England, they'd had to bring him to the ship on a wagon. By the time they'd rounded Liverpool and headed out to sea, he strolled up on deck with no assistance. And while Mary and Sarah were below decks with motion sickness, he was the healthiest of the bunch and kept an eye on the younger children. Now he carried luggage and kept up with the stevedores. Sarah was overcome with gratitude for her father's recovery. She hadn't thought it possible, but, she reminded herself, with God all things are possible.

The Williams' followed the stevedores over to the building called Castle Gardens, where they found beds made up for the travelers. Mary moved quickly to mark their places with handkerchiefs on the pillows so the other travelers would know those spots were taken. They sat down on their suitcases next to their beds to rest a moment.

"The train leaves day after next," Evan announced after checking in with the dock master. "The station is right here, so we won't need to travel to get there."

"That's a blessing," Mary said.

"How long will it take us to get to Utah, Father?" Gwilym asked.

"I'm not sure, son. But it's nearly across the entire continent, so we should be prepared for a long journey."

"While we're here in New York City, I'd like to see a bit of the place," Mary commented. "I've heard it's the greatest city in America."

"We could go for a walk, then, and take it in," Evan said.

"Are you sure, Father? Aren't you tired?" Sarah asked.

He smiled. "You're always concerned for me, aren't you, daughter? I'm feeling all right. Let's go and have a look at New York."

Sarah took Gwilym's hand in hers, and the family walked out of Castle Gardens and away from the boat docks. As soon as they left the shipyard area, they found themselves right in the hustle and bustle of a city larger than Sarah could have even imagined. And the noise! Horse hooves clipped the roads all around them, voices shouted, children here and there and everywhere—she held Gwilym's hand even more tightly, afraid of losing him in the crowds.

"Sarah! You're hurting my hand!"

"Oh, I'm sorry, Gwilym. I'll let you go a bit."

After a short time, her neck began to hurt from looking up at so many tall buildings. She focused her attention on the people around her, how they dressed and how they walked. They seemed so sophisticated. Her own plain dress and shoes were serviceable enough, but nothing like what the ladies in New York were wearing.

And the hats! Big, beautiful hats with ribbons and feathers. She reached up to make sure her handkerchief was still in place. She would have a hat before the day was out or die from embarrassment.

Up ahead on the sidewalk, she noticed a group of very fancy ladies and gentlemen gathered together in conversation. As they passed, one of the ladies said something, and the rest laughed. Sarah glanced back to see that woman was looking right at her. She didn't understand all of what was said, but she had caught the word "foreigner." Sarah held her chin up a little higher. She was a foreigner, that was true. But what was wrong with that? America was entirely made up of immigrants!

An hour later, wearing a new hat she had finally been able to locate at an accommodating store, Sarah led the way back to Castle Gardens. Her father had worn out at last and was ready to nap. Even Jane's enthusiasm had waned a bit, and she was quiet—a strange thing for a little girl who loved to talk so much. New York was certainly exciting, but big and busy and far too much for people just coming off a ship from a small village who, aside from the old Welsh castles, had never seen a three-story building in their lives.

* * *

The Train West
May, 1878

Evan took his seat on the train and carefully pocketed the coins he received as change from the telegram office. "I wired Ben to let him know which train we're on," he said. "With any luck, he'll be at the station to meet us."

The locomotive started up with a hiss of steam and slowly pulled out of the station.

"We're on our way," Richard unnecessarily announced, bouncing up and down on his seat.

"And soon we'll see Mary Ann!" Jane joined in.

"I don't remember Mary Ann," Gwilym said.

"Silly, you weren't born when Mary Ann left," Jane poked him.

"Children, please keep your voices down," Mary said. "You're disturbing everyone."

"What's Mary Ann like?" Gwilym asked, more quietly.

"She's very pretty and very kind. You'll like her," Sarah told him.

The train moved westward with measured speed. Many of the other passengers were also immigrants, most coming to seek their fortunes in the gold mines. More mines. Sarah sighed. Was there never to be an end to mining?

The farther west the train moved, the more dust it kicked up. Although they kept their windows closed, the passengers soon found themselves covered with a fine layer that seeped in through the cracks between the windows and walls. Sarah gave up brushing herself off after the third attempt.

Evan's breathing became difficult as he inhaled the dust-laden air, and soon he was coughing violently with no way to stop.

Richard ran down the aisle, where a water bucket sat on a bench. "Drink this, Father," he said, pressing the dipper to Evan's lips. It worked for only a moment, then Evan began to cough again. Mary gave him her scarf, which he tied over his nose and mouth to filter out the dust, but for the remainder of the journey, he coughed constantly, doubled over with his hands pressed against his chest. His asthma simply couldn't handle all the debris in his lungs.

After several days of riding in hot and dusty conditions, the train pulled into the station at Salt Lake City. Sarah was immensely relieved. For a time she had been worried that her father would choke to death on all the dust.

As he stepped off the train, Sarah said a silent prayer of thanks that her father had lived to see the Salt Lake valley.

"Where's Mary Ann?" Richard asked, looking in all directions.

"I don't know," Mary answered. "Let's gather up our things. I'm sure she'll be here soon."

Several minutes passed, but Mary Ann was nowhere to be seen. Sarah was beginning to worry that the telegram had been misdirected, when a young man approached them.

"Excuse me, are you the Williams'?" He spoke in Welsh, which sounded heavenly to Sarah's ears.

"Yes, we are," Evan said weakly, his voice strained from the coughing.

"I'm Hugh Griffin, Ben's brother-in-law. He was detained and couldn't come right away, but my wife and I would be delighted if you'd come stay with us until Ben gets here."

"We certainly appreciate it," Mary said. "Thank you."

Hugh helped load their things into a wagon, placing the trunks on the wagon floor. Mary, Sarah, and the children climbed in and sat on top of the luggage. Evan climbed up beside Hugh, and they were on their way.

"Ben will meet you at the train station in York in two weeks," he said over his shoulder so all could hear.

"Two weeks! Surely we can't trespass on your home for so long," Mary objected.

"It's not trespassing, Mrs. Williams. We're more than happy to have you."

"Where is York?" Evan asked.

"It's south, by Nephi." Hugh laughed. "But you don't know where Nephi is, either. It's not too far by train."

"It's good to hear Welsh, isn't it, children?" Mary said. "The last leg of our journey, we were the only Welsh people on the train, and it was hard to communicate with the other passengers. Speaking with you makes me feel like I'm home again."

"You'd best be learning a few words of English, even so, Mrs. Williams. There aren't as many Welsh immigrants around as we'd like," Hugh said.

"Time enough for that, I hope."

The wagon bumped along the road, jarring Sarah with the impact.

"I never thought the day would come when all my earthly belongings would fit in the bottom of a wagon," Mary said in a small voice that only Sarah could hear.

"It will be all right, Mam. Truly it will." Sarah touched her mother's shoulder. "Father felt healthy until the dust came up, and as soon as it clears out of his lungs, he'll be all right again, much better than he was in Wales. Doesn't that make the move worth it?"

"It does," Mary said. She smiled at Sarah. "Your father's health is a blessing indeed. I wonder sometimes what the Lord meant by letting him get so sick. But I'm now starting to wonder if He didn't allow it so that we could be reunited with Mary Ann."

Sarah merely smiled and nodded.

Whenever she heard her mother talk of the purposes that God had for the family, she felt a little uncomfortable. Her parents had been members of the Church of Jesus Christ of Latter-day Saints for as long as Sarah could remember, and although her father had drifted away from the Church, her mother was a staunch believer. She was always looking for God's hand in their lives and commented on His mercies and miracles.

Sarah believed in God, but didn't have such a close, personal relationship with Him as her mother did. She sometimes wished she did. Her mother spoke of God as though He were a friend.

A group of missionaries on the ship from Liverpool, returning home after serving in England, had taught several hymns to the passengers, and the group passed the time by singing together up on deck. Something about the music of the hymns touched Sarah's soul. She had always loved music—the stirring rhythms of a jig or the slow melody of a waltz—but the Saints' hymns were different. It was as though Sarah possessed a harp deep within her, and the hymns reached inside and plucked the strings, making her sing all over.

The horses gave a whinny as the wagon stopped in front of a small house. Hugh leaped down from the high driver's seat and came around to give Mary and Sarah a hand down. Then he returned to the front of the wagon to help Evan. His voice had slowly returned, but he was weak from the coughing spasms and kept his arm curled around his midsection.

Hugh's wife Ruth came to the door and greeted them as they walked up to the house. "Welcome! Welcome to our home! You must be exhausted. I have some hot bread ready for you." She looked much like her brother Ben, with dark hair and eyes. Two small, dark-eyed children ran out into the yard, pushing past their mother's skirts and nearly knocking her over.

Sarah washed up at the pump before she ate. She had so much dust and grime on her face and hands that it turned to mud when it first hit the water. She tried to shake out her dress, but only succeeded in raising a cloud that made her choke. Ruth came up behind her with a towel and a bar of soap.

"I've told Hugh that you'll all want baths tonight. He's prepared to fill the washtub as many times as you like."

"Thank you, Ruth," Sarah said. She wiped her face, and was dismayed to see the mark she left on Ruth's clean white towel. "I'm sorry."

"You're not to worry about it. I can get it clean." Ruth laughed. "Traveling certainly does wear a body out."

"Yes, it does." Sarah looked around at the yard and the flowers that had obviously received much care. "You have a beautiful garden."

"Thank you. It wasn't this beautiful when we first came, though. It's taken years of cultivation and weeding to bring it to this point. And the house! I don't know who lived here before us, but they left it in terrible condition. I was glad to have a home ready made so we didn't have to worry about building, but it was filthy. I believe we used four coats of paint just to make it look bright."

Sarah glanced around at the land that surrounded them. "Do you like Utah, Ruth?"

"I love it here. You'll soon make friends and find things to do and grow to love it as I do."

"Even though I'm not a Mormon?"

Ruth looked surprised. "I didn't realize you weren't."

"My parents are, and most of my brothers and sisters. But I was never baptized. I've been attending the Methodist church."

"Well, believe it or not, there are plenty of people in Utah who aren't members. You may have to look a minute to find one, but you will. Don't worry, Sarah. You'll find a place for yourself here."

Sarah certainly hoped so, but at that moment she wasn't sure.

CHAPTER TEN

Salt Lake City, Utah
May, 1878

Sarah had planned to wake up early the next morning to help Ruth with breakfast, but she slept late. Delicious smells coming from the kitchen seeped into her consciousness, and she stretched, opening her eyes to see a strange ceiling overhead. For a moment she didn't know where she was. Not the train or boat, and certainly not home. Then she remembered and got up quickly, fumbling her buttons in an attempt to dress and get ready for the day.

"I'm sorry, Ruth," she said as she came into the kitchen. "I meant to come help you, but I couldn't wake up."

Ruth laughed—a happy, frequent sound. "I would have sent you back to bed if you had tried. You've had a long journey and I don't expect you to cut yourself short of sleep on my account."

The family soon gathered for breakfast, and Ruth placed several large plates on the table. One plate was filled with little cakes—or at least that's what they looked like to Sarah. A little strange to have cakes for breakfast, she thought. She picked one up and set it on her plate, and after the blessing, she took a bite. A strange, acrid taste filled her mouth, and she couldn't swallow.

Glancing around the table, she lifted her napkin to her lips and spat the food into her hand as discreetly as she could. She folded the napkin around the morsel so no one would notice.

A few moments later, Ruth caught sight of the untouched remnant still sitting on Sarah's plate.

"Don't you like your baking soda biscuit?"

"Baking soda?" Ah, so that was the strange taste. "It was very . . . different."

Ruth laughed. "I know it's different from what we used to eat in Wales. But baking soda biscuits are quite a favorite in these parts." She stood up and fetched a bowl from off the counter. "I have a surprise, a special treat for your arrival."

The children all brightened up at the word "treat," and Sarah was eager, too. The baking soda had left an aftertaste, and she wanted to chase it down with something better.

"This is called a banana." Ruth placed a crescent-shaped yellow fruit in Sarah's hands.

She turned it over and over. She had never seen anything like it and wasn't sure what to do with it.

"You eat it like this," Ruth explained, peeling down the sides. Hugh helped the younger Williams children with theirs.

Sarah studied her banana. She carefully removed the rest of the outside portion, placed the lighter yellow part on her plate, and took a bite of one of the strips Ruth had removed. It was tough and fibrous, and she couldn't get her teeth through it. She glanced around the table to see everyone else eating the inner part. She quickly pulled the skin out of her mouth, but not before Ruth saw her.

"Sarah!" Ruth laughed. Sarah had enjoyed her laugh at first, but it was beginning to grate on her nerves. "You eat the inside. It's delicious."

Sarah picked up the fruit and took a bite. It *was* good— mellow and sweet, unlike anything she'd tasted before. But that didn't change the fact that she had made a fool of herself.

She excused herself before breakfast was over, claiming a headache. She went into the room she was sharing with Kate, Jane, and Ruth's little girls, and collapsed on the bed.

Her mother came in a moment later. "Are you all right, Sarah? You look tired."

"I don't really have a headache, Mother. I'm just so frustrated."

"With what?"

Sarah sat up and wiped her eyes. "I looked like such a fool, eating the skin of that banana. And I thought those biscuits were little cakes. How am I ever going to learn about America? I'll never be able to speak English. And what kind of word is *banana*?" She sniffed. "I should have stayed behind and married Tom."

"You regret coming with us?"

"No, not really. I'm just feeling sorry for myself." Sarah pulled out her handkerchief and pretended to smile. "I'll be all right, Mother. You know I will. I just feel so foolish after breakfast this morning." She wiped her nose. "I really should have stayed to help Ruth clean up."

"No need," Mary told her. "Kate and Jane are helping, and I set Richard to sweeping the floor. You rest for a while. I'm sure you'll feel better in a little bit."

"I don't think resting will make me feel like less of a fool."

"No one thinks you're a fool, Sarah. When Hugh and Ruth first came, they had to get used to things around here too. They understand how you feel. And after we've been here for a time, these strange things will seem second nature to us, too."

"You're right. You'll not hear one more word of complaint out of me, I promise."

Mary kissed her daughter's forehead and left the room. Sarah leaned back on the pillows and stared at the ceiling. Tom Wilcox was somewhere across that ocean. She wondered if he was thinking of her, too.

* * *

The Trip to Cedar City
June, 1878

The day arrived for the Williams family to meet Ben and Mary Ann. Kate, Jane, and Richard had been chomping at the bit, wondering why they couldn't have gone directly to Mary Ann's house when they got to Utah. Sarah wondered that herself. Why such a long delay?

The family boarded the train and headed south. The land around them was brown and dry, looking as though a raindrop would vanish in the heat before it could even reach the ground. The wheels of the train kicked up a fair amount of dust, but not nearly as much as they had on the ride across the states, and Evan fared better than the first time.

The train chugged south past a small town called Nephi, then pulled up to a stop at a tiny station. The only thing there was a wagon with two people in it—a man and a woman.

"Mary Ann! Mary Ann!" Richard ran down the aisle of the train and nearly bowled the conductor over. The boy dashed off the train in a flash and ran over to the wagon, where the woman waited with outstretched arms.

"That must be them," Evan commented sardonically. "Either that or some strange woman is hugging my son."

The rest of them disembarked, but not as quickly or as loudly as Richard. Mary Ann had tears streaming down her cheeks as she took them all in.

"You've all grown so much, I hardly recognize you! Evan Edward! And I don't know you at all," she said to Gwilym, taking his hand. "I'm your oldest sister."

"I know," Gwilym answered. "They've told me all about you."

"They've told me about you, too." Mary Ann turned to Sarah. "Oh, it's so good to see you. Look at you! You're all grown up."

Evan had been helping Ben load the luggage into the wagon. Mary Ann caught her father's sleeve as he turned back for another load. "Father, it's so wonderful to have you here."

Evan cleared his throat, and Sarah could see that he held back emotion, perhaps the reason why he had not greeted Mary Ann until that moment. "It wasn't just my illness that brought me here, Mary Ann. I had to see you again. You look wonderful."

"Thank you, Father," Mary Ann said, stepping into his arms for a hug.

"Where are my granddaughters?" Mary demanded to know.

"Hiding in the back of the wagon. Girls!" Mary Ann called.

"Come out here and meet your grandparents."

Three small faces peeked out from behind the canvas wagon cover.

"That one is Mary Jane, that one is Catherine, and this is Delia." She turned slightly and lowered her voice. "Her father keeps coming to pick her up, but every time she sees him, she starts to scream. Finally we decided we should just keep her, and her father agreed. If he'd insisted on taking her, I don't know what I would have done. She's like one of my own."

Mary Ann urged the girls to come out, but they wouldn't, casting shy glances at the newcomers.

After everyone had hugged everyone else several times and shed many tears, Ben announced that it was time to go.

"I'm sorry we didn't come to get you sooner," he said as the family piled in the back of the wagon. "I was hired to help clear some land, and I couldn't get away until the job was done."

"No harm," Evan replied. "Ruth took good care of us."

"It's a couple days' journey down to Cedar City," Ben announced as they drove. "We'll be camping along the road."

The children thought that sounded wonderful, but Mary looked doubtful and couldn't keep the hesitation out of her voice when she spoke. "Camping?"

"Yes. I brought a tent for the women, and us men folk can sleep under the stars. Isn't that right, Richard?" Ben cast a playful look at his young brother-in-law.

"Can we, Mother? Can we?" Richard pled.

"Well . . ."

"I'm afraid we don't have a choice, Mother Williams," Ben explained. "In some patches, there's not another soul for miles. If we counted on a house to spend the night, we'd be out of luck for sure. There are a few settlements along the way, but we'd still have to rough it in tents. There isn't room for them to put us up in beds."

Mary folded her hands on her lap. "Very well, then."

Sarah pressed her lips together, trying to hide a smile. She couldn't picture her mother sleeping in a tent, and she wouldn't have believed the day would ever come.

The sun slid down behind the horizon, and Ben pulled the horses to a stop. The Williams' piled out of the back of the wagon, and the children immediately set to work, obeying Ben's request that they gather firewood. They had taken to Ben immediately. Sarah vaguely remembered him from Wales years before and had always found him to be good and kind, but the younger children didn't know him at all. They had been shy at the start of the journey but soon followed him around like puppies, doing everything he asked. Before long, a fire ring had been built and a blaze was started, a tripod set up and a kettle on the hook.

Mary reached in the back of the wagon and pulled out a bundle.

"What's that, Mother?" Mary Ann asked.

"My feather tick. I may have to sleep out of doors, but I won't sleep like an animal." Mary disappeared into the tent.

Sarah didn't bother to hide her smile; her mother couldn't see her, anyway. She could understand how Mary felt. It certainly wasn't Sarah's idea of civilization, either. She had never seen a covered wagon before coming to Utah, and now she was to understand that they would be living out of one for the next few days. She had never camped out or cooked over an open fire. The look on Kate's face said that she felt much the same as Sarah.

The boys loved it, though, and Sarah could see that there was fun to be had. After a moment of feeling sorry for her mother, she went and joined her younger siblings as they danced around the campfire under the starry sky.

* * *

Cedar City, Utah
June, 1878

"This is our house," Catherine said, taking Mary by the hand and pulling her into the small sod house that was surrounded on all sides with flowers. "I helped clean it."

"I'm sure you did a good job," Mary replied. She had cheered up considerably when Mary Ann's children had finally warmed up to her, and once she was distracted by their little lisped confidences, her complaining about the wagons and insects had stopped. Ben soon had the children busily unloading the wagon and bringing in the luggage.

After dinner, the children in bed and snoring, Mary Ann came over to where Sarah stood at the fireplace and placed an arm around her shoulders.

"You can't imagine how good it is to see you," Mary Ann said. "I know you've missed me, but you've had the family to keep you company. Ben's wonderful, but it's not like having a sister nearby."

Sarah returned the hug. "I'm glad to be here," she said. Her heart gave a pang at the words. Despite her joy at seeing Mary Ann, she hadn't decided yet if she was truly happy to be in Utah. The whole experience had been so strange, the people so different, and her thoughts kept wandering off across the ocean to a tall scamp of a fellow named Tom Wilcox.

"Tell me all the news from Wales," Mary Ann said. She sat in a wooden rocker next to the fire and pulled out some sewing.

Sarah tried to think of all that had happened since Mary Ann left, but had difficulty remembering everything. Mary Ann kept her going with questions, one right after the other.

"And what about Tom Wilcox?" Mary Ann asked at length. "He always was a smart, handsome fellow. What happened to him?"

"He's still in Treboeth." Sarah couldn't help the sad note that entered her voice.

Mary Ann's eyebrows came up. "Sarah, did something happen between you and Tom?"

Sarah smiled. "He asked me to stay and marry him."

Mary Ann laughed. "That's wonderful, Sarah! He would make you a fine husband."

"I know. But it just didn't feel right."

Mary Ann instantly sobered. "I can see this hurt you."

"If only there had been some way . . ." Sarah shook her head. "That's behind me now. It's time to move on."

"But still, I'm sure you miss him."

Sarah shook her head. "I'm not letting myself dwell on it. I made my decision, and I can't exactly go back on it now."

* * *

"We won't trespass on your home for long," Evan said to Ben. The two men had been out walking around the property Ben and Mary Ann owned, and now they stood by the fireplace, one arm each up on the mantle as they faced each other. From Sarah's vantage point across the room, they looked like bookends.

"You're welcome here, Father Williams. We want you to stay."

"No, Ben, we need a place of our own. We'll find some land and build, and we'll be out from underfoot before you know it."

Evan hadn't tried to disguise the fact that he was displeased with Ben Perkins for whisking his daughter halfway across the globe. Even though he was now reunited with Mary Ann, the words he spoke were edged with his disdain for the young man. Sarah felt sorry for Ben. All he had done was fall in love and follow his dream. What harm could there be in that?

Mary Ann had done a beautiful job of setting up house. Everywhere Sarah looked, she could see the love her sister had put into her home. Even though it was small, it was clean and comfortable. The curtains were embroidered to match the tablecloth. A handmade quilt covered the large bed in the corner, made from fabric that Sarah recognized as being from dresses Mary Ann had when she left home nine years before. She knew the material because she had helped Mary Ann hem those dresses. Plates lined the shelf in rows. It truly felt like a home, and while not filled with possessions, it was filled with love, and Sarah could sense her sister's happiness.

Early the next morning Sarah took a walk around the property. The dirt was reddish brown, and she bent down to touch it. It fell through her fingers like dust.

"I know exactly what you're thinking," Mary Ann said, coming up behind her. "You're wondering where the grass is."

"You're right," Sarah replied. "I'm sure you thought the same thing."

Mary Ann raised her shoulders. "We're in a different world now. Everything, from the land to the people, is different. But that doesn't mean it's bad."

"No, I don't think it's bad. I'm just wondering how long it will take me to get used to it." Sarah raised a hand to her head. The wind had blown several strands of dark hair out of her bun and into her face. "How long was it until you felt you truly belonged here?"

Mary Ann smiled. "Sometimes I still don't feel like I belong. I'm Welsh, through and through. But here in my home, with Ben and the children—that's where I belong." She glanced over at the house. "You could pick up this house and set it down anywhere in the world, be it in Utah or Africa, and I would be happy."

Sarah thought about that long after Mary Ann returned to the house. Her sister had truly made a life for herself, one that was not dependent on a country. Instead, she had surrounded herself with people she loved, and they comprised her world and her sense of belonging. Sarah needed to follow that example. She had been blessed to grow up in Wales, but now it was time for her to learn about new places and broaden the scope of her knowledge. She supposed she must do that by first learning English.

* * *

Cedar City, Utah
August, 1878

Sarah sighed and closed her book. "I don't think I'll ever learn this language. It's been three months, and I feel as ignorant as ever."

"Of course you'll learn English. But you need to start speaking it all the time," Mary Ann told her. "I suppose it doesn't help that we speak Welsh here at home. If you keep lapsing into Welsh every time you get frustrated, you will never learn."

"Can't I just keep taking Kate with me every time I go somewhere? She's picking up on things fast enough, and she can help me."

"You can't rely on Kate forever. You certainly can't take her to work with you."

Sarah had a new job helping Mrs. Davis, a woman in town, with her housework. She didn't enjoy the work particularly, but she wanted to make a contribution to the family now that her father had purchased land and a home was being built not too far from Mary Ann and Ben's.

"I know, you're right. But the language doesn't make any sense."

"You'll learn it, Sarah. I did."

"You've been here for nine years."

"And if you don't keep studying, soon you'll have been here nine years and not know a bit more than you do now."

Sarah nodded. It wasn't in her nature to complain, but here she was doing it again, despite her promise to her mother. She opened her primer book and began to read again, sounding out the letters and knowing she sounded terrible.

Sarah finished her lesson and set the book aside. Mentally straightening her shoulders, she told herself that she could do it. She knew she could.

PART THREE

THE MISSIONARIES

CHAPTER ELEVEN

Cedar City, Utah
December, 1878

"Mary Ann?" Ben called out as he stepped into the house and pulled the door shut behind him. Catherine came running up, her little feet slapping against the hard wood floor. Ben swung his daughter into his arms and called for his wife again.

"I'm right here," Mary Ann answered, coming from the back bedroom.

Ben crossed the room, Catherine still dangling from his arm. Mary Jane and Delia sat at the table, drawing chalk pictures on their slates. Sometimes he couldn't believe his good fortune, that he had three beautiful daughters and a loving, thoughtful wife. He smiled. In the spring there would be another child. Nothing could make him happier than he was at that moment.

"I have some news," he said, after kissing Catherine's forehead and sending her off to play. "I ran into a few of the brethren on my way home."

"And got to talking, I'm sure," Mary Ann interjected with a smile. "I thought you were a little late."

"I'm sorry," he said.

"I'm not nagging you," she explained. "I just missed you."

He stepped over and laid his hand on her arm. He had never gotten over the wonder of loving his wife even more now than he had the day he married her. He had heard other men express similar feelings, but had never believed them until it happened to him.

"What did the brethren have to say?"

"A few years ago, before President Young passed away, he met with some of the apostles, and they talked about sending some Saints over to the San Juan area to build a new settlement. But President Young died before anything was done about it. Now President Taylor has decided to press forward with the idea."

"San Juan? Where is that?"

"Straight east from here, about two hundred and fifty miles or so."

Mary Ann frowned. "Isn't that Indian territory?"

"Yes, it is, and that's partly why President Young wanted a settlement there, to act as a buffer between the Saints and the Indians. I've also heard tell of some outlaws who hide out in the area. There are Mormon settlements on all the other borders of Zion, but nothing down in that corner, and the brethren fear that we're leaving a back door open for the Indians and outlaws to come in and attack us—or at the very least, to cause trouble."

"But I thought all the Indians around here were friendly."

"They are, for the most part, as long as we keep with the Church policy and feed them, not fight them. But you never know when that might change."

Mary Ann shook her head. "I feel sorry for the Indians. I know I wouldn't like it if someone took over my land."

"That's part of the problem, right there. Remember what Kit Carson did?"

"Of course. He told the Indians that they all needed to move to the reservation."

"Well, some of the Indians aren't taking too kindly to that. There's been unrest, and the brethren want us to be prepared for whatever might happen."

"So they want to set up a Mormon town over there?"

"Yes, a strong one. President Taylor feels as President Young did, that it would help ensure our safety."

"That sounds like quite an undertaking."

"It would be. But it sounds exciting."

Mary Ann looked at Ben, surprise on her face. "Ben Perkins, are you thinking of going on this expedition?"

"It all depends on what the Lord wants me to do. If He wants me to stay here, I'll stay, but if He asks me to take part of this mission to the San Juan, I'll go. Think of it, Mary Ann. A chance to explore the territory, to go where no one else has been before." It sounded so right to him—he wanted her to feel that way too. "I'm not going to make any plans as of yet. We'll just wait and see what the Lord has in store for us."

She moved off to start dinner, but Ben remained where he was. He didn't know anything about the San Juan area other than what he had just told Mary Ann, but something inside seemed to tell him that's where he belonged.

* * *

Parowan, Utah
December, 1878

The Saints in the Southern Utah area crowded into the meetinghouse in Parowan for stake conference. Rumors had been circulating that a group of missionaries would be sent over to the San Juan, and an equal number of rumors had flown about who would go and who would stay behind. Ben sat tall in his seat, sure that he knew what was about to happen. It was no surprise to him when the names of the selected missionaries were read over the pulpit and his was one of them. Mary Ann, sitting to his left, gasped.

"I can't believe it," she said as they walked to their wagon. "I just can't believe it."

"Don't you want to go, Mary Ann?" he asked.

Her face was pale. "I'm just surprised, that's all. Of course, if that's where the Lord wants us, that's where we'll go." She took his arm and looked him hard in the eye. "Ben Perkins! Did you know we were going to be called? Did someone tell you?"

"No one told me, but I've felt for several days that we would be, ever since I told you about the plan."

They loaded the little girls into the wagon, then climbed in themselves, Mary Ann accepting some help from Ben. She placed a hand on her stomach.

"Do you know how soon they'll want us to leave?"

"I don't know. They didn't say."

"I can't imagine having a baby out on the trail somewhere."

He reached over and took her hand. "I wish I knew for sure, but I believe the child will be born here. Surely the brethren will give us more than a few months to get ready."

"I hope so." She looked away, toward the houses and trees they passed on their way out of Parowan.

"But we won't be alone," Ben continued. "You heard them read Hyrum's name too."

"I did." She smiled. "Your brother and his wife will be a good help to us, I'm sure."

Shortly after they arrived back in Cedar City, the Williams family came over to Ben and Mary Ann's house. They had been at the stake conference as well, and heard the announcement from the pulpit. Mary was in tears.

"We've only been reunited for such a short time, and now you're leaving again," she said, taking her daughter in her arms.

"San Juan is much closer than Wales, Mother," Mary Ann said with a laugh. "We'll see each other for holidays and birthdays."

"I know," Mary said with a sniff. "And I know this is what you're supposed to do. But you're taking away my grandchildren."

Evan reached out and shook Ben's hand. "Best of luck," he said. "May all go well."

"I believe it will," Ben said. "Now, it's a matter of finding out when we leave. We'll need to sell the house and get organized."

Mary Ann turned quickly to face her husband. "Sell the house?"

"Of course. We won't be living here anymore."

She sank into a chair. "You're right, of course. How silly of me. We'll need to sell the house." She looked around with an expression of loneliness that grabbed Ben's heart. He took her by the elbow and led her outside, then closed the door and wrapped his arms around her.

Her shoulders shook as the tears began to flow. "Ben, I'll be all right, I really will," she said into his shirt. "I just . . . when I thought about leaving the house—the house we worked so hard to build—"

"I know," he said, squeezing her a little closer. "It will be difficult to leave. But I'll build you another house, twice the size of this one."

"Twice?" Her voice was muffled.

"Okay, three times the size. And I'll build two barns. And we'll have two clotheslines and two—"

She laughed, pulling back to look at him. "Now you're just being silly."

"I'm serious. You shall have a new home. I'll build it however you like." He reached out a finger and wiped away a tear that rested on her cheek. Oh, how he hated to see her cry, especially when he was the cause of it. She didn't cry often, so when she did, he knew her heart was breaking.

"I told Sarah that my home was with you, regardless of where it was built, and I meant it. We'll go to the San Juan, and we'll make a new home for ourselves. And I will be happy there, I promise you, as long as you're there too."

Ben held his wife another precious moment, then they returned to the house, where the rest of the family sat discussing the great wilderness to the east and wondering what an Indian ate for breakfast. The children were sure it was pancakes, but the adults, not quite so sure.

CHAPTER TWELVE

Cedar City, Utah
April, 1879

Do you know when you're leaving, Mary Ann?" Sarah asked.

"No, but an exploring party left yesterday to find a trail for us to take. They aren't certain when they'll be back, but the baby will probably be here before we go." She rested her hand on her stomach, now larger than ever.

"I'm glad about that," Sarah said. "It would be terrible for you to leave us before we've had a chance to see the baby."

"Actually, I've been meaning to talk to you, Sarah," Mary Ann said. She leaned forward to take some of the pressure off her back. "Ben and I have been discussing it quite a bit. The trip will be difficult for us, with three small children and a new baby. We wondered if you'd consider coming with us to help me with the children as we travel."

"Oh!" Sarah blinked. She paused a moment, tracing the pattern on the tablecloth with her finger. "Well, if it means that I don't have to say goodbye to you so soon, yes, I will come."

"Thank you, Sarah! You don't know what a burden this lifts from me." Mary Ann's heart felt lighter at Sarah's words. "Truly, you've been an answer to prayer."

They talked for a few moments about what Sarah would need to do to get ready, then she rose. "I'd best get back to the house. Mother asked for help finishing some mending."

"I'll come with you," Mary Ann said. "I've some things to mend myself, and I'd much rather do it with company." She pushed herself up, placing both hands squarely on the table. "It gets harder to move every day!"

They gathered up the little girls and Mary Ann's sewing basket, then walked the short distance to the Williams' home. They were just entering the yard when a tall young man turned the corner onto their street. Mary Ann didn't pay him any heed until he drew closer and caught her attention. Something about him . . .

"Sarah, do you know him?" she asked quietly, closing the gate.

"No, I don't think so."

"He looks familiar." Suddenly Mary Ann realized who it was, and she unlatched the gate and ran through it, her skirt flapping behind her. She flung herself into his arms, throwing him off balance.

"Whoa there!" he said, returning her hug. "Are you going to bowl me over right here in the street?"

"I'm sorry. It's just so good to see you."

Sarah walked up slowly, a look of confusion on her face. "Mary Ann?"

"Sarah, don't you know who this is?" Mary Ann tucked her arm through the stranger's and turned him to face Sarah.

"She might not. It *has* been a while," he replied.

Sarah shook her head. "I'm sorry, I don't . . ." She took a step closer and looked him in the eye. "Thomas?"

He let out a great booming laugh. "Yes, little sister, it's me."

"I thought you were still in Australia."

"Well, as it turns out, I was on my way home to Wales when you sailed for America. Our ships must have passed each other on the ocean. When I got home, the neighbors told me where you'd gone. I had to save money for another passage, so I've been working for the last while. And now I'm here."

"Why didn't you write that you were coming?"

"And ruin the surprise?"

He had grown much taller since Mary Ann saw him last, and wore a full beard. It was no wonder Sarah didn't recognize him.

But his eyes were the same. Mary Ann would know those eyes anywhere.

"Come in," she said, taking his arm.

He looked up at the house. "I don't know if I'll be welcome," he said softly.

"Of course you will," she said with a tug on his elbow.

"After the way I left? What if Father doesn't wants to see me?"

"You'll have to face him sometime," Mary Ann told him. "Come."

Sarah took his other arm, and the two women led him into the Williams house. Mary sat at the table, her mending spread out in piles in front of her. Evan stacked wood at the fireplace. Neither of them glanced up at first.

"Sarah, did you borrow the sugar from Mary Ann?" Mary asked.

"I'm sorry, Mam. I forgot. But I have something you'll like better."

Mary turned, and her face grew white and slack. She narrowed her eyes. "No, it can't be."

Thomas took off his hat as he stepped farther into the room. "Hello, Mother."

Mary stood, knocking over the chair in her haste. "Thomas?"

"Yes, Mother. It's me."

She took the floor in three steps, then pulled her son into her arms. "I can't believe it," she said over and over again, not releasing her hold for several seconds.

Mary Ann went to her father's side. "It's Thomas, Father," she said.

"I know who it is," Evan replied. "I have eyes in my head."

Thomas wrapped his arm around Mary's shoulders and turned to face Evan. "Father?"

"Hello, Thomas." Evan nodded, a sharp bob of the head.

"It's good to see you." Thomas took a step forward and held out his hand, but Evan ignored it.

Thomas looked a little hurt, but kept talking, sounding hopeful. "I went home to Wales and found that you had left. I'm glad to finally catch up with you."

"Are you hungry?" Mary interjected.

"I'm all right for now, Mother. Thank you." Thomas looked at Evan. "It's been a long time," he added.

"Yes, indeed." Evan turned his back and finished stacking the wood, creating an elaborate pattern of short and long pieces.

"Tell us all about your travels," Mary Ann said, sinking into the chair Mary had vacated after first setting it to rights. "Mother wrote and told me about your shipwreck."

"It was very frightening," Thomas said off-handedly, not taking his eyes off his father. "We were lucky to have survived."

"Luck had nothing to do with it, boy," Evan said from the corner. "The prayers of your mother kept you alive."

"I don't doubt that," Thomas said. "I know you were all praying for me."

"Some more than others, perhaps," Evan said. "I believe I prayed for myself most of all."

"Sir?"

"First I prayed that I would be forgiven for chasing you away. Then I prayed to forgive you for leaving your mother and the small ones the way you did, especially with your mother in her condition."

"I don't understand," Thomas said, taking a step forward. "What condition?"

"Your mother was with child when you left."

Thomas' eyes darted over to his mother. "You were?"

Mary nodded.

"I'm sorry. I didn't know. Why didn't you say anything?"

"It's hardly something I could just talk about, Thomas."

"But I never would have left if I had known. And with Father gone. How did you manage?"

"We sold the house and started a bakery," Mary answered in a matter of fact voice. "You're back now, Thomas. That's all that matters."

"No, it's not." He knelt by her side and picked up her hand. "Can you ever forgive me? I've been irresponsible and selfish. I can't believe all that I left you to endure alone."

Mary reached out and touched her son's face. "I admit I struggled, Thomas. But there's one thing you can do that would make everything right again."

"Tell me. I'll do it."

"Trim your beard."

Thomas blinked. "What?"

Mary smiled. "It's far too bushy for your face."

Thomas rocked back on his heels. "I'll do better than that. I'll shave the whole thing off."

"Then I have nothing to complain about."

Thomas stood and faced his father. "And you, sir? What can I do to make things right?"

Evan studied the floor for several long seconds before lifting his head to look at Thomas. "You can forgive me for chasing you away," he said, his voice thick with emotion.

The two men embraced. Mary Ann could see tears in their eyes, but knew that neither one of them would admit to any such thing. They were far too much alike.

* * *

"Where's Ben?" Thomas asked a few hours later, after one of Mary's delicious dinners.

"He's out working on the farm," Mary Ann replied. "It's been a challenge for him, but he's never shirked from a challenge in his life. He's managed to make that soil produce beautifully."

"I didn't think I'd ever see Ben Perkins as a farmer," Thomas laughed.

"We didn't farm when we first got here," Mary Ann said while wiping crumbs from Delia's face. "He found a job on the Union Pacific Railroad, along with his brother Hyrum. He's also helped build several of the buildings around here, including the temple in Manti."

"Impressive," Thomas said. "I'd like to see it someday."

"It's beautiful," Mary Ann told him. "There's another temple in St. George that's much closer."

Thomas sat back. "It's so good to see you again, Mary Ann. You always were pretty, but I think the years have made you beautiful."

She blushed. "I can't possibly be beautiful in this condition, Thomas," she protested, placing a hand on her stomach.

"I think you are. And I can hardly wait to hear all your news and get reacquainted."

"I don't know how much time there will be for such things," she said. "We'll be leaving for the San Juan in the fall."

"San Juan?"

"Ben was called as a missionary to go and settle that area," she explained.

"You're leaving just as I get here?"

"I'm not sure when we're leaving. An exploring party left yesterday to go and scout out a road. Once they've chosen the best route, then we'll be able to decide a departure date. Sarah will help with the children on the journey."

"So there's not a road where you're going?"

"That whole area is unsettled. We'll have to build roads, no matter which route we take."

Thomas nodded thoughtfully. "It sounds exciting. Is there room on this journey for one more?"

"You'd go with us?" Sarah asked hopefully.

"I believe I would. I can't send my two best girls out into the wilderness alone."

"We'll hardly be alone," Mary Ann said. "Over fifty families were called to go."

"Be that as it may, I'd still like to come along and help out. What say you?"

"I would love it," Mary Ann said, and Sarah nodded.

"Then it's settled. I'm coming too."

"You can't all go." Mary placed a dish in the basin with a clatter. "I can't send all my children off into the desert to face the wild Indians out there."

"I won't be staying there, Mother," Sarah reminded her. "And it sounds like Thomas would be coming back as well, wouldn't you?" She nudged her brother's elbow.

"Of course," Thomas assured their mother.

"Well, you'd better," she replied, tying on her apron with an extra tug at the strings. "But I don't like this one bit. You've only been home for a few hours, and already you're planning to leave again."

"I make you a promise," Thomas said, coming to his feet. "I'm never going to leave the family again. I'll see my sisters safely to the San Juan, and then I'm coming right back. I swear it."

CHAPTER THIRTEEN

Cedar City, Utah
October, 1879

George Hobbs stopped by the other night," Mary Ann said. She placed a glass of water on the table for Sarah, then took a seat. "Ben worked with him clearing land a while back, and he's been a friend to us. He was on the exploring party that went to the San Juan."

"He's a good man," Ben offered from across the table.

"Did he tell you anything about the journey?" Sarah leaned forward, her eyes alight with interest.

"He did, enough to have me worried."

"What did he say?"

Mary Ann rubbed her temples. "He says that the exploring party took the southern route by way of Kanab, and then over the Colorado River on Lee's Ferry. They went through a place called Bitter Springs Desert, where they sometimes went for fifty miles without water."

"Fifty miles?"

Mary Ann nodded. "They lost about a third of their cattle crossing the desert, and suffered for thirst themselves. And they ran into Indians!"

"Truly?"

"He said the Indians demanded a toll for crossing their land. We're not going to be able to get a large group of people to the

San Juan that way, Sarah." Mary Ann shook her head. "Between the lack of water and the Indians . . . it's just not possible. George and his group were lucky to have made it at all."

"Up around the north is still a trip of over four hundred miles," Ben supplied. "Silas Smith, the leader of this expedition, thinks that if we went straight across, we'd cut our traveling time in half."

Sarah straightened in her chair. "But I heard someone say that the land drops off in a cliff."

"Silas says there has to be a way down the cliff," Ben said. "In fact, George was telling me that down south of Escalante there's a notch at the top. One of the men thinks we could widen it a bit with some blasting powder and get through."

"Has anyone else been down there?" Sarah asked.

"It's never been explored. It will be a rough trip, but it should only last six weeks, and then we'll be in San Juan." He walked over to the cradle. Naomi's eyes opened, and she screwed up her mouth, the first sign that she was going to cry. He bent down and scooped her up, holding her close against his chest. "We have a good life here, but out in San Juan, we'll have the chance to do some real good, to make a difference."

Mary Ann shrugged. "I'm going because you are, Ben. But couldn't the Lord use us just as well here?"

"He can use us any old place. But sometimes He needs us to go somewhere else so we can do an even greater work." Ben rubbed the baby's back as he swayed from side to side.

"I'm a little nervous after hearing what George had to say," Mary Ann admitted. "But I have faith in our leaders. And I have faith in you."

Ben was so tender with their little girls—it brought tears to her eyes sometimes. His lips were pressed against the baby's soft head and she wished she had a way to capture that moment forever. Her fears paled as she looked at her husband. She might not know what lay in their future, but she knew that no matter what happened, Ben would always keep her and the girls safe.

CHAPTER FOURTEEN

Cedar City, Utah
October 22, 1879

The two Perkins wagons stood in front of their home, loaded and ready to go. The early dawn light brought no warmth, and Mary Ann reached into the back of the wagon to make sure her three girls were warmly wrapped. The baby she held close to her chest.

She turned and took a step toward her house. It looked lonely. The new owners would be moving in later that week, and she knew her home would be cared for. But her heart broke to leave it. Ben had worked hard to build it, and she had spent hours making it a home—sewing curtains, planting the garden. She had always thought she would live there forever. She turned back toward the wagon, unable to look at the house any more. If she dwelled on it a single minute longer, she would lose all her nerve.

Sarah came up the street, a small bag in her hand. Ben had picked up the rest of her things at the Williams' house the night before. She looked cheerful, despite the early hour.

"Oh, Sarah, I don't know if I can do this," Mary Ann said as her sister drew closer. "We've worked so hard to make a life for ourselves here."

"You can do it again," Sarah said. "You're taking everything you need with you—your heart and your husband's hands."

Mary Ann smiled. "You're right. Leaving just seems so final, so impossible."

"Mother's been crying ever since you left last night," Sarah said. "It was hard on her to say goodbye."

"Mother cried?" Mary Ann blinked. "I don't think I've ever seen her cry."

"She's been known to do it once or twice," Sarah said. "In fact, she cried the morning you left to come to America."

"I didn't know that," Mary Ann said softly.

"She didn't want you to know."

Ben came striding up to the wagon. "The rest of the livestock is corralled until Mr. Davis gets here," he said to Mary Ann. "He gave us a fair price. Good morning, Sarah."

"Good morning, Brother Perkins."

Ben clapped his hands together and rubbed them for warmth. "I believe we're all set to go. Where's Thomas?"

"Here," Thomas said, coming up behind them. "Mother had a hard time letting me out the door. Thinks I'll get shipwrecked again or something. I tried to explain to her that there's no ocean where we're going."

Thomas threw his bag into the back of the second wagon and climbed up into the driver's seat, Sarah beside him. Ben helped Mary Ann up onto the seat of the lead wagon and then took the reins.

"Ho for the San Juan!" Ben shouted, urging his team forward.

"Ho for the San Juan!" Thomas echoed, and both wagons lurched down the street.

Mary Ann wouldn't look back. She promised herself that. She wouldn't look at her home. She wouldn't glance down the street toward her parents' house. She would look only forward, to the new life ahead. But it was hard. She closed her eyes tightly, preferring not to see anything at all.

* * *

The wagons rolled until they reached the spot where they would meet the other missionaries who were coming with them.

Sarah glanced around and saw that Ben's brother Hyrum and his wife Rachel were already there, along with Kumen and Mary Jones. After a quick headcount, the wagons fell into line, and they headed north toward Parowan and Paragonah, picking up more missionaries along the way. The rattling of the wagon was already getting to Sarah, but she held on to the edge of her seat and pressed her lips firmly together.

As they drew close to the six mile mark, Sarah heard a voice calling out from behind them. Thomas slowed the wagon as George Decker brought his horse alongside.

"Can I talk to you a minute?" he asked Thomas.

Thomas nodded and pulled the wagon off to the side of the road. Up ahead, Ben turned and noticed, pulling his wagon over too. He hopped down to see what the trouble was.

"I could sure use your help with the livestock," George said to Thomas. "We've got some skittish animals, and we'll be picking up several more along the way, to the tune of eighteen hundred head. We'll be better off once we're out in the open, but the animals are going to be out of control when we pass through the towns. I need a few more hands on horseback."

"If you're willing to go, Thomas, we'll be all right," Ben said.

"I'd like to help," Thomas replied, sliding off the wagon seat.

"I've got a spare horse you can use. She's over there," George said, and Thomas turned to follow him.

"Sarah, move over, please." Ben motioned her to the driver's side of the seat, putting the reins in her hands. "This is your wagon now."

"What?" Sarah looked down at the long leather strips in her hands. "I've never driven a team in my life!"

Ben grinned. "No better time to start. Let's get going. We'll be left behind."

He climbed back up on his wagon seat and urged his horses forward. Thomas looked back and laughed.

"Thomas, this isn't funny," Sarah called out, trying to untangle the reins that had somehow bunched into a knot. She was furious with him. "You should be up here driving this wagon!"

"Would you rather herd eighteen hundred head of cattle?" Thomas asked, retracing his steps to the wagon.

"No," she admitted. She took a deep breath. "How do I get these things going?"

Thomas talked her through it, then mounted George Decker's horse and rode off. Sarah shook the reins, and the horses began to move. Terrified for the first three miles, her hands clenched so tightly on the lines that her knuckles hurt. What if the horses got it into their heads to take off on their own, and she went bumping through the desert on a runaway wagon? What if they stopped walking and she couldn't make them go forward? It took a while for her to realize that the horses knew what they were doing, and all she had to do was let them know that someone—anyone—held the reins.

They stopped at Parowan to meet the other missionaries. They had come twenty miles—fourteen of that with Sarah driving—and so far, they were none the worse. Ben came back to see how Sarah fared.

"How are you, Sarah?"

"I'm quite well, Brother Perkins. How are you?" She couldn't help but be cool toward him. She was not amused at having the wagon handed over to her in that fashion.

He laughed. "I see you haven't lost your dignity, even on top of that wagon box. Good for you. Good for you."

Thomas rode up to the wagon and tied his horse's reins to the back. "Some of the other help has arrived, and we're taking shifts with the animals," he explained. "I go back in a few hours."

"Thomas Williams," she fumed, "take these reins!"

"You're doing very well, Sarah, and it's not a bad idea for you to learn how to handle a team," Thomas told her seriously. "What if something happened to Ben or me?"

Sarah nodded. She could see the wisdom in what he said, even though she didn't like it much. "Very well, then," she said, lifting her chin. "I shall consider this my wagon."

A few moments later, Sarah caught sight of another woman driver. She sat confidently at the head of her team of horses, holding the reins as though it were second nature.

"We aren't leaving just yet, are we, Thomas?"

"I don't think so. I believe we're waiting for a few more wagons."

"I'll be right back." She handed him the reins and climbed down, straightening her skirt as she walked.

"Hello," she said to the sister perched high on the wagon seat. "My name is Sarah Williams."

"I'm Ann Rowley," the woman replied. Her accent easily defined her as British.

"You must be from England. I'm from Wales," Sarah said.

"Yes, I thought so," Sister Rowley replied. "It's good to meet you. My husband is over there." She nodded her head to indicate a man with a full, dark beard rethreading the harnesses over the backs of the oxen on his wagon.

"I must confess, I was so relieved to see another woman driving, I had to come meet you," Sarah said. "My brother and my brother-in-law forced me into taking over a team."

Sister Rowley laughed. "They did, did they?"

"Yes. I believe they thought I wouldn't do it."

"I hope you're proving them wrong."

"I think I am."

Brother Rowley approached just then.

"Samuel," Sister Rowley said, "This is Sarah Williams. Sarah, this is my husband, Samuel."

"It's a pleasure, Sister Williams," he said. "Oh, it looks like we're about to pull out."

"I'll see you again soon, Sarah," Sister Rowley said as she gathered up her reins. Sarah walked quickly back to her own wagon and climbed into the seat, grateful that at least she was not the only lady making a spectacle of herself.

* * *

Ben laughed as he climbed up on his wagon seat.

"What's so funny?" Mary Ann asked, shifting Naomi in her arms.

"Your sister is angry at me for making her drive the wagon. She's quite a spitfire, isn't she?"

"Only when provoked. I see you've been provoking her."

"It's for her own good." Ben looked over at his wife. "What would you do if I handed you these reins?"

"I'd most likely hand them right back."

Ben laughed. "You Williams girls. You're a handful, the whole lot of you."

The caravan continued on, picking up wagons here and there, until it reached nearly two miles long. As they passed through the small communities that dotted their path, Saints turned out to stand along the roadside and cheer them on. It did Ben's heart good to see faithful members and to know that he and the other missionaries would be in their prayers.

They camped that night at Paragonah Fields. Sarah and Thomas slept in the supply wagon, arranging the cooking pots and other needed items to make room. Thomas settled in the front of the wagon, but Sarah preferred the back. Mary Jane decided to sleep with Aunt Sarah, so they made a bed for her as well. Ben, Mary Ann, and the other three girls bedded down in the first wagon. The sounds of crickets and howling animals filtered in through the canvas wagon cover, making them all a little nervous. But soon the sounds that had frightened them became friendly and lulled them to an exhausted sleep. Sarah drove the wagon in her dreams, white-knuckled, the sound of the wheels crunching the road beneath her constant in her ears until she woke up the following morning.

CHAPTER FIFTEEN

Little Creek Canyon
October 25, 1879

You'd better let me take over, Sarah," Thomas said, reaching for the reins. "Look at the road up ahead."

Sarah squinted her eyes and made out a sharp incline, the first of many leading up a switchback that would take them to the top of Little Creek Canyon.

"I think you're right." She passed the lines over to him and wiped her forehead with her handkerchief. She had grown completely comfortable with the team, but the canyon had proven tricky, and she was more than happy to let Thomas take over. Thank goodness it was his day off from livestock duty.

The horses plodded on, oblivious to the steep grade. But Sarah hung on to the edge of her seat, willing herself not to slide off. Her hands began to hurt after a few minutes, and she inwardly laughed at herself for being silly. She let go and allowed herself to relax. It was only a steep road, after all. She wouldn't think about the danger, she'd pretend that everything was just fine. She swallowed. The knot in her throat didn't believe the story. She didn't open her eyes until Thomas said they were almost at the summit.

The wagons pulled to a stop at the top of Little Creek Canyon and prepared to make camp for the night. The first task was to unhitch the team. Ben and Thomas had done it alone the first couple of nights out, but Sarah wanted to be as useful as possible.

"Thomas will you show me how to unhook the harnesses?"

He raised his eyebrows but didn't question her. A moment later, her hands full of leather and metal, she turned to see Ben approaching.

"What are you doing?" he asked.

"If I'm going to drive the horses, I might as well know how to take care of them."

She saw a smile begin to twitch at the corners of his mouth as he nodded. "Very wise." He gave Thomas a wink as he walked away.

"Why did he wink at you?" Sarah asked Thomas.

"We're very proud of you, Sarah. You're quite a woman."

He finished showing Sarah how to loosen all the buckles and straps, then brought out brushes and blankets for the horses and showed her how to use them. By the time they finished, her cheeks were bright red with exertion, and her hair flew every which direction, but she felt satisfied with a job well done. When she stopped to examine her feelings, she found that she felt happier than she had in a long time.

* * *

The fire had burned low, and many of the pioneers had gone to bed. But some still remained, sitting on the fallen logs that circled the fire ring and talking about the day.

"I think we'll arrive before Christmas," one of the men commented.

"I would like to get our house built before the really heavy snows start to fall," said another.

Ben sat with his feet stretched toward the fire. The night had grown chilly, and he was enjoying the feel of the heat through his boots. He looked across the diminishing flames to where Sarah sat and had to stifle a laugh.

She certainly looked a sight. Her cheeks were rosy, and her hair had come loose from her bun, framing her face and making her a picture. She was pretty—in a different way than Mary Ann, but pretty nonetheless.

Mary Ann came and sat down by him a moment later, and he scooted over a bit to make room for her on the log. "The children are finally asleep," she said. "I thought they would never settle down."

"It must be hard for them to sit still for so long," Ben replied. "They're used to running free."

"I wish we could let them walk a bit each day, but it's far too dangerous with the steep slopes." She tried to stifle a yawn behind her hand, but it didn't work.

"When we camp tomorrow night, let's encourage them to run around and look for firewood. That's useful, and it should help them tire out."

The two of them stood a moment later and walked off to their wagon. Ben turned and looked back. Sarah still sat at the fire, looking more tired than Ben had ever seen her. He opened his mouth to speak to her, then changed his mind and went to bed.

* * *

Bear Valley Creek
October 28, 1879

Three days later, the wagons pulled in to Bear Valley Creek. Sarah climbed down from the wagon and rinsed her handkerchief in the cold water, then wiped it across her face. Dust filled the air, churned up by the feet of so many animals, and it clung to her cheeks and forehead. She tried to remember what it was like to immerse herself in a warm tub. Even though they had only been on the trail a few days, a bath seemed like a distant memory.

Thomas knelt beside her and took a long drink. "This is good," he proclaimed.

"It feels good, too," she replied, wiping her face again. "I'm half-tempted to jump in headfirst."

The missionaries made themselves busy setting up camp, then refilled their barrels with water from the nearby creek. Beautiful mountain peaks rose around them, and Sarah thought it one of the prettiest places she'd seen since coming to Utah. She wondered if she was a little bit prejudiced, though—it was the nearest thing to Wales she'd seen. She'd have to learn to appreciate Utah for its own beauty instead of comparing it to Wales all the time.

They pulled into Panguitch at the first of November, where they were joined by another group of missionaries. It seemed that everywhere they went, they picked up a wagon here and another wagon there. All the missionaries were in good spirits and ready to face the road ahead of them.

Or, the lack of road.

Mary Ann had told Sarah that, according to George Hobbs, much of the way would be difficult, as there *were* no roads. Sarah mentally squared her shoulders. They would face that when the time came. In the meantime, she still found it exciting to sleep under the stars, and the newness of the journey had not worn off. There would be time enough to worry later.

They passed through Red Canyon and refilled their water barrels at Sweetwater Spring. It was a beautiful spot, quiet and secluded. The fresh water roiled up out of the ground and tasted wonderful. Sarah drank her fill, then washed her face and hands. A breeze kicked up and dried the moisture on her cheeks, cooling her down. She raised her face to the sun and enjoyed the warmth for a moment before turning to her other chores. Sometimes it just felt good to be alive.

* * *

Escalante Mountains
November 8, 1879

Sarah swayed back and forth by the fire, a fussy Naomi swaddled in her arms. Mary Ann had a hard time getting the other girls to settle down in their wagon. Sarah couldn't help but feel sorry for the little girls. She didn't want to sleep either. The day had been long and hard, at times frightening.

They had come up the Sweetwater Canyon into the Escalante Mountains, and run into snow. It was deep and slick, icy in some patches, and the teams were struggling to keep their footing. Thomas had the reins, and even with his skill, had a hard time encouraging the horses to keep moving. Near the crest, the grade became so steep that they had to put four horses on each wagon to make it to the top, then go back to collect the wagons left at the bottom.

Sarah held her breath the whole time during that last bit of the ascent, letting it out a little at a time, then inhaling sharply each time one of the horse hooves slipped. As soon as they reached the top, she ran over to Mary Ann's wagon to see how her sister and the little girls had fared. The girls had been frightened, looking out the back of the wagon to see the ground dropping sharply out from under them. Mary Ann did her best to calm them, but it took a good hour before they felt safe again, and now they refused to sleep.

Sarah didn't mind watching Naomi while Mary Ann struggled with the older girls. The baby was sweet and delicate, only five months old, and an angel. Sarah paused a moment in her rocking to tuck the blanket more firmly around her niece, then began to sway again. The baby's eyes were growing heavy, and it would only be a matter of time before she dropped off.

Ben came up to the fire out of the darkness. "The livestock has all been bedded down," he said. "The horses were a little skittish tonight."

"So are your daughters," Sarah said, nodding toward Ben and Mary Ann's wagon. "Mary Ann's having a hard time putting them to sleep."

"I'll go and see what I can do to help." He walked off in the direction of the wagon, only to return a moment later. "The girls have gone to sleep, and Mary Ann right along with them. It certainly has been a hard day." He reached out his arms. "I'll take the baby. Thank you for putting her to sleep."

"My pleasure." Sarah gently transferred the sleeping bundle into Ben's arms, making sure that the blankets stayed snug around her. Then she wandered off to the wagon she shared with Thomas and three hundred pounds of flour, feeling alone—even though she was surrounded by people.

She wondered what it would be like to have a husband and children—Mary Ann seemed utterly content. Had Sarah left behind all chance for love in Wales? Was her choice to come to America also, by default, a choice to take care of other people's children, but never her own?

She frowned at her foolishness. She wasn't an old maid yet. But late at night, when the loneliness set in, it was hard to remember that she had plenty of time—especially when faced with the prospect of snuggling up with a cold sack of flour.

CHAPTER SIXTEEN

Escalante, Utah
November, 1879

Mary Ann reached up with both hands and attempted to smooth her hair back into its bun as they drove into Escalante.

"You look beautiful," Ben told her, glancing at his wife out of the corner of his eye.

"I look a fright," she said. "It's been days since we've been in an actual town. I'll probably scare the people out of their wits."

"I doubt that," Ben said. "I'll wager you're the most beautiful woman they've ever laid eyes on."

They pulled their wagons to a stop and clambered down. Mary Ann lifted the little girls out of the wagon and told them that they could run around, but only if they stayed in sight. Mary Jane took Catherine's hand very solemnly and told her mother that she would take care of her sister. Delia followed, a silent shadow.

Mary Ann paused in the shade of the wagon and rubbed her head. The glaring sun had bored into her eyes for most of the day, and she had a headache. The shade brought some relief, but she knew it wouldn't last.

"How are you faring, Mary Ann?" Sarah asked, coming up beside her.

"Well enough," she replied, "although my head hurts."

"Perhaps this break will help," Sarah said.

Ben came out of the general store with a sack over his arm. "I bought some pork and molasses. This should see us through until we reach the San Juan."

Thomas was nowhere in sight when Sarah returned to their wagon, so she walked down the row a bit until she reached the Rowley's two rigs. Samuel wasn't there, but Ann was busy in the back slicing some bread for her children.

"Hello!" she called out to Sarah. "I'll be out in a minute."

Sarah walked to the front of Sister Rowley's wagon and rubbed the horses' ears. A moment later, Ann joined her.

"This one is Prince, and this one is Polly," Ann said, pointing out the horses to Sarah.

"They look like nice horses."

"They are. They've been very patient and gentle. My children James and Hannah are riding our other two horses to herd the cattle."

"I don't understand horses very well yet," Sarah said, "but I'm learning."

"I've kept an eye on you, Sarah Williams. You're doing very well indeed."

Samuel returned to the wagons with his sack of provisions. "How do you do, Sister Williams?"

"Quite well, thank you."

"I've heard that from here on out, we're making our own road."

"I've heard that as well. It should be . . . interesting."

Samuel laughed. "Yes, it should."

The call came to move out, and Sarah walked back to her rig and climbed up. The wagons rolled on, changing their heading from east to south. The two Perkins wagons pulled in behind the Rowleys, and Sarah had the opportunity to see how Brother Rowley's oxen fared, compared to the horses. The large animals frightened her a little bit, but she could see now that they were hard-working and diligent.

The land south of Escalante was hard and dry, and for the first little bit the wagons progressed with ease, although no track laid ready for them. After a mile, the party hit Alvey Wash, which they would follow to the south.

Night drew near, and the group decided to make camp. The children went to sleep early, so Sarah wandered over to the Rowley's wagon, where Ann and Samuel greeted her warmly.

"What do you think of Utah?" Samuel asked her after a moment of chit-chat.

"It's very different from Wales," she said. "It's taking me a little while to get used to it, and to the language."

"You're doing very well," Ann told her.

"Thank you. At first, I thought I would never learn English. But it's getting easier, and I'm not looking for grass anymore."

"What?" Ann asked.

"When I first got here, I couldn't believe how brown and dry everything was. I kept expecting to see grass."

"Up in the northern part of Utah, it's much greener," Samuel told her. "It doesn't look like Wales, but it's certainly greener than here."

"Where are you from?" Sarah asked.

"I'm from Worcester, and Ann's from Nottingham."

"And why did you come to America?"

"To be with the Saints, of course," Samuel answered with surprise in his voice. "Isn't that why you came?"

"I'm not a Mormon. I came here to be close to my family."

"I'm surprised you aren't a member, Sarah. You have the spirit in your eyes," Ann said.

"The spirit?"

"Yes, a portion of the light that Heavenly Father gives to His children. You may not be a member, but you are one of His chosen daughters."

Sarah thought on that for a long time after she went to bed. Thomas had long since been asleep on his side of the wagon, and she could hear his snores over the wall of flour that divided the wagon front and back. She lay on her side, staring out the back at the stars. What did that mean, to have the spirit in your eyes? And why did she feel Ann had paid her a great compliment when she said that?

* * *

Alvey Wash
November, 1879

Sarah's fingers were stiff with cold the next morning as she harnessed the horses. She stopped working for a moment and clapped her hands together, trying to warm them up so they would work properly.

"Good morning," Samuel Rowley called out, approaching the wagon.

"Good morning," she replied.

"The mineral content in this area must be very high," he said. "Did you try any of the water from the wash? It's so hard, we couldn't cook beans or peas in it."

"We had gruel for dinner and couldn't taste the water."

"You're lucky, then. Where's Brother Perkins? I promised to let him use some axle grease."

"He's over at the other wagon."

The rest of the morning's preparations went smoothly, and soon it was time to move on. The pioneers followed Alvey Wash down to Ten Mile Spring. The land was cut across by numerous gashes of canyons ten miles apart, almost exactly—hence the names of the landmarks they encountered.

"It almost looks like God took a ruler and measured this part of the land before He created it," Thomas chuckled.

"Why did He do that, do you think?" Sarah asked.

"I don't mean He really did measure it," Thomas said.

"I know you were joking, but I'm serious. Look around us. We come from Wales, where everything is green and fresh. The mountains are gentle and sloping, the air is humid, and there's a more peaceful feel. Here, the land is harsh. The sun glares down on us, the air is hot and dry, and I feel a sense of challenge in this land, a need to survive. Why did God make the two lands so different? Why didn't He make the world all the same?"

Thomas laughed. "You're a poet, Sarah."

"Only when I speak Welsh. Now, what is the answer to my question?"

"I don't know." He looked off to the hills that surrounded them as they descended the canyon. "Perhaps God loves variety. He doesn't have just one favorite kind of climate or terrain. So, in order to create a world that contained all His favorites, it had to be varied from one place to the other." He fell quiet again for a moment, then added, "Maybe that's why people are all so different from each other, too. When I was in Australia, I met some Aborigines. They're a very dark people. I guess they're like Australian Indians. They look different and live differently than we do, but they were some of the kindest people I've met. I can see that they're God's children, just like we are."

The wagon tipped sharply downward as they reached the last stretch before the end of the canyon, and they didn't speak for several minutes except for necessary words. When the wagon leveled out again, Sarah asked, "What is it like in Australia?"

"Very different from Wales. It's dry, like it is out here, and the ground is dusty and sandy. It's hot."

"Did you like it?"

"I liked it a lot, but I missed home. And Mother's cooking."

"I'm glad you came back, Thomas." She reached out and put a hand on her brother's arm.

"I am too. In many ways, I wish I'd never left."

* * *

Twenty Mile Wash
Mid-November, 1879

The wagons rolled in to Twenty Mile Wash, and Ben pulled his team to a stop. He looked back to the second wagon. Thomas was on break from his cattle-driving shift and held the reins loosely in his left hand. Sarah was nowhere to be seen.

"Did you lose your sister?" Ben yelled.

"She's in the back lying down," Thomas replied.

Ben slid down from the seat and walked to the back of the second wagon. He stuck his head inside to see Sarah lying down, her head resting on a flour sack.

"Are you all right?"

She opened her eyes. "Yes. The sun is a little bright, and I have a headache."

"Mary Ann doesn't feel well either. I suppose both of you are sensitive to the glare."

"Does she need help?" Sarah started to sit up, but Ben held up a hand.

"She's all right. She says she just needs to get out of the wagon and walk around for a while. You can rest."

Ben helped Thomas unhitch the teams, then went to check on his wife. She sat on a blanket on the ground, holding Naomi, watching the three other little girls chase each other around the wagon.

"Sarah's down with a headache. How are you feeling?"

Mary Ann smiled up at her husband. "Better. It feels good to be sitting on something that's not moving."

"I know how you feel." Ben squatted down on his heels next to her and reached out to touch Naomi's cheek. She reached up and grabbed his finger.

"Very smart girl," he said. "Are you going to be as smart as your mother and aunt?"

Naomi grinned and tried to stick his finger in her mouth.

"Oh, no, you don't. My hands are dirty." Ben pulled his hand out from his daughter's grasp.

* * *

Finding clear patches of land for the wagons to pass through became increasingly harder. It took days to get to Thirty Mile Hollow, then on to Forty Mile Camp. Ben's shoulders were weary from hour after hour of holding the reins. Every so often he had to leave his wagon to help clear a spot up ahead so they could continue. Wielding shovels and picks, the men would chop the trees that stood in their way, sometimes pushing boulders aside with their shoulders. Each night when they camped, Ben would pull out his map and mark how far they'd come, but some nights he wondered why he even made the effort when the progress was so slight that any mark on the map would be too small to see.

At last they pulled into Forty Mile Spring, their animals coming to rest after a long weary pull. Several wagons sat waiting for them.

"It's the rest of our group!" someone called out. Ben craned his neck to see. Sure enough, many of the wagons were filled with provisions, and he saw Silas Smith walking forward to greet them.

That night they held a camp meeting. Silas introduced the newcomers to the rest of the company, saying, "And this is Platte D. Lyman. He brought these good Saints all the way from Oak City to join us."

A thin man with a serious face and moustache raised his hand. "It's good to be here."

Ben had to admire the new addition to their group—the journey from Oak City must have been difficult.

The mood in the camp was merry that night. Some of the missionaries had brought instruments with them, and they played music while the others danced.

Ben couldn't help himself. Even though he felt tired, the music got to him, and his feet began to tap. It had been too long since he had been to a real dance. He got up and performed a Welsh jig, his feet flying in the familiar steps and patterns he had danced so many times as a young man. He was still a young man, at that! He found no reason to believe thirty-five was old.

He glanced over and saw a smile twitching around the corners of Mary Ann's mouth, and his daughters' eyes were wide. "Didn't know I could do that, did you?" he asked Caroline. She shook her head, not removing her thumb from her mouth.

"Your mother and I used to dance together, back in Wales," he said. "Sarah, do you mind watching the girls for a moment?"

Mary Ann handed the baby over to her sister, and Ben took his wife in his arms. Round and round they went until Mary Ann laughed breathlessly.

"It's been so long," she said, gasping. "I can't dance like I used to."

"You've never looked better," he told her, swinging her around again. He loved the touch of color that sprang to her cheeks, the merriment in her laugh. If nothing else came from their journey into the wilderness, he'd be forever grateful for that moment under the stars.

* * *

Forty-Mile Camp
Mid-November, 1879

"We can't go any farther," Ben announced to Thomas, Mary Ann, and Sarah the next morning. "I just spoke with Silas Smith and Platte Lyman. Apparently the land is impassible from here on out."

"But didn't the exploring party come this way?" Mary Ann asked.

"They didn't have eighty wagons with them, nor did they have eighteen hundred head of cattle."

Mary Ann nodded.

"So, what will happen now?" Thomas asked.

"I don't know. We'll have to wait and see." Ben couldn't believe they'd come all that distance, just to be stopped. There had to be a way.

George Hobbs came wandering by their wagon that afternoon. He looked tired and worried.

"George, it's good to see you," Ben greeted him.

"Likewise." George took his hat off and nodded toward Mary Ann. "Sister Perkins."

"George, have you met my sister-in-law, Sarah Williams?" Ben asked. "And this is my brother-in-law, Thomas Williams."

George stepped forward and shook Thomas's hand after nodding at Sarah.

"What brings you over?" Ben asked. "A hankering for some of Mary Ann's pie?"

"I would travel a distance for some of your pie, Sister Perkins, but I'm here for a different reason today," George said.

"That's just as well, Brother Hobbs. I haven't figured out a way to make it in the wilderness," Mary Ann replied with a smile.

"Have a seat, George."

Both men sat on a log that Ben had placed near their wagons as a bench. "Well, I guess you've heard that the path from here on out is extremely rough."

"Yes, we heard that."

"Jens Neilson is sending me and some of the other men on an exploring party to see if there's a better way to get to the Colorado River. We'll be leaving in the morning."

"Who's going with you?"

"William Hutchings, Kumen Jones, and George Lewis."

Ben nodded. "All good men."

"Yes, they are. We should get along well. The reason I'm here is I would like to ask you to keep an eye on my rig for me, if you don't mind. I pulled it up just over there." He nodded off to the right.

"We can do that."

"Thanks. That takes a load off my mind." George stood up. "I'll be taking the bay horse with me, but the rest will need to stay here."

"We'll see to it, George." Ben rose and shook his friend's hand. "I wish you luck."

George looked off into the distance. "I can't help but feel we'll be taking the route we originally chose. I've been over this ground before, on the first exploring party in April. I think this is the only way to go."

"It never hurts to look things over another time."

"You're right about that, Ben. I'd rather be wrong than waste precious time." He squinted up at the sky. "Who knows how long we have until the snow flies. Those clouds are getting heavy."

Ben looked up too. "With any luck, we'll be snug in our new homes in the San Juan before it builds up."

George nodded to the ladies again and went on his way. Ben watched him for a moment, then turned his gaze back to the sky. The breeze picked up with a chilling gust. He didn't know how to read the weather, but even to his untrained eye, those clouds looked like snow.

CHAPTER SEVENTEEN

Forty-Mile Camp
Late November, 1879

Ho the camp!"

Sarah lifted her head from the fire, where she was adding beans to boiling water. She shielded her eyes from the sun and could make out four men on horseback.

"Mary Ann! Brother Perkins! The scouts are back!"

Ben scooted out from under the wagon, where he had been working on an axle. He dusted himself off and looked in the direction Sarah indicated. "Sure enough, there's George Hobbs. I wonder what news they've brought us."

A young boy ran up to their camp site a half hour later. "Brother Smith says to gather for a meeting!" He didn't stop but continued on his way, shouting the news to every family.

When all had assembled, the scouts gave their report. Sarah listened with interest to everything said, trying to imagine a land more rough than the one they had already been through.

"I say it can't be done," one man called out after hearing what the scouts had to say. Many others added their voices to his, saying that they should all just turn back and go home.

"And I say it *can* be done," George Hobbs said. He stood before the group, holding his hat in his hands. "We brought tools with us, and we're all hard workers. The Lord called us to this mission, and I say we go as planned."

"But the terrain is too rough," said another.

Sarah listened to the murmurs of the people around her. They were discouraged. "I feel like we've been misled," said one man behind her. "First they tell us there's a way, and now they say there's not?"

"Hush," said the man's wife. "Let's hear them out."

George Hobbs was still speaking. "If we turned back every time we ran into something hard, there would be no Church."

"I agree with George," Andrew Schow called out. "Rueben Collett and I were there. We'd have to do some blasting to get through that rock, but then it's on to the river and away we go. Let's move forward."

The discussion continued for several more minutes. Silas Smith looked worried, and Sarah wondered what was going through his mind. What a responsibility, to be in charge of an expedition like that! All the people under your care, needing your guidance on everything from where to go to how to resolve issues with your fellow travelers. She shook her head. She didn't envy his task in the slightest.

After hearing the arguments on all sides, Brother Smith stood. He held up his hands to signal for silence. The group hushed, anxious to hear what their leader would say.

"This is too great a decision to make in a rush. I feel the need to send out one more exploring party." He looked around at the assembly, his eyes roving the faces of those seated before him. "Joseph F. Barton, you're going. Andrew Schow, you and Rueben Collett." Andrew nodded. "Samuel Rowley."

Sarah glanced over at where the Rowleys sat. Ann's shoulders were held straight, but Sarah caught a glimpse of her face, and she looked apprehensive.

Brother Smith continued to call out names. "Samuel Bryson. George Hobbs. William Hutchings. Cornelius Decker. Kumen Jones. Platte D. Lyman. Joseph Nielsen. James Riley. John Robinson." Brother Smith scanned the audience once more, and nodded. "That will be all. Be prepared to leave the morning of the twenty-eighth. I want you to look at the land, not only with your eyes, but with the spirit of discernment. We need the

Lord's help on this errand, and we need to prepare ourselves to do whatsoever He tells us to do."

The men who had been assigned to go gathered together for a few minutes after the meeting to discuss their preparations. Sarah caught Ann's arm as she herded her children toward the wagons.

"You look worried, Ann."

Ann smiled. "I'll be all right. Thank you for being concerned."

"Bring your children over to our wagon to play while your husband is gone. It will give our little girls something to do," Mary Ann invited.

"That's very kind of you, Sister Perkins. I may do just that." One of the Rowley children tugged on Ann's arm, and she sighed. "The children are hungry. I'd best go."

Mary Ann waited until Ann walked out of earshot, then asked Sarah in Welsh, "I've lost count. How many children do they have?"

"Seven. And little John Taylor was born just the month before we left home."

Mary Ann shook her head. "She certainly has faith to come on this journey with so many small ones. If she doesn't come visit us, we shall go over there."

* * *

Forty Mile Camp
November 28, 1879

The morning of the twenty-eighth arrived, and the scouting party left. They took with them two wagons—one loaded with supplies and one carrying a boat to explore the Colorado River, should they get that far. Ann Rowley had kept herself busy baking bread for her husband to carry with him, and Mary Ann and Sarah made several loaves as well, hoping to aid the men's journey.

"I hope this scouting party agrees with the first. We can't go back now," Mary Ann told Sarah. "We've invested too much in this. I feel we would disappoint the Lord to give up so easily."

"Disappoint the Lord?" Sarah asked. "I've heard of the Lord being angry with His people, but disappointed?"

Mary Ann motioned Sarah over to the fallen log near their fire, and they sat. "Most people think of God as being vengeful," she said. "Mormons have a different view. Because we believe He is our Father, we see Him as having fatherly feelings toward us. Yes, He becomes angry with us, much as we do when our children will not obey. But mostly He feels disappointment. He knows what we are capable of becoming, and when we don't strive to grow and become all that we are meant to, He is sorrowful for our misguided choices."

Sarah felt overwhelmed. She had never heard such a thing before and looked at her sister in amazement. "I don't know what to say," she said after a long pause. "The things you are telling me are joyous to my soul, but they go against everything I've heard at church. God is wrathful toward those who don't obey."

"You've been going to a different church," Mary Ann said, placing her hand on her sister's arm. "Perhaps it's time for you to learn what I believe."

Sarah sat by the fire for a long time. She was confused and uplifted at the same time. She had attended the Mormon meetings in Cedar City frequently, there being no Methodist church in the area, and enjoyed the singing of the hymns very much. But the sermons were given in English, and she didn't understand many of the words. Perhaps out here, in the midst of the beauty of God's creations, she would be able to understand why her family felt the way it did about the Mormon Church, especially with her sister to explain it to her in Welsh.

* * *

Forty Mile Camp
December, 1879

After another long wait, the scouts returned, and again a meeting was called. They didn't have a favorable report. Thick snow covered the ground, and the people were cold and numb, not in a very good mood to begin with. Added to the news that the path ahead was too rough to travel, a spirit of despair and unhappiness hung over the camp.

Sarah had bundled herself from head to toe in all her skirts and scarves, not used to such cold. She looked around at the other travelers. Heads were bowed and shaking back and forth, feet were scuffing the dirt. She had never seen such a discouraged-looking group. It was December third, and they had been on the road for over six weeks. They thought they would be all the way to the San Juan by then, and here they were, not even halfway. They once hoped to be in their new homes by Christmas, but that dream had suddenly vanished in the harsh light of reality.

"We can't go back," one of the men spoke up. "The path behind us is blocked with snow."

"The cattle are starving," Thomas said. "We have to either go forward or back. We can't stay here."

Jens Nielsen was a strong man, mighty in his faith. A Danish convert, he had crossed the plains with the Martin Handcart Company. Sarah had always admired his clear thinking and deep spirituality. He rose and said, "The final decision on this matter shall be left to President Smith and to the Lord." He dismissed the meeting.

Thomas poked up the fire with a stick when they returned to their little camp. "What do you think?" he asked Ben.

"We'll go forward," Ben replied. "The Lord has a purpose in this mission, and a rough road won't stop Him."

"I'm worried about the livestock," Thomas said. "They haven't had a good meal since we left Cedar City. They've been making do on whatever they can find along the way, and it isn't much."

Ben shook his head. "This is no place for man or beast."

The bugle sounded the next morning, and word spread through the camp that they were to meet to discover what answer the Lord had given to Silas Smith. He stood up in front of the group, dark circles under his eyes and looking as tired as Sarah had ever seen him.

"Brothers and sisters," he said, looking out over the crowd, who seemed to hold their breath until they heard what he had to say. "I spent the night supplicating the Lord for an answer to our dilemma. He has heard my prayers."

Sarah leaned forward, eager to hear.

"Peace spoke to my soul concerning the route we have taken. We will go forward as planned. The company must go on, whether they can or not."

One of the men rose and addressed the group. "I know you are right, Brother Smith. I feel in my heart that the Lord wants us to take this route. God lives. Hosanna!"

"We must go forward," another brother said. "We are called of God and must do His bidding."

Several others bore their testimonies throughout the group. Sarah sat in wonder, listening to the voices calling out all around her. The Saints had received a direction from their leader and rallied to the cause, believing he was called of God and spoke with Him the previous night. A warm burning began in her chest, swelling out until it brought tears to her eyes.

She couldn't help but notice that several of the men who had borne their testimony were men who had gone on the exploring party and said it couldn't be done. They had seen the land with their own eyes and formed an opinion, but were ready to lay aside their own desires and obey the word of God.

Suddenly, voices rose in song, coming from all around her. The Saints stood and lifted their heads to the sky, singing from the depths of their souls, "The Spirit of God like a fire is burning."

The sound carried out across the wilderness and rang in Sarah's ears. She could believe in that moment the music carried up to God's throne itself, to be heard by His angels. She wiped tears from her eyes—tears she didn't know were coming until they were on her cheeks. She didn't understand the Mormon religion, but she knew it was speaking to her in a way nothing ever had before.

CHAPTER EIGHTEEN

Dance Hall Rock
December, 1879

The reins felt hot and sticky in Sarah's fingers, despite the chill in the air. She let go one hand at a time, wiping first one and then the other on her skirt. Up ahead she could make out a huge rock of some kind, looming up out of the ground.

The wagons creaked and groaned all the way to the rock and stopped, almost with a sigh.

"This is the fifty-mile mark," Silas Smith announced. "We will camp here."

The Saints parked their wagons for the night, unhitched their teams, and started their fires in record time, after first clearing away patches of snow. It was becoming second nature to them, as though they had lived all their lives on the prairie.

"Thank goodness for the supplies we bought in Escalante," Mary Ann said to Sarah. "We're running low on the food we brought from home."

"I feel as though we've reached the exact middle of nowhere," Sarah replied. She turned and looked around. There was nothing in any direction but sandstone, a few tufts of dried grass, and various rock formations scattered here and there.

"Hello," Ann Rowley called out, approaching their wagon. "The children wanted to come for a visit before dinner."

"You're always welcome," Mary Ann told them. The children immediately invented a game and began to play, and the women took seats on the log arranged as a bench.

"They've been so restless," Ann said, wiping her forehead with the back of her hand. "I can't help but feel sorry for them."

"Ours too," Mary Ann told her. "I feel like I'm trying to control a litter of puppies, they're so frisky."

Ben came back to the Perkins' camp, wiping his hands on a handkerchief. "I talked to Silas Smith," he said. "The cliff we'll be blasting through is eight miles ahead." He nodded to Ann. "Hello, Sister Rowley."

"Hello, Brother Perkins. I've been meaning to tell you how much I enjoy the Welsh music you favor us with each morning."

Ben blushed. "Thank you. Not everyone in the camp feels that way."

Sarah pressed her lips together to keep from smiling. Every morning, bright and early, Ben would get up and start moving around the camp, the happy strains of a Welsh tune coming from between his lips. Although often greeted with groans, the Saints couldn't help but smile at the cheer he brought to the camp. He was something of a Welsh rooster.

The Saints gathered that night on the long, flat rock, a broad piece of sandstone that formed a perfect dance floor. It rose up in back and provided a shelter of sorts in a lip that hung down over the top, looking somewhat like a bowl turned on its side. They named it Dance Hall Rock, and the musicians brought out their instruments. Mary Ann, Sarah, Ben, and Hyrum sang a Welsh song for the group, and other more popular tunes, joined by Kumen and Mary Jones. Then Ben and Hyrum harmonized on *Will You Love Me When I Am Old*. Their voices blended together beautifully, and Sarah pulled out her handkerchief to wipe a tear out of her eye. She had so loved the men's choirs in Wales. Listening to the men sing tonight filled her with nostalgia and homesickness. But beneath all that lay a feeling of joy, knowing that she was helping in a worthwhile cause. She glanced around and saw expressions of contentment on the faces of the Saints that surrounded her.

Ann came up beside her and took her elbow. "I'm so relieved we're nearly at the hole," she said. "Just think—once we're through, the hard part of our journey will be over and we can begin our mission in earnest."

"That will be wonderful," Sarah replied. She too looked forward to reaching the end of the trek. But at that moment, she felt as though she could stay beneath that starry sky and listen to the music forever.

* * *

Hole in the Rock
December, 1879

Sarah's shoes threatened to slip right out from under her as she approached the narrow slit in the canyon rock. The ground lay smooth and hard, and it was all she could do to remain upright. Finally making it to the edge of the cliff, she paused for a minute to catch her breath.

She stepped forward and looked down the hole. The ground on the other side dipped down so sharply that it almost could not be seen. Far below, she could see the blue of the Colorado River, but from her vantage point, it appeared to be almost a free-fall down to that level.

She sank down to her knees and rested her head on her hands. How would they ever get the wagons through that slit, and from there, down to the river? It was impossible. The Saints all believed they had been called of God, and that He would provide a way for them to make it to the San Juan Valley in safety. Sarah believed in God and in His mercies and miracles, but the mission seemed like foolishness. Her God was more logical than that. If the Saints were following a true religion, wouldn't God have led them on a different path? Maybe it was a sign that the Saints were wrong about the way they chose to worship. Maybe her old Methodist minister was right after all.

Even as she had those thoughts, crouched at the top of the hole, a warm feeling began to fill her heart. She recognized it as the same feeling she'd had while listening to the Saints decide to continue their journey, and the testimonies they had borne. In her thoughts, she had been showing a lack of faith. She might not worship God the way the Saints did, but she did believe they worshipped the same God, and surely He watched over them all. They would find a way to bring the wagons through the rock, lower them down to the river, and continue on their way to San Juan—in the Lord's way and time. She felt as sure of it as anything else she'd ever experienced.

She straightened as those thoughts filled her mind. Was God speaking to her, Sarah Williams, out there in the middle of that lonely desert? She looked around. Although alone, she felt someone near. Doubt left her mind as she contemplated what she had just experienced. Suddenly the Saints didn't seem so foolish in their determination to forge ahead. She still didn't know how they were going to do it, but she knew they would.

* * *

Hole in the Rock
December, 1879

"There's not enough room for all of us to camp together, so we're going to split the group. Half will camp at Dance Hall Rock, the other half will camp here, at the Hole." Brother Smith made the assignments, and the Saints regrouped. Sarah was sad to see that the Rowleys were amongst those who would camp at Dance Hall Rock, as she and the Perkins were staying at the Hole.

"It won't be for long," Ann reasoned. "And when we reach the other side, we'll see each other frequently."

The children were sad as well, but brightened when Ann told them they might come for a visit.

Ben set up the two wagons on a flat piece of land below the Hole, and Mary Ann unpacked some of their things and went about making it as homey as possible.

"Who knows how long we'll be here?" she said. "I went up and looked at that rock. It's going to take a great deal of work to make it passable."

"I looked at it too," Sarah said. "I'm still a little dizzy, just remembering it."

Ben laughed. "It is steep, at that. But we'll figure out a way."

"How deep is the crevice, Brother Perkins?" Sarah asked.

"The explorers said it's about two thousand feet from the top of the cliff down to the Colorado River. The slit there at the top is barely wide enough for a thin man to pass through, so we'll have a bit of blasting to do. From there, we'll bring the wagons through the slit, down the incline, and to the river. Hyrum and I have been asked to teach the other men how to use blasting powder, since we have experience with it."

"So perhaps your time in the mines wasn't wasted after all," Mary Ann said, smiling at her husband.

"I suppose not." Ben returned his wife's smile and scooped up Catherine, who hung on his leg. "What do you need, little miss?"

"When is Father Christmas coming?" she asked.

Ben looked at Mary Ann over their daughter's head. Sarah knew Mary Ann had tucked away some treats for the special day, but they had planned to be in their new home, not celebrating Christ's birth out in here in the wilderness.

"He's going to come on Christmas, just like he always does," Ben told her.

"But what if Father Christmas can't find us? What if we don't get any presents?" Catherine was clearly worried.

"You shall have presents, my girl. Don't you worry about that." Ben kissed her on the forehead and set her back on the ground. He walked over to the wagon and started fiddling with the wheel spokes, whistling a Welsh tune, the look on his face anything but cheery.

"He wanted so much to have us in a home before Christmas," Mary Ann said in an undertone to Sarah. "He hasn't complained, but I know the delay is bothering him."

"It has worn on everyone," Sarah replied. "But how were the leaders to know how long the journey would take?"

"Six weeks was a guess," Mary Ann agreed. "They couldn't have known about all we would encounter. We'll be in a home soon enough. But Ben didn't want the children to celebrate the holiday in a wagon."

"He's a good husband to you," Sarah said.

Mary Ann nodded, a little smile on her face. "He's been wonderful."

Ben's melancholy seemed to have disappeared by the time dinner was served, and he played rollicking games with the children until bed time. Thomas came riding in from his work with the cattle and kissed the little girls good night.

"Any dinner left?" he asked.

"I have a bowl of beans right here," Sarah said.

He lifted the bowl to his nose and sniffed. "I never thought the day would come when plain beans would smell so good."

"You've been working hard, Thomas. That will build up an appetite."

Silas Smith approached the wagon, and they switched from speaking Welsh to English, for his benefit.

"Brother Perkins, we'll be meeting in the morning to discuss how best to blast through that rock," he said.

"I'll be there," Ben replied.

"I must say, I'm glad to have you along on this expedition. Your experience is going to prove invaluable."

"I'll do the best I can." Ben motioned toward the fire. "Will you sit a while?"

Silas pulled off his hat and ran a hand through his hair. "I wish I could but I've got a lot to do. Another time." He nodded to Sarah and Mary Ann, then walked off into the darkness.

"I wouldn't trade places with him," Ben said, resuming his seat by the warm fire. "He's carrying a big load on his shoulders."

"We'll be there soon, and then we can all rest." Mary Ann dunked Thomas's empty bowl in the pot she was using as a dishpan. "Another few weeks and it will all be over."

CHAPTER NINETEEN

Hole in the Rock
Mid-December, 1879

Ben and Hyrum stood at the top of the cliff, peering through the slit in the sandstone that the leaders of the expedition had named The Hole in the Rock.

"What do you think?" Hyrum asked Ben softly in Welsh.

"We'll have some fun," Ben replied, then turned to Silas Smith, Jens Nielsen, and Platte D. Lyman, who were waiting to hear what the brothers had to say.

"We can do it," Ben told them. "We'll need to set blasts here, here, and here," he said, motioning with his hands. "But we're going to need more blasting powder. What we have is not sufficient."

"I'm sure we can get some," Silas said.

"It may take some time to make the crevice large enough," Ben continued. "When you're using blasting powder, you have to be precise. Slow and careful—that's the ticket."

The leaders nodded. "I'll see what I can do about getting more powder from Salt Lake City," Silas said, and the men went back to their wagons to get their lunch.

Ben gave Mary Ann a kiss on the cheek before sitting down to eat. "It's going to be hard work, but nothing we're not used to," he said. "Brother Smith is looking into getting us more blasting powder from the Valley. We'll be drilling holes into the rock and blasting it out, bit by bit. It will take a while, but we'll make a notch big enough for a wagon to go through. And we'll be out in the fresh air instead of underground." He grinned. "Should be fun."

"Your definition of fun is a little different from mine," Mary Ann told him with a fond smile.

"You don't think it's fun to blow things up?"

"No, I don't."

Ben tucked into his lunch, feeling better than he had for a long time. At last he had a direction, a purpose. He could hardly wait to get his hands on that powder and truly begin to make a difference.

* * *

Hole in the Rock
December, 1879

"Hello!" The familiar voice carried on the wind. "Hello!"

Mary Ann looked up to see the Rowleys approaching the camp on horseback, the larger children riding with the smaller ones to hold them in place. She waved her hand as they drew closer.

"It's a beautiful morning to be out for a ride!" Samuel said, sliding off his chestnut gelding. "We thought we'd come and see how you all were faring."

"Brother Smith left this morning to go to Salt Lake City," Mary Ann told him. "He thought it would be faster to get the powder himself instead of sending a letter and waiting for it to be delivered."

Samuel nodded. "Very good thinking. He'll save quite a bit of time that way."

"That's what we're hoping."

Ann sat down on the log near the fire ring, holding baby John Taylor on her lap.

"And how is this big fellow?" Mary Ann asked, reaching out to tickle the baby's feet.

"Colicky," was Ann's one word reply. "Between the cold nights and his colic, it's a wonder we've had any sleep at all."

"Does he like to sleep on his stomach?" Mary Ann asked.

"I've tried that, but he cries harder," Ann said. She turned the baby to face Mary Ann more directly. "During the day, he's just a lamb."

"I can see that," Mary Ann replied.

Mary Jane, Delia, and Catherine ran up to the fire ring, out of breath and full of high spirits. Sarah followed them more slowly, sitting down on the log with the other ladies when she reached them.

"They've got more energy than is fair," she said to Mary Ann in Welsh. Then she said to Ann in English, "I am so tired from chasing them. I'm sorry. I'm still learning all the words I want to say."

"You're not to worry about it," Ann said to her. "I've spoken English all my life, and sometimes I still can't figure out what I want to say."

Samuel left the camp shortly thereafter and went up to the Hole. The children played happily for some time, then little Naomi woke up and wanted her lunch, so Mary Ann climbed in the wagon to care for her.

"While we were on our walk just now, I spoke with some of the other women in the wagon train," Sarah said to Ann after the children were out of earshot. "They told me that a few of them are plural wives. I don't understand the principle of polygamy. It doesn't seem to fit in with the other teachings of the gospel."

"I know how you feel," Ann said softly. "I'm not sure where I stand on it, either. My husband's brother, John, has several wives. In fact, two of his wives are sisters."

"Sisters?" Sarah sat up straighter, surprised. "Do they get along well?"

"They seem to. But that's not the whole story." Ann leaned forward. "They are sisters, but their mother is another one of John's wives. They are her daughters through her first husband."

Sarah's eyes opened wide, and she gasped. "He married two of his step-daughters?"

"He did, and they seem to be living the principle righteously. They all look happy."

Sarah shook her head. "That's unbelievable."

"It is, rather. We were quite surprised when John told us."

"I don't know if I'll ever understand," Sarah admitted. "It all seems . . . wrong."

"I don't fully understand it either, Sarah. I don't know how I would feel if Samuel were commanded to take another wife. But I have learned one thing, and perhaps it's a valid point in this, as well. The more we learn about the gospel, the more we come to understand that what doesn't make sense to us today, will make sense tomorrow."

"And you think that someday plural marriage will make sense?"

"I certainly hope so. It has caused me many sleepless nights, wondering if I could endure such a challenge in my own life. Thankfully Samuel has not been asked to take another wife. I truly don't know if I could accept it."

"May I ask you a question?" Sarah said a moment later.

"Certainly."

"You told me that you came to America to be with the Saints."

"Yes, that's right."

"Now that you're here, is it what you were hoping for?"

Ann shifted the baby on her lap. He slept, one finger hooked in his mouth. "I don't really know what I expected, to be honest with you. I didn't have any picture in my head about what it would look like or what we would find here. All I knew was that this is where God wanted us. So we came."

"That was enough for you? To just know God wanted you here?"

Ann nodded.

"I think I understand," Sarah said after a moment. "I didn't know if I should stay in Wales, but I felt like I belonged with my family. It was the right thing to do."

"I'm glad you came," Ann said, reaching out and touching Sarah's shoulder.

"I am too," Sarah told her.

The conversation shifted to other things, but Sarah's mind kept wandering back to the story of John Rowley and his plural wives. How could such a thing be? All those women, married to the same man, and yet living in happiness? It sounded like a twisted fairy tale, and not real at all.

* * *

Hole in the Rock
December 16, 1879

"It looks like I'm off on another scouting trip," George Hobbs told Ben. He squatted down by the Perkins' fire and held his hands out to warm them. "George Sevy and Lemuel Redd have arrived with their families, and they want to push through to the San Juan while we're stalled here at the Hole. Platte thinks that George and Lemuel should go ahead and scout, and he's asked me and George Morrell to go along with."

"You've certainly done a fair share of scouting," Ben said.

"It's probably because I'm so good at it." George laughed.

"We wish you luck. Bring us back some good news."

"I'll do my best."

The scouts rode out first thing the next morning. They took two pack horses, carrying enough food for eight days, planning to restock in Montezuma. They also took along two riding horses, which they would take turns using. Ben watched them go until they were out of sight, wondering if the scouting party would bring back a positive report.

* * *

Hole in the Rock
Mid-December, 1879

"You've got to cover your ears," Ben shouted to the men nearest the blast. The men obeyed, barely protecting themselves before the powder detonated. They turned away as rock chips blew everywhere, many flying down the hole and into the crevice, bouncing down the drop toward the river. Smoke and dust filled the air and hung suspended for a moment before vanishing in the breeze.

The gap got wider by the day. Jens Nielsen was a great help to Ben and Hyrum, soon becoming nearly as proficient in the use of blasting powder as they were. The two brothers had been dubbed, "The blasters and blowers from Wales," a nickname they enjoyed. But they were going to run out of powder soon, and Silas Smith had not yet returned. A rider had brought a letter from him, saying that he had arrived in Salt Lake City and made the request for the powder, but he had gotten caught in a snow storm on the way and contracted pneumonia, so it would be some time before he could travel. That left Platte D. Lyman in charge for the time being.

Ben felt the pressure of waiting. He wanted to get through the rock and on to the San Juan, building a home for Mary Ann so she wouldn't have to sleep in a wagon any more. Several of the men he worked with expressed their frustrations as well, but there was nothing they could do about it.

"Here you go," Ben said, handing some small twists of wick to Jens. "Let's get this set off and break for lunch."

"Sounds good to me," Jens said, turning back to his work.

"Ben, would you come look at this, please?" Platte called. Ben walked over to the leader, who had spread a piece of brown paper on a rock and studied it intently.

"What is it?"

"I had a few of the men slip through the Hole and climb down. They took some measurements and made this sketch." He ran his hand along the figures. "This is pretty rough, but you get the idea. Right on the other side of the Hole, the ground breaks away, creating a steep and slippery chute. Then it practically disappears, right out from under foot. Toward the bottom everything levels out, but right here, in the middle, we're going to have some problems. There's nothing for the wagons to hang onto. The men climbed down all right with a rope, but there's no way to get a wagon across there."

Ben rubbed his chin while he looked at the drawing. "When you say the ground disappears, what do you mean?"

Platte took up his pencil and began to sketch a new line. "It slopes down so sharply and at such an angle that you can hardly maintain a foothold along here," he pointed. "A wagon couldn't possible make it."

Ben took another look and said, "I'd like to see for myself."

"Go ahead."

Ben waited until the last charge went off, then walked over to the top of the Hole. "I'm going down," he said.

"Do you want me to come with you?" Hyrum asked.

"I'd like that."

The two brothers slid through the Hole. They had made some progress in widening the space, so it wasn't a tight squeeze, but it was still nowhere near large enough for a team and wagon. Ben looked up as they went through. The walls of the cliff on either side were so close that he had to bend way back to see the sky. Once through the Hole, it opened up naturally and dropped, like Platte had said.

Ben and Hyrum slid down fifty or sixty feet, practically on their backsides. When they reached the end of the slippery chute, they paused to look over the section of path Platte had told Ben about.

"I see what he means," Ben said. "The ground practically drops right away."

"It's a steep cliff," Hyrum replied. "I don't see how we're going to get wagons down here."

Ben sat down on the ground and looked things over. It had to work. There had to be a way. They had been told by the leaders and by the voice of the Spirit that whispered in their own hearts that this was the way to go.

"What do you think?"

Hyrum shook his head. "I don't see a way to do it."

"What if we piled boulders up here and here . . .no, wait." Ben scratched his head. "There's not enough level ground."

The two brothers tossed ideas back and forth, first one and then the other. It wasn't getting them anywhere.

After a while Ben lapsed into silence, staring at the wall in front of him. He didn't say anything for a long time, and Hyrum said nothing to break his train of thought. Everything Ben had learned at the mine ran through his head, all the tricks of the trade. Finally he stood up. "I know what we need to do."

He climbed up to the base of the crevice and hollered, "We need a hand up."

A rope came tumbling down through the Hole, and Platte's head stuck over the rim. "Here you go," he called out.

"Thanks," Ben said, grabbing hold of the rope and using it to hoist himself up the rest of the way. Once on the top, he held it anchored for Hyrum, and soon they were both speaking with Platte and Jens about what they had seen.

"I have an idea, brethren, but you may think I'm mad," Ben said.

"We'll decide after we've heard you out," Platte replied.

"We need to build a dugway." Ben picked up the pencil and began to create his own lines on top of the sketch Platte had been using. "We can drill some holes in through here, on the north side of the cliff, and shove staffs into the holes, sticking out and creating a sort of shelf, which we can then cover with brush to make a road. Just above the holes, we blast out a groove that runs down the length of the dugway. The right wagon wheel rides on the staffs, and the left wheel runs down this groove."

"So what you're saying is, we stick some poles out of the wall of the cliff, like this." Platte held up his hand, palm down, fingers splayed.

"Yes."

Platte looked at his fingers a moment longer, then back at the drawing. "How will you drill that many holes into the face of the mountain without actually chipping out pieces of the wall? If the holes broke into each other, the whole thing would fall apart."

"That's why we proceed slowly and carefully."

Platte looked back and forth between Hyrum and Ben. "What do you think?" he asked Hyrum.

"This is the first I've heard of it, but I say it will work," Hyrum replied.

"Have you seen something like this before?"

"Nothing. But I trust Ben."

Platte turned his attention back to Ben. "Why are you so sure about this?"

"I feel that it will work." Ben met Platte's eyes squarely, not sure how to explain the deep conviction he felt within his heart. It was a feeling, nothing more. He couldn't explain how the idea had come to him or why he was so sure . He just knew.

Platte turned to Jens. "What do you say?"

"We should do it," the Dane replied.

Platte shook his head. "What you're suggesting is that we essentially hang a road out in midair." He studied Ben's drawing for a minute, and nodded. "You may be just a little bit mad after all . . . but this might work. In the meantime, I think we should assign the men camped at Dance Hall Rock to come and start making a road on the other side of the river. We'll need a workable destination once we get through."

Ben presented his idea for a dugway to the other men, and after explaining just how it would work, they nodded their heads in agreement. Ben felt relieved to see they were enthusiastically accepting of his plan. No one else had come up with an idea to top his, so they agreed and started to discuss ways to carry it out.

"What kind of staff should we use, Ben?" Jens asked.

"I think oak would work the best. It's strong, and we can haul it in. All the trees around here are too small."

"How far apart will the holes have to be?" someone else called out.

"I'll do some measuring," Ben replied.

Once again the men took his word for it, and Ben suppressed a smile. He appreciated working with men who listened to his opinion and trusted his expertise. He might not know everything, but he was good at what he did.

Over the next few days, the men got busy preparing to carry out the plan. The blasting powder hadn't arrived yet, but they chiseled away at the Hole, widening it a bit every day. From time to time as they worked, they'd accidentally drop their tools down into the crevice. They would put one of the older boys in a half bucket and lower him down on a rope to collect the tools, then haul him back up, hand over hand.

Wilson Daily, a blacksmith who was not a member but traveled along with the Saints, moved his forge to the Hole so he could be of help. Ben met him there as soon as he had set up his equipment.

"Morning, Mr. Daily."

"Good morning, Mr. Perkins. I understand you're the man in charge of this madness."

Ben laughed. "Well, I'm not in charge of the overall project, but I guess I'm in charge of the crazy aspects of it. What we're proposing will not be simple."

"Or possible."

"Oh, it's possible. It just won't be simple."

Mr. Daily smiled at Ben's easy-going attitude. "What can I do for you?"

"I need some drill bits that will create holes two and a half inches wide."

"I can do that."

Ben stayed with the blacksmith for a little while, answering questions about the proposed dugway and what would be needed to bring it about, then he returned to the Hole.

He looked down the steep incline toward the spot on the north wall where the dugway would be built. He shook his head. It didn't seem possible, and that was a fact. But there was no other answer, and he had to believe that the Lord would bless them for trying. "Please, Lord, make this work."

CHAPTER TWENTY

Hole in the Rock
December 24, 1879

"My hands are so cold I can barely grip my hammer," Hyrum said. He rubbed his hands together and slapped them against his thighs.

"We're making fairly good progress," Ben replied. "I just wish that blasting powder would get here."

Hyrum pulled his worn-out glove more snugly over his hand. "What's your family doing for Christmas tomorrow?"

"Mary Ann is planning to make some cookies over the fire tonight after the children are asleep. She's not sure it will work, but she wants to try anyway. We're hanging their stockings off the wagon wheel, since they don't have beds to hang them from. Catherine's sure that Father Christmas will never find us out here in the middle of nowhere."

Hyrum laughed. "He should be able to follow us, all right. We cleared the road for him."

"Why don't you bring your family over for breakfast?" Ben invited.

"We will. Thanks."

Ben turned at the sound of some rocks bouncing down the Hole. A moment later Samuel Rowley hoisted himself up and over the lip of the rock.

"How are things down below?" Ben asked him.

"It's hard work, building a road," Samuel said. He looked around at the progress that had been made on the opening in the Hole. "No harder than chiseling through solid rock, though."

"Just a little bit more and we'll have those wagons through," Ben assured him.

"Is Mr. Daily around? I need some help refitting my tools." Samuel held up a worn leather tool bag.

"I think he's over there," Ben nodded.

"Thanks, Ben." Samuel walked off to find the blacksmith.

Hyrum sat down on one of the nearby rocks and rewrapped a bandage he had on his hand.

"Are you hurt?" Ben asked him.

"Oh, I'm all right. This rag keeps getting in the way, though." He gave the bandage one last tug, replaced his glove, and rejoined Ben at the cliff. "I'll be glad when this is over."

Ben laughed and started singing a Welsh tune. Hyrum soon chimed in, and the happy sound echoed down the Hole to the Colorado River.

* * *

Hole in the Rock
December 25, 1879

"Did he come? Did he come?"

"Did who come, Catherine?" Mary Ann asked sleepily.

"Father Christmas," Delia replied. "Catherine woke me up four times."

Mary Ann sat up and rubbed her eyes. Everyone else still slept, but Catherine was sitting up in bed, wide awake and impatient.

"Yes, Catherine. Father Christmas came. But you must wait until everyone else is awake first."

Catherine crossed her arms and looked grumpy, but a slow smile passed across her face. She reached out her hand and started poking Naomi in the side.

"Catherine! It's not fair to wake the others."

"Sorry, Mam."

Mary Ann tried to go back to sleep, but Catherine was restless and wide awake. She finally gave up and got out of bed. "Now, little miss, if I go and wake up Aunt Sarah and Mary Jane, will that make you happy?"

Catherine bounced up and down.

"I suppose that's my answer," Mary Ann said with a yawn.

After everyone woke up and dressed, the children got their presents. They each got cookies, a handful of parched corn, and a doll that Ben had made late at night by whittling sticks and fastening them together. Mary Ann found scraps of material in her sewing basket to create dresses for the dolls. The girls were delighted.

Hyrum and Rachel arrived a short time later, carrying baby George wrapped in a blanket. Mary Ann served a delicious treat she had created by taking dried plums, grinding them up with water and spreading them out, then letting the mixture dry.

"This isn't the Christmas I had planned for you," Ben told her, putting his arm around her shoulders while they watched the girls play with their dolls.

"I know, Ben, but I don't mind. Look at the children. They're so happy."

Ben nodded. He still looked disappointed, but the children were far from it, and in Mary Ann's mind, that's what Christmas was all about.

* * *

Hole in the Rock
January 4, 1880

"Here you go, Mary Ann," Ben said, setting an armload of coal down by the fire.

"So it's true? Dick Butt really discovered coal in the cliffs?" Mary Ann picked up a piece and turned it over in her hands, not really believing what she saw. "This is truly a blessing. It's been difficult to find enough shadscale to burn."

"A detail of men has been assigned to mine out the coal. Hopefully there will be enough to last us a while." Ben wiped his forehead and gave his wife a kiss. "I'll be back for supper."

Sarah climbed out of the back of the wagon, bringing a freshly-diapered Naomi. "Is that coal?"

Mary Ann turned, still holding the piece she had picked up. "It is! And it's a miracle."

Sarah straightened her back, stretching muscles tired from stooping over fires and sleeping babies. "Back in Wales, we had more coal than we knew what to do with. Things are certainly different out here."

Mary Ann reached out and took the baby. "They certainly are."

Rachel appeared around the tongue of their wagon. "Hello!"

"Hello, Rachel. Come, have a seat by the fire," Mary Ann invited. "How are you?"

"We're doing well. A bit cold at night, but I'm so glad we're sleeping in a wagon and not on the ground."

Mary Ann and Sarah both nodded in agreement.

"I've come to ask if you have any extra axle grease. Hyrum's hands are blistering, and I've been rubbing them with grease every night. But we've nearly run out."

"We do," Mary Ann said. She rose and fetched some out of the back of the supply wagon. "Do you have a way to carry it?"

Rachel pulled a small tin from her pocket. Mary Ann dug out a portion and put it inside.

"Thank you," Rachel said. "Hyrum was accustomed to doing this kind of work in Wales, but since we arrived here, he's been doing other tasks, and the skin on his hands has softened."

"I hope the grease helps," Mary Ann told her sister-in-law.

"It should," Rachel replied.

She had just barely left when Ann Rowley came riding up, carrying John Taylor in a little bundle strapped to her waist.

"Hello, ladies. I've come to share the news."

"What news?" Mary Ann asked.

"Lizzie Decker delivered a baby girl. They named her Lena."

"That's wonderful!"

Sarah reached up to take John Taylor so Ann could climb down from her horse.

"She's a beautiful baby. Looks quite a bit like her mother."

"How does Lizzie feel?" Sarah asked.

"She's tired, but relieved that the baby's healthy."

Mary Ann shook her head. "So much could go wrong out here. I'm glad it all turned out for the best."

"In this cold, in the back of a wagon, without her mother?" Ann shook her head. "I can't say it was for the best. The baby's doing well, and so's Lizzie. But I wonder how they're going to keep warm enough in this weather."

"I do struggle to keep Naomi bundled," Mary Ann agreed. "I must wake up three times a night to make sure everyone's covered."

"It's hard enough to keep a house warm. These wagons are impossible." Ann took the baby back from Sarah and straightened his hat. "I'm surprised we're all as healthy as we are."

"It's a blessing, that's for sure," Mary Ann said. "The hand of the Lord must be in this. There's no other explanation."

* * *

Hole in the Rock
January, 1880

George Hobbs lowered himself onto the log by the Perkins' fire. He pulled off his hat and set it on his knee, then passed both hands over his face.

"Where have you been all this time, George?" Ben asked. "We were worried about you."

George shook his head slowly. "We had a time of it, that's for sure."

"What happened?"

George accepted the plate of hot food Mary Ann offered him, and told his story between bites.

"We took turns walking and riding, each man riding for an hour and walking for an hour. Things were going all right until we discovered we were stuck up on top of some slick rocks and we couldn't find a way down." He chewed and swallowed, then continued. "Have you ever seen a llama, Sister Perkins?"

"A llama? No, I never have. What's a llama?"

"It's an animal. It looks sort of like a small camel with no hump and it's covered with hair. Well, we saw what we thought were some llamas out there, and I tried to lasso one, but it didn't work. I felt a little foolish, but as the animal ran off, it showed us the way off the rocks."

Mary Ann rose and refilled his plate.

"Thank you, Sister Perkins. On the fourth day we found an old trail which led us to a remarkably well-preserved Indian cliff dwelling. I'd like to go back sometime and take a closer look at it—I've never seen the like. Then we came to Grand Gulch. Ben, those cliffs were over two thousand feet high. It was the most incredible thing I've ever seen."

"Two thousand feet?" Ben whistled. "That's a mighty high cliff."

"As you can imagine, we couldn't find a way over, so we changed our planned route a bit. Christmas Eve we camped at Grand Flat. Eight inches of snow fell on us in the night.

"Come morning, we had a hard time finding our horses. They had wandered off, and the snow had covered their tracks. After we finally found them, we made a flapjack for breakfast out of the last of our flour, and cut it into fourths to share."

"The last of your flour? But Brother Hobbs, you hadn't even reached your destination yet." Mary Ann refilled his plate again—she couldn't bear the thought of anyone being hungry.

"It was a hardship, to be sure. All day we wandered around, trying to figure out where we were. We were near frozen, and very hungry We began to wonder if this Christmas Day would be our last." George leaned closer to the fire. Ben felt chilled too, just hearing George's tale, and stood to put several more sticks on the fire.

"I saw a hill up ahead, and climbed it to get a better look at things. From there, I could see the Blue Mountains about ten miles. We knew Montezuma lay to the south of the Blue

Mountains, so we followed the next canyon east. We found a cave to sleep in that night, out of the elements. I named that hill Salvation Knoll, for without it, we would have never caught sight of the mountains and known where we were.

"We came to Comb Ridge the next day, and followed it south to Butler Wash. We were exhausted, near dead from hunger. I didn't know if we'd live to see morning, so I carved my name in the rocks, hoping that someone would remember me." He paused a moment.

Ben remained silent, seeing the emotion that passed over George's face before he resumed his tale.

"The morning of the twenty-eighth, we climbed out of Butler Wash and passed Comb Wash by sliding our animals down a steep mountainside. One of the burros fell. I confess I hoped that it had broken its back so we could eat it. But the plucky little fellow was fine."

"A shame for you," Ben said.

George laughed. "I was pretty disappointed."

Ben threw another armful of brush on the fire. "What happened next?"

"Finally, after four days without food, we staggered into the Harris cabin in Bluff. We were never so happy to see other human beings in our lives. Sister Harris and her mother-in-law, Sister Warren, set about feeding us. I believe I ate twenty-two biscuits, I was so hungry."

"I don't blame you one bit."

"They were good biscuits, too. That woman can cook." George paused, a blissful smile on his face. "The next morning we set off to Montezuma. I felt greatly relieved to see my sister. She and the Davis's were sorry to hear that the group was having difficulty getting through the Hole. They were hoping we'd be there by now."

"How are they doing? It can't be easy for them, out there by themselves."

"They were in pretty desperate straights. Their canals had been washed out, and their crops had all burned in the heat. All they have left is some wheat they've been crushing in a coffee grinder. They think they have enough food for sixty days, but they are counting on us to come quickly."

Ben shook his head. "I wish I could make a promise, George, but I don't know how long it's going to take to finish the road. Charles Hall and his sons have been working hard to get the ferry ready on time, but the Hole . . . I don't know."

George nodded. "There's no way to predict such things."

"So if you weren't able to restock your supply in Montezuma, how did you fare getting home?"

"We passed a trapper named Peter Shurtz heading through that way. He sold us a bag of flour for twenty dollars. It saw us through until we got home. It's lucky we happened upon him."

"Lucky indeed."

"Harvey Dunton, one of the Montezuma men, came back with us. He'd like to help us finish getting through the Hole."

"Every man is welcome." Ben reached out and poked the fire. "Was your return trip uneventful?"

George laughed. "I should say not! We took a different trail back and found a short cut to Grand Flat. From there we found the old Indian trail without difficulty and thought ourselves rather clever. We searched for another route through Grand Gulch, and after wandering around in several false canyons, were finally able to get out. We ran out of flour, and we were again facing starvation.

"When we reached the Slick Rocks, they were so covered in snow and so slippery we couldn't get up them. We knew of no other way to get back here than over the Rocks, so we packed snow footholds onto the sides of the rocks and waited for the chill of night to freeze them. By next morning they were frozen tight, and we climbed up them to the top."

"Very good thinking," Ben said.

"We felt pretty clever, at that. But by that time we were so tired, we couldn't walk any more. Instead of taking turns on the riding horses, we rode the pack animals as well. One of them had worn through its hooves and left a circle of blood in the snow with every step—a pitiful sight. We hated to ride him but we had to, or perish ourselves. And that is the story of our return."

Ben sat back and looked at his friend. "It's a miracle you came back to us."

"I believe it is."

"Do you feel that we can take wagons through to the San Juan?"

"We have to do it, Ben. The lives of the families in Montezuma and Bluff are depending on us for their very survival."

"But what about the food?" Mary Ann looked from one man to the other. "They're counting on us to bring food, and our rations are starting to run out as well. How can we feed them when we won't have food ourselves?"

"I don't know, Sister Perkins," George said, handing her his plate. "But I believe the story of the loaves and the fishes in the Bible. God can create food out of nothing. We'll need to trust that He'll do it for us."

* * *

Hole in the Rock
January 26, 1880

Ben picked up the last of the oak staffs and shoved it into the hole he had created. To his left, the rest of the staffs stretched along the wall of the cliff eighteen inches apart, and all that remained was to cover them with brush. Hyrum and some of the other men brought armload after armload of shadscale and laid it on top of the poles, then they all stood back and looked at what they had done. The groove for the inner wheel had been chiseled and smoothed out, and Ben couldn't think of another thing that needed to be done to prepare.

"All right, men, we're ready to use the road." Ben dropped his chisel into a bucket. "Come daybreak, we'll be heading down."

He climbed up the rope, hand over hand. Once at the top, he turned to look down. The dugway looked sturdy, but he knew as well as anyone that looks could be deceiving.

Ben couldn't sleep that night. He tried not to toss and turn, knowing that any movement in the wagon disturbed Mary Ann.

But she sensed that he lay awake. She reached over and took his hand. "What's the matter?" she asked softly.

"I'm worried about tomorrow," he replied. He rolled onto his elbow and looked at her. "I've done everything I can, and I have felt the hand of the Lord guiding me as I planned the dugway, but we have yet to see if it works."

"It will work," Mary Ann told him. "We're supposed to be doing this."

Ben leaned back and stared at the roof of the wagon. "I know the Lord is directing us, but people could die if this fails. My mind is playing tricks on me, telling me to doubt."

"Tell your mind to be quiet and go to sleep," Mary Ann said. She turned on her side and gazed into his eyes. "The dugway will work. I know it will."

The strength of her faith comforted him, as it always did. He fell asleep minutes later, his wife's hand against his cheek.

The Saints were up before dawn, packing up their wagons and securing their belongings with rope. Word had been sent to the Saints at Dance Hall Rock that it was time, and their wagons began pulling in shortly after daybreak. Ben situated the heaviest items on the bottoms of the wagons, centered carefully and surrounded by blankets and other soft items. Mary Ann dressed her girls in their sturdiest dresses and shoes, and wrapped an extra blanket around Naomi. Sarah offered to make breakfast, but both Ben and Mary Ann said they weren't hungry, so she fed the little girls and packed the rest of the food away.

The wagons were lined up and ready to descend, but there was some discussion as to who would go first. Many men wanted to, and others said that they wanted to see how it worked before attempting it themselves.

Ben listened for a few minutes, then spoke up. "I think my wagon should be the first to go down," he said. "After all, I'm the one responsible for this, and if it doesn't work, it's only fitting that I be the one to find it out." The other men nodded.

"I'll drive Sarah's wagon down first, and be back for the others," he told Mary Ann.

Ben climbed up in the seat of the second wagon and looked down at his little family, huddled close together.

"You don't mind if I drive your wagon, do you, Sarah?" he joked, looking at his sister-in-law.

"You'll have to, if you want it to go down that hole," she replied. "I won't drive it down there."

Ben laughed and turned to his wife. "I'll be right back," he promised. He studied her eyes, trying to convey to her how much he loved her. Who knew what was about to happen, and he couldn't go without telling her one last time.

Mary Ann didn't say anything. She nodded, biting her lower lip. Ben could see from the way her arms were crossed that she struggled to maintain control. Her eyes were bright, but dry.

Ben took a deep breath and urged the horses to go forward. He stopped them at the top of the Hole.

"Are you ready?" he called out.

"We are." Men standing on either side of the notch had tied ropes to the back of the wagon. "We'll pull on these so you don't go down too fast," one of them said to Ben.

Ben and Kumen got down under the wagons and wrapped heavy chains around the wheel felloes. Then they secured the running gears. "I've got to go as slowly as possible," Ben called out to Kumen. "If I spin out of control, who knows what will happen."

Ben climbed back up onto his driver's seat. He urged his team forward, but they wouldn't go. They crept to the edge and looked over, then took several steps backward, clearly terrified.

"I'm going to need some help," Ben called out after several attempts. "They won't move."

Several men came forward and grasped the wagon, pushing it forward until the neck yokes pushed the collars up to the horses' ears, and they had no choice but to go forward.

"Ben, be careful," he heard Mary Ann call out. He raised his hand in response, took a deep breath, and forced his animals over the top, with help from the men behind.

When the front of the wagon tipped down, for a split second Ben wanted to turn back. The trail below him dropped out from under him, sixty feet of virtual freefall. But there was no way to stop now.

Before the thought could even process, he was going down, holding onto his teams with all his might. He planted his feet and leaned back, trying to keep from falling out of the wagon. The horses screamed as they plunged down the chute, their hooves sliding out from under them as though they were trying to run on ice. The sound of the wheels scratching on the rock filled Ben's brain, and he wished his hands were free so he could plug his ears. After a few seconds of absolute terror, feeling as though his head would explode, Ben reached the dugway.

Those who had worked on the project had affectionately named that stretch "Uncle Ben's Dugway." Ben felt honored to be remembered in such a way, but at the moment, the weight of responsibility sat on his shoulders. If it was a success, he would be a hero. If it failed, he would be culpable for whatever tragedy took place.

Until Ben had tested it out for himself, he couldn't be confident that it would really hold. He flicked the reins, and the team walked out onto the oak staffs that had been pushed into the holes in the cliff wall. He maneuvered the wagon until the left wheel nestled in the groove, and they went forward. The wheels crunched on the brush that had been laid out over the staffs. They proceeded with caution another fifty feet to the end of the dugway, where the ground rose up to meet them and carry them the rest of the way to the river. The horses were much relieved to be back on solid ground, and so was Ben.

He raced back up the trail, pulling himself up the chute with the help of the rope they had placed there. Mary Ann waited for him at the top, and he swept her up and kissed her, heedless of who else might be watching.

"It worked! It worked!" he told her, swinging her around.

"Of course it did," she said. She reached up and brushed his hair back from his forehead. "Now, we'd better get the rest of these wagons down."

* * *

The rest of the day was spent moving one wagon after the other and ushering down the women and children who had walked—sometimes sliding down the chute on their bottoms. The wagons lined up at the top, each man with his heart in his throat. Although afraid, the missionaries turned to God and sang His praises as they approached the Hole, singing "Come, Come Ye Saints"—a song they knew would give them comfort.

A crew was organized at the base of the Hole to keep the wagons rolling out from the path of those who had yet to come down, and get them over to the ferry, where Charles Hall and his sons loaded them as quickly as they could and got them to the other side of the river, three hundred and fifty feet away.

Ben guided the teams down and helped those horses who had fallen to get back on their feet. He watched anxiously for his family, grinning from ear to ear when he saw them emerge from the Hole.

Sarah and Mary Ann walked carefully, holding hands with the little girls, and reached the bottom in safety.

The sun started to set. Stanford Smith had been working at the ferry, helping get the wagons on board and across the river. Suddenly he wasn't there anymore, and Ben wondered where he'd gone.

After a few minutes, he realized that Stanford's wagon must still be at the top. He hadn't seen it come through, and he hadn't seen Arabella, Stanford's wife.

"Stanford's still at the top," he called to some of the men who were loading the last of the wagons on the ferry. "Let's go and get him down."

"Be there in a minute," came the answer.

About ten minutes later, Ben headed toward the Hole with four helpers. They had barely begun the uphill climb when Stanford's wagon came rushing past, nearly running them over. They followed it to the river, where it came to a stop on the bank.

"We're sorry we didn't get there sooner, Stanford," Ben began, but Stanford cut him off.

"Forget it, fellows, we managed fine." He looked at them with obvious disgust on his face and glanced at his wife, who sat on the wagon seat. "My wife here is all the help a man needs."

The five men didn't know what to say, and followed Stanford as he drove his wagon on to the raft. He gently laid Arabella down on a pallet near the raft's edge, and she went to sleep.

As the last of the rigs touched the bank on the opposite side of the river, Ben looked across the blue expanse and gazed up at the notch they had created. What they had just done was impossible. But with God, nothing is impossible.

CHAPTER TWENTY-ONE

Colorado River
January 26, 1880

The Saints were exhausted.

The day had not only been physically demanding, but it had taken every speck of emotional strength they could muster to face that hole. Now they were on the other side of the river, and things would ease up from there. The hard part of the journey was over.

Ben needed to talk to Stanford. He took Mary Ann with him, hoping that with her gentle ways, they could find out what happened and soothe Stanford's feelings. They approached the Smith's wagon with trepidation, not sure what sort of welcome they would get.

Stanford sat alone outside his wagon, staring up into the night sky. Ben did not see Arabella or the children anywhere.

"Stanford, I've come to apologize," Ben said. "I don't know why no one was there to help you, but I'll see what I can do to find out."

"Never mind," Stanford said. He sounded tired. "It's not important."

"I want to do what I can to make it right," Ben insisted.

Stanford motioned for them to sit. "I'd like to tell you a story, if you have a minute."

Ben and Mary Ann both nodded.

"Well, as you know, I'd been at the bottom all day, helping. Word came that all the wagons were down, but I didn't see mine anywhere. I cropped my shovel and climbed to the top of the crevice.

"My wife sat at the top waiting for me, wrapped in blankets and holding our baby. She told me she thought I'd never come.

"Our wagon had been pulled off to the side, and our two children sat in it, waiting for me. I took off my hat and stomped on it a few times. I thought that with me down there helping to get the wagons on the raft, someone would bring the wagon down for me. I felt pretty angry to find we'd been forgotten. There was no one at the top to hold the ropes for us, either."

The fire snapped, and Ben felt Mary Ann startle. The sound was a harsh intruder into their quiet conversation.

"Belle told me she had the horses harnessed and the things all packed. Sure enough, she had done everything she could to get ready. I tied our old horse Nig to the rear axle, and then Belle helped me cross-lock the wheels.

"I told her I feared we couldn't make it. She was calm as she could be. 'We have to make it,' she said.

"I told her that if we had someone to hold the wagon back, we might succeed."

Stanford paused and rubbed his face. He resumed talking, his voice thick with tears.

"Belle said she would hold the wagon back."

"Oh, no!" Mary Ann exclaimed.

"She told me she'd pull back on Nig's lines and that we'd leave the children at the top, and come back for them. I worried we wouldn't come back, but she said we would. We wrapped the children up in blankets and set them on a snow bank. Roy, he's our three-year-old, sat down, and Belle put the baby between his legs. She told him to hold his little brother until we came back for them. She put Ada, our oldest, in front of the two boys and asked her to say a little prayer, and told them not to move and not to stand up." Tears ran freely down Stanford's cheeks.

"Ada asked me if we were going to come back. I nodded my head. She said, 'Then I'm not afraid.' She said a little prayer, the sweetest prayer I've ever heard. She said, 'Bless me and Roy and baby until our father comes back.'

"I climbed onto the seat and took up the reins. Belle pulled back as hard as she could, but the momentum of the wagon pulled her off her feet, and she was thrown under. Her foot caught between two rocks. A jagged rock tore her leg open."

Mary Ann reached out and grasped Ben's hand.

"The wagon struck a boulder at the bottom of the chute, and it flung her up on her feet. When I looked back, she was standing upright.

"The team had wedged under the tongue of the wagon. I got down and loosened the tugs to free the team, then turned to Arabella. There she stood, her face white against the red sandstone.

"She was the most gallant thing I've ever seen as she stood there, defiant, blood-smeared, covered in dirt, and her eyes flashing. She had the look on her face that always tells me she doesn't want my sympathy.

"I asked her how she made it, and she said, 'Oh, I crow-hopped right along!' She didn't tell me until we had crossed the river just all that had happened to her on the way down.

"I looked her over and saw the gash on her leg. She admitted Nig had dragged her all the way. I asked if her leg was broken." Stanford laughed harshly. "She kicked me and asked if the leg felt broken to me. I knew then that she would be all right."

He wiped his eyes. Mary Ann's fingers held on to Ben's tightly.

"I climbed up to the top and found the children right where I'd left them. The baby had gone to sleep, and Roy complained that his arm was almost broken from holding him. Little George woke up and gave me a toothless smile. Ada told me they had waited right there with God until I came back for them."

Stanford bowed his head and wept, his shoulders heaving. Ben glanced at Mary Ann and saw that tears ran down her cheeks as well. Ben wasn't immune to the spirit of the story, and he swallowed several times lest he cry himself.

"I took the children down the chute to the top of the dugway, where I had left the wagon," Stanford said after several minutes.

"We came down the rest of the way without a trouble, and that's when we encountered you and the other men coming up to help. I was angry, Ben, and I shouldn't have been. I was scared, rightfully so, and shaken, but I shouldn't have lashed out at you. I'm sorry."

"We're the ones who need to apologize," Ben said, but Stanford held up his hand.

"I realized, coming down the Hole, how much my family means to me. I might not have learned that lesson if I hadn't come so close to losing them. I think the Lord wanted to teach me today. I'm ashamed of how I acted toward you. Please forgive me."

Ben reached out to shake Stanford's hand, and held it in a tight grip for several seconds.

"How is Belle?" Mary Ann asked.

"She seems to be fine, but she's worn out. She's lying down with the children in the wagon."

"May I peek in at her?"

"Certainly."

Ben waited at the fire with Stanford while Mary Ann checked on the sleeping family in the wagon. He was shaken, listening to Stanford's story. They almost lost Sister Smith that day, but instead, she made it down, and not one member of the party had perished. It was as if God Himself had stretched forth His hand and brought the wagons down by the strength of His power, and yet found the time to sit with three scared children atop a snow bank while they waited for their father.

* * *

Thomas sat at the Perkins' wagon, his head in his hands. "My head aches," he said. "Have you ever tried to drive eighteen hundred head of cattle down a cliff?"

Sarah smiled as she handed him a cup of hot broth. "No, I don't think I ever have."

"The animals were frightened, and so were we. The last thing we wanted was a whole herd of scared cows angry with us. We couldn't get them to move on their own, so we had to push them over the top of the cliff. Their hooves were going everywhere. Once we finally got them all down, it took us twenty river crossings to get them all over here." He pulled at the blanket he wore. "Hence my fashionable attire." His clothes hung near the fire to get dry, and Sarah poked at them to see if they were getting close. Not yet.

"Where are Ben and Mary Ann?"

"They went to pay a call on another wagon. Apparently something scary happened on the way down the Hole."

"Only one? I would have thought that a great many scary things happened."

"It all went remarkably well, as near as I can tell. The girls and I walked down with Mary Ann, holding hands all the way. We didn't have a bit of trouble."

"I'm going to hear the bellows of the cows in my dreams tonight," Thomas said. He stood up and checked his clothes. "These will have to stay here 'til morning. I'll get some clean ones out of the wagon, and then I'm going to bed."

"Good night," Sarah called after him and sat back down by the fire, holding her hands out to the warmth.

She had purposely tried to sound cheerful while speaking to Thomas, wanting to keep the conversation light. But truth be told, she had been terrified. When the moment came to approach the top of the cliff and start down the other side, her feet had refused to move for a moment. But with Mary Jane tugging on one hand and Delia pulling at the other, their little faces turned up toward hers, she knew she had to put on a brave front for their sakes, if not for her own. She had noticed that several of the horses wore blinders to keep from seeing what they were about to do, and she wished she had a pair as well.

Once on the bottom, she had to admit it wasn't as bad as she'd feared. It was certainly easier walking than to drive one of the wagons. She had seen the looks of fear and anxiety on the faces of some of the men as they approached the Hole, and she felt grateful beyond expression that Brother Perkins had driven her wagon and not asked her to do it. He had just enough gall that

she wouldn't have been one bit surprised if he'd asked her to lead
the team through that crevice. But she would not have agreed,
not for anything.

* * *

Western Bank of the Colorado River
End of January, 1880

A two hundred and fifty foot wall of sheer cliff formed the
eastern barrier of the Colorado River. The men from Dance Hall
Rock who had been assigned to build the road during the work
on The Hole had done a fair amount of blasting, and a narrow
dugway had been created that angled diagonally across the face
of the cliff to the top. From her perch on the wagon seat, Sarah
looked up and shuddered at the fearsome road.

But hadn't they just come through the Hole? They could do
anything.

She drove the wagon to the base of the dugway, then willingly
turned the reins over to Ben.

"You're saving all the fun for me, aren't you, Sarah?" Ben said
as he took the reins from her.

"There are some kinds of fun I don't want to have."

The wagons moved up the dugway slowly and carefully. Those
with more than one wagon either asked someone else to help
them drive, or left one wagon at the base and came back for it.
After what seemed like an eternity, all the wagons were finally at
the top, and they could move on. The horses were exhausted
from pulling up such a steep incline and seemed grateful for a
stretch of flat land.

Day after day the wagons moved east, up hill, down hill, over
crevice and down into gulleys. Sometimes the terrain was so
slick, the horses and oxen could barely keep their footing.

The pioneers passed the broad and slippery expanse of
Register Rocks. They camped at Cottonwood Creek, enjoying a
ten-day respite from the glaring sun as they relaxed under the
cottonwood trees, mended their wagons, and washed their

clothes—only to load back up and continue their journey. Sarah's hands were growing calloused, but she no longer cared. One look at the hands of the men who went ahead to build the road erased any complaint she might have had about her own skin.

CHAPTER TWENTY-TWO

Cottonwood Hill
February 11, 1880

Sarah guided the horses to the base of Cottonwood Hill and looked up. Those were cliffs of limestone, not sandstone, as the other cliffs had been. Seventy road builders and a thousand pounds of blasting powder had come from Panguitch, arriving on the first of February. She felt grateful for the additional help and supplies, but couldn't help shaking her head as she looked up at the seemingly insurmountable obstacle.

The men had gotten to work right away, now more than familiar with all that went into blasting a road. Chisel a hole, place the powder, insert a wick, tamp with mud, set it off. They worked automatically, tasks that they had never even tried before, now performed in rhythm.

The women had their rhythms, too. Build a fire, cook the food, tend the children, and mend the clothes. After a time it was as though they had always lived out on the trail. But despite the confidence they had in their tasks, it still took over two weeks to build a road up that cliff.

Thomas drove the wagon to the base of the hill. Sarah sat beside him, thankful he wasn't on duty with the livestock, and holding on to the seat with all her might. She could see Mary Jane's head poke out the back of the wagon ahead, and she called out for the girl to get inside and hang on tight. The wagons tipped upward, and the horses climbed, their hooves slipping even though they had been newly shod. Sarah clenched her eyes tight and wouldn't open them again until Thomas said they were stopping.

"What's the matter?"

"The horses can't do it. It's too steep."

He climbed down and went to confer with the other men. Sarah pulled out her handkerchief and wiped her face and hands, which were sticky with sweat and coated with grime that clung to her like honey.

Thomas came back. "We're going to need to back up." He urged the horses to retreat, leaning to the left and looking back to see where they were going.

He parked the wagon and handed the reins to Sarah. "Wait here. I'll see what's going on."

He was gone a long time. Sarah had dozed off and awakened again before he returned.

"The men have to hitch the teams up seven strong to get the wagon to the top," he said. "They've named the upper portion of this hill Little Hole in the Rock. The men had to do quite a bit of blasting up there—that's why we were camped for so long."

"Seven teams?" Sarah asked. "Fourteen horses to get a wagon to the top?"

Thomas nodded. "We're in for quite an adventure. I'm going to go back and see if there's anything I can do to help."

He returned fairly soon and took the reins. "If ever you've closed your eyes before, now's a good time as well." He flicked the reins on the horses' backs, and they were off.

The grade rose at an extreme angle, the other Perkins wagon now behind them instead of in front. The wagons ahead of them moved slowly, the horses straining against their shoulder harnesses.

Sarah closed her eyes but kept opening them as sounds from up ahead distracted her. She heard a scream as the wagon in front of them went off the side of the road, despite the two solid weeks of blasting that had been done to try to prevent such things from happening.

Some of the brethren came and tied ropes to their wagon to try and keep them from tipping over. The road became steeper and more treacherous by the minute. Six additional teams were brought to haul them over the top. All this Sarah saw through brief glimpses as she covered her face, her eyes sometimes flying open of their own accord to take in surroundings she'd rather not see. An ache in her stomach grew more fierce by the minute as her anxiety mounted.

Finally they reached the top of the Little Hole in the Rock at Cottonwood Hill. The horses were exhausted and covered in foam, their legs scratched and bleeding from all the times they had gone down on their knees. The men were worn out and drained from all the effort. As they rolled forward, the wagon wheels sank into thick sand that lay everywhere, threatening to bog down their rigs. They pulled through to the other side and gratefully made camp.

Sarah lowered herself from the wagon seat, her knees nearly collapsing beneath her. She made it to the fire ring, but just barely, her strength gone.

"Did you hear about the beehive?" Mary Ann asked as she placed the kettle over the fire.

"No. What happened?"

"One of the wagons that tipped had a beehive on the side. When the wagon fell, the beehive broke, and all the bees came out. They were practically frozen by the cold and didn't fly away, and all the owners had to do was pick the bees up and put them in a sack."

Sarah smiled, too tired to laugh at the funny story. The children went to bed that night without any fuss. Naomi drifted off in Sarah's arms, which were sore from the strain of holding herself on the wagon seat. Too exhausted to carry her niece to the wagon bed, she sat by the fire, staring into the flames, relishing the warmth of the sleeping baby against her chest. The trip had proven to be more than she had ever anticipated—more difficult, surely, and more challenging. But the Saints in the group seemed to be up to the task. It was her own strength she doubted.

* * *

Grey Mesa
February 13, 1880

Sarah automatically pulled her team to a standstill when she saw the wagon ahead of her slow. "Grey Mesa!" the call came back through the group. "Camp here."

She pulled her wagon off to the side and slid off the seat. Her muscles were aching from the drive. She walked around for a moment to work the stiffness from her legs, then set to work unhitching the horses. She was nearly through when Ben came back to check on her, carrying Naomi in one arm and holding on to Delia with the other.

"How are things back here, Sarah?" he asked.

"Just fine."

He nodded, looking around. "This is a good spot for a camp." He brought his attention back to the task she performed. "You're doing very well, Sarah. Thank you for your help."

His voice was very soft, and she looked up, surprised. His eyes were bright with frank friendship, and she smiled. "You're welcome."

Riders approached that evening, hailing the camp from a distance. Platte Lyman went out to greet them and returned with the news, "It's a supply delivery from the tithing office in Panguitch." The riders delivered two hundred pounds of pork and forty pounds of cheese. Platte distributed the pork to the families, but there wasn't enough cheese to go around fairly, so he held an auction and sold the cheese to the highest bidders.

Sarah watched the proceedings with interest. The men called out their bids cheerfully enough to start, then with more frustration as they were outbid and had to raise their price. Ben walked up and stood beside her, chuckling a little bit.

"They're trying so hard to outdo each other," he said. "I'm going to be grateful for my own bit of pork and leave them to their squabbling."

Sarah agreed, and they began to walk back to their camp. George Hobbs was approaching, and stopped to talk.

"Ben, Sister Williams."

Sarah didn't bother to correct him. She had been called Sister Williams nearly from the start of their journey, and it didn't seem to make any difference to the Saints that she wasn't a baptized member of the Church. They called her Sister all the same.

"I'm heading out in the morning. I promised my sister that I'd be back with supplies, and I'm running out of time to keep that promise. I thought we'd be there by now."

"I did too, George," Ben said softly, his dark eyes solemn.

"If I don't take some food to Montezuma, I'll have my sister's blood on my hands. I'm taking a pack train and a few men out with me at first light."

"Good luck and Godspeed." Ben shook hands with George, who tipped his hat to Sarah and disappeared into the dark.

"George Hobbs is a good friend," Ben commented as they neared their own camp. "He hired me to help clear some land a few years ago, and we worked well together. I surely hope he reaches his sister in time."

"And if he doesn't?" Sarah asked.

"He'll never forgive himself."

* * *

Wilson Canyon on top of Grey Mesa
February 17, 1880

Sarah had never seen anything like it. They were up on top of a mesa, and yet they were approaching another crevice in the land. Wilson Canyon stretched out ahead, a deep gash that cut straight across their path with no way to go around it. The wagons would have to go down into it and up the other side. Thomas was on duty with the herds, and Sarah didn't know what to do. She had been blessed so far in not having to take the wagon on the more treacherous slopes, but with Thomas gone . . .

"I'll take the first wagon down and come back." She didn't know Ben was approaching until he stood right beside her. She looked at him with relief. She had more confidence with the team now than ever, but the thought of driving the wagon down that incline filled her with dread.

"Thank you, Brother Perkins," she said. "I'll wait here."

She watched as the wagons disappeared one at a time over the top of the canyon. Ben and Mary Ann's wagon passed from view, as did the Rowley's, and Hyrum and Rachel Perkins'. Finally Ben returned and climbed up onto the wagon seat.

"Is it bad?" she asked.

"It's bad enough," he replied, and urged the horses forward.

Sarah had purposely not gone to the edge to look over, although tempted to while waiting for Ben to return. She knew that it would only make her nerves worse. As they neared the edge, she could see the path before them, a steep and smooth slope entirely made of sandstone. The men had thrown small rocks and sand along the path, trying to provide some traction. Ben pulled out the chains and wrapped them around the back wheels and put on the brakes.

"Here we go," he said.

Sarah grabbed the edge of the seat, and they were off. The wagon skidded down the path, the rocks in their way doing very little to slow their descent. They arrived at the bottom breathless, but safe.

The only way out of the canyon was up a smooth watercourse they dubbed The Chute. It looked impossible, as had many other parts of their journey. The Saints paused for a short time to rest and regroup.

"I thought once we got through the Hole in the Rock, everything would be fine," Ann Rowley said, walking up to the Perkins' wagon with John Taylor on her hip.

"I believe we all thought that," Mary Ann replied, Sarah nodding in agreement.

"I would say that the Hole in the Rock has actually been one of the easier things we've had to do," Ben said. "But we'll do this as well, never you fear."

"I'm not afraid," Ann said, a little fire in her eyes. "I'm just wondering what you're going to blow up now, to get us there."

Ben threw back his head and laughed. "I'll blow up anything that gets in our way, Sister Rowley."

The Saints gathered around for a prayer, then scattered sand and rocks over the surface of The Chute. They put two teams of horses on each wagon, leaving many rigs at the bottom and coming back for them later. Sarah stayed with her wagon until Ben returned, having taken Mary Ann and the children to the top.

He climbed to the seat and took the reins. "Hold on," he said, gathering up his whip.

They approached the Chute, but the horses wouldn't go up. Ben raised the whip, and it came down with a crack, hissing off the backs of the animals. They crept forward, but halted again. Over and over he whipped them, bringing the lash down whenever they stalled.

Sarah felt sorry for the poor animals, but she knew Ben had no choice. The wagon must get to the top, and the horses must pull it.

When they reached the top, they saw Mary Ann standing just off the path, anxiously waiting for them. Her face relaxed when she saw them.

"We had a hard time getting up," she told Sarah. "Ben had to whip the poor horses several times before we crested. I'm glad you made it."

"So am I," Sarah said, rubbing her temples.

She turned in time to see Samuel Rowley bring his team of oxen over the ridge. They seemed to be able to hold their footing better than the horses, and for a moment she wished that she had a pair of oxen on her wagon, too.

But no—if she did, she'd have to drive them, and she had no desire to try to control those ornery animals. The team of horses was bad enough.

* * *

Grey Mesa
February 28, 1880

The cold bit through the canvas wagon cover with icy teeth. Sarah wrapped another blanket around Mary Jane and put her arm around her, trying to give both of them some heat. She didn't want to put her head outside the wagon, sure it was even colder outside. To think that in the middle of all that, Olivia Larson had just given birth to a baby boy. She wondered how Sister Larson managed.

They had reached the edge of Grey Mesa. It ended abruptly with sandstone cliffs reaching down a thousand feet—a smooth, almost oily surface. They had been there for seven days, huddling together in the cold and wind as the road builders tried to create a path down to the valley floor. They were only partway down the cliffs when the engineers from Panguitch gave up and went back home.

Sarah watched with amusement. Those Mormon Saints, bullheaded in their stubborn loyalty to their religion, were accomplishing more than the professionals brought in to help them. They had already chiseled and blasted a narrow passage partway down when the engineers left, and they just kept on working after their help was gone. They gouged out a series of steps to fill with sand to give the horses some footing. That had been only the day before, and the road had already been pronounced ready to try.

Finally Sarah knew she could not lie in bed any longer, and she got up before she could change her mind. The camp moved through its morning routine numbly, joints stiff from the cold. Mary Ann cut a loaf of bread she'd baked the night before, and they ate standing up, anxious to get the descent behind them.

Twelve men stood ready with ropes to hold back the wagons. The road before them was steep, but no more so than any of the others they had successfully navigated.

Thomas was on hand to help Sarah with the wagon. At first she had thought it a nice coincidence that either he or Ben was always there to help when there was a steep incline to traverse, but then she realized they had worked it out that way. She was still a little bit irritated that they had given her the job of driving the second wagon in the first place, but it warmed her heart to realize they were watching over her and wouldn't allow her to do anything that might bring her harm.

The road was slippery, but all the wagons got down safely, with no incident, and passed over Slick Rocks—the very spot where George Hobbs had seen the strange animal. Once they reached the valley floor, they found guide stones placed by the scouts and followed the marked trail to a beautiful lake, edged with stones and trees, arriving there just at the beginning of March.

"What is this place?" Sarah asked.

"The scouts say it's called Lake Pagahrit. That means *standing water*," Thomas said. He brought the horses right down to the edge of the unusually blue water and let them drink their fill.

"It's like an oasis out in the desert," Sarah said. She climbed down from the wagon and washed her face and hands. Again she was filled with the desire to jump in face first, holding herself back by the force of will.

"We'll be staying here for a few days to rest the horses," Ben said, coming up to them. "I'm looking forward to the break."

"How's your rig holding up, Ben?" Thomas asked.

"The axles are worrying me a bit. I'll have to do some repairs while we're stopped."

"This wagon needs some attention too," Thomas said.

"I'll see to it," Ben promised.

Sarah and Mary Ann pulled every stitch of clothing and bedding out of both wagons and plunged them into the lake. Everything they owned was covered in dust, the pernicious stuff having filtered in through every gap in the wagon cover. Ben chopped down a small tree and made a drying rack, and they spread the wet laundry on the branches out in a rare patch of sunshine— a small piece of civilization in a very uncivilized land.

"Now it's our turn," Mary Ann announced. "Ben, keep an eye on the girls."

Ben raised a hand in acknowledgement, and the sisters walked along the edge of the lake, looking for a secluded cove. They found one after several minutes, and Sarah gave in to her instincts and threw herself into the water. It was just warm enough to keep her from getting a chill, but not warm enough to keep her from gasping as she surfaced. She let down her braid and scrubbed her hair, rinsing out the days and weeks of dirt and grime that had accumulated.

No bath had ever felt more wonderful.

CHAPTER TWENTY-THREE

Clay Hill Pass
March 12, 1880

N ot again." The words came involuntarily to Sarah's lips as she looked at the gully ahead. The Saints had rested by the lake for several wonderful days, but they couldn't stay there forever, no matter how badly they wanted to, and they had continued on their way. Since then it had been nothing but hills and gullies, up and down, forcing their poor, tired animals down one incline after another. Sarah drove the teams down the more mild grades, and one of the men took over when things became potentially dangerous.

She wondered how the animals were faring. They looked tired, almost resigned, and she wished she could read their thoughts. Surely they were even more weary of the monotony than she was—they were the ones doing all the work.

The wagons passed over the last of the sand hills and reached Castle Wash, which they followed to Clay Hill Pass. The snow blew in sideways, covering everything with a thin glaze of white and chilling Sarah's fingers through. She and Mary Ann did everything they could to keep the children warm, especially Naomi, still so small.

Sarah worried about Thomas when he was out with the livestock and not in camp. The wind gusted strongly enough to take her breath away, and was cold enough that she almost didn't care if she got it back. It numbed her mind and all her senses. Out in the foraging areas, there was little cover, and she wondered how her brother was managing not to freeze.

They pushed forward. Sarah wrapped strips of cloth around her hands to ward off the cold, but her fingers still felt frozen after a few hours of driving the team. They reached Clay Hill Pass and stopped. The mountain plateau ended in a sheer drop of almost twelve hundred feet.

"Everyone stay here," came the word. "We're sending scouts."

Platte D. Lyman, George Sevy, and Samuel Bryson took a pack horse with them and set out to find a way down the cliff. Everyone else set about keeping warm—a hard task that took nearly all their time. The men of the camp knew that they would have to clear a road, and decided to get to work on that while the scouts were gone.

Mary Ann and Sarah took care of the camp while Ben and Thomas worked on the road with the other men. When the scouts came back five days later, they said the words everyone had been expecting, and yet dreading. They would have to build another dugway—but at least the road was almost done.

Sarah marked the date in her journal that morning, March 12th. She had walked to the edge of the road and seen what they were up against—a narrow, slippery chute just wide enough for one wagon. It would be so easy for the wagon to go off the side and tumble down to the bottom. She closed her eyes. They had come that far and been successful. Surely the Lord would see them through the rest as well.

She almost laughed at the thought. She was starting to sound like a Mormon. She had spent so much time in their company that their phrases were starting to creep into her own vocabulary. She remembered how her minister had warned her to be careful lest the Mormons lure her in a little at a time, slowly making her one of their own. It was happening already. But she didn't find it as objectionable as she once had.

"There you are," Thomas said, coming up behind her and standing at her side on the top of the cliff. "I've been looking for you."

"Are you going to drive it for me?" she asked, nodding at the trail.

"Yes, unless you want to do it yourself."

"I will do no such thing."

"I didn't think so. Yes, I'll be driving."

The sun started to peek over the rocks. "You were up and out of camp so early, I was worried about you."

Sarah turned and gave her brother a smile. "Thank you for caring about me. Truly. Not just this morning, but through this whole trip."

He wrapped his arm around her shoulders. "You're welcome. Now, what's bothering you?"

"You can read me that well?"

"I can."

Sarah looked down at the road again, trying to put her words into thoughts. "When the scouts told the Saints that another road would have to be created, I heard a sigh of disappointment. But I didn't hear anyone complain or give up. They were all resigned to what they must do, and they did it."

"I noticed that, too."

"Why are they pressing forward like this, Thomas? Given my own choice, based on what knowledge I have, I would have given up the expedition at the Hole in the Rock. It was impossible. But Brother Perkins found a way, and we all came down without a single death and only one bad injury. And what did the Saints do? They packed up the very next day, kept moving, built another road, and did the whole thing all over again. I've seen them do this for five months now, Thomas. Get up, blast a hole, drive through it, do it again the next day. I don't understand."

"They're a stubborn people, that's a fact."

"They aren't just stubborn. They're devoted."

A horse whinnied and a man shouted. Sarah and Thomas turned at the sound of commotion behind them. "It sounds like it's time to go harness up the teams," Thomas said. "Come on, let's go down this mountain. We'll have to solve the mysteries of the Mormons later."

* * *

Whirlwind Bench
March 15, 1880

Three days later, all the wagons were at the bottom of Clay Hill Pass and camped at Whirlwind Bench. It had been a very long and frightening two days. They had locked the wheels on the wagons and tied ropes to the back, much as they had done on all the other steep roads. Slowly and carefully, one wagon at a time, they came down the cliff. Each teamster breathed a sigh of relief and a prayer of thanks as they pulled in to the camp.

Sarah's wagon was one of the first down, and she watched the rest make the descent. Surely it was not the hand of men alone. She began to feel that if only she looked close enough, she would see angels guiding those wagons down the mountain.

That night was the coldest Sarah had ever known. She put all her clothing on in layers and took Mary Jane to bed with her, piling the blankets over the top of them both and holding her niece close, trying to share the heat between them. She had seen Mary Ann put Naomi's feet down the front of her dress, trying to keep them warm.

Sarah shivered so badly, she didn't think she'd ever fall asleep, and wasn't sure that she wouldn't freeze to death. The cold was a monster, reaching into the wagon and threatening to tear her limb from limb.

She had just started to doze when she heard voices. She lifted her head to listen.

"Platte?" It was Ben's voice. "What's the matter?"

"I didn't mean to wake you, Ben. Nothing's the matter. I'm walking around, trying to stay warm. It's impossible to be comfortable in bed, or anywhere else."

A moment later, Sarah heard Platte Lyman bid Ben good night, and she laid her head back down. Her eyes were just closing again when she heard a sound like a bear under the wagon.

"Thomas!" His head appeared over the top of the flour sacks. "Thomas, I think there's a bear growling outside. No, more than one bear."

Thomas grabbed his rifle and slowly stuck his head through the canvas flaps. "Sarah, get Mary Jane and go over to the other wagon. Quick."

She didn't question. She snatched up the sleeping child and all the blankets she could carry and ran the hundred feet to the wagon where Mary Ann slept with the other little girls. Ben was still awake and took his daughter from Sarah's arms, tucking her in between Caroline and Delia. Thomas came right behind with the rest of the blankets.

"It's a wind storm," he told Ben. "I've got to go see to the livestock."

"Thomas, don't!" Sarah reached out and caught his arm. "They're just cows. Stay here where it's safe."

"They may just be cows, but we need them, Sarah. I'll be all right." He kissed her forehead. "Snuggle down here with everyone else. I'll be back as soon as I can."

He had only been gone for a few minutes when the wind came descending on them in a horrific maelstrom. Despite Sarah's efforts to keep Mary Jane asleep, she woke up, screaming.

Mary Ann and Sarah each took two of the frightened children on their laps. Ben crouched at the rear, holding the canvas flaps closed with his hands. The wind sounded as though it meant to destroy them. Even with all their weight, the wagon rocked from side to side. Soon they heard a large crash, and Ben peeked out.

"It's the other wagon," he said grimly, looking at Sarah. "Tipped clean on its side. If you and Mary Jane had been over there on your own, you would have been thrown onto the ground. I'm glad Thomas brought you here."

Sarah wrapped her arms more tightly around the children, wondering how Thomas knew to bring them over. Was it just for the comfort of being all together, or had he somehow known their wagon sat in danger's path?

The wind finally died down after several hours, and Ben went out to check on the damage and to see if Thomas was safe.

Mary Ann and Sarah worked hard to get the little girls to go back to sleep They spoke words of encouragement, but could not promise that the wind wouldn't come back—they didn't know if it would or not. They certainly prayed that it wouldn't.

"Tents are down all over the place," Ben reported back. "Wagon covers are ripped, and the animals are spooked. Thomas is all right. There are some caves in the hills, and he ducked into one when the wind picked up. He says he'll be by in the morning to help set things to rights. He's going to stay and try to calm the animals for now."

Sarah lay back, relieved to her core. She had already lost Thomas once. She couldn't lose him again.

"I checked on Hyrum and Rachel. They're pretty shaken, but they're all right. I also anchored the other rig. It will be all right until morning." Ben took his place at the head of the wagon bed and pulled the blankets over him. Slowly, everyone went to sleep. It was a little crowded with all of them in there, but Sarah didn't want to be anywhere else on that frozen and frightful night. The sound of everyone else breathing lulled her to sleep, knowing that she was not alone.

The next day it felt much warmer. Ben and Thomas, with help from Hyrum, Kumen Jones, and Samuel Rowley, got the wagon turned back up on its wheels and found that nothing had been ruined inside. They spent the day in repairs and recuperation.

Early the next morning they were off again. The trail ahead lay mostly clear, and for once they were able to travel a good piece without having to stop and build a road. They pulled into Grand Gulch, grateful for a day of peaceful travel.

CHAPTER TWENTY-FOUR

Elk Ridge
March 20, 1880

The wagons were surrounded on all sides with majestic cedars. The air blew cool and pleasant, and Mary Ann inhaled deeply. "It's so fresh here."

Sarah glanced up from where she worked, stirring flour into boiling water over the fire. "It does smell good," she agreed. "The gruel is almost ready. Do we have any molasses left?"

"Just a little bit. This will be the end of it."

"Should we save it for a special occasion?" Sarah asked.

"No, let's just use it now."

Sarah spooned the mixture into bowls for the little girls, then took a fussy Naomi from Mary Ann's arms. "You sit down and eat," she told Mary Ann. "You look tired."

"I was up with the baby quite a bit during the night," Mary Ann said, grateful to relinquish the baby. "I think she's teething."

Sarah turned the baby to face her. "I think you're right," she said. "She looks a little swollen here in front."

Mary Ann took a bite of the hot food. It wasn't the most delicious lunch she had ever eaten, but it warmed her and would be filling. She looked over at Sarah, who crooned to Naomi and made her laugh.

"I'm so glad you came, Sarah," she said impulsively. "I don't know what we would have done without you."

"You would have found a way," Sarah replied. "You always do."

"I'm glad that way was you." Mary Ann reached out and touched her sister's sleeve. "Truly, thank you."

"You're my sister," Sarah said. She hoisted Naomi a little higher on her hip. "How could I have said no?"

Ben, Hyrum, and Thomas came into the camp, covered in sweat and looking weary. "We've chopped down enough trees to go forward about half a mile," Ben said.

"Only half a mile?" Mary Ann asked. "How long is this going to take?"

"We have no way of knowing. But, at least we have enough fuel." Ben smiled, and his eyes twinkled in that special way reserved just for Mary Ann. Ben never ceased to amaze her. Clear out here in the middle of nowhere, living off what they could find or carry, he still found ways to make her feel like the only woman in the world. She would kiss him for that as soon as they had a quiet minute.

Getting the wagons down from the forest plateau to the floor of the canyon was a remarkable feat of road building. After spending days chopping wood and preparing a trail, the men finally announced that the way had been cleared, and they could go forward.

Ben was exhausted. Mary Ann could see it in the little lines around his eyes and the set of his mouth. She tried to get him to rest, but he stubbornly refused until the job was done.

The road was winding, because of the contour of the canyon wall. They dubbed it The Twist and approached it with the same mixture of faith and apprehension as they had every other time they had a new road to try. Again they were blessed with no incidents.

They traveled with relative ease for the next stretch. Ben was starting to relax and sang several Welsh tunes as he drove. Mary Ann felt pleased to see him looking so happy, but she wondered how long it would last. The journey had presented trial after trial. Would her husband have a rest before he was faced with the next challenge? Would there be time to regroup for the next onslaught?

They reached Comb Wash. Behind it loomed Comb Ridge, a thirty-mile-long line of vertical, one thousand-foot-high cliffs that stretched from north to south, completely blocking off those who wished to travel east and west, as the Saints did. Mary Ann had never seen anything so forbidding in her life.

"Don't think about it for now," Ben advised. "We'll cross that mountain when we come to it." He laughed at his own joke because Mary Ann didn't do it for him. "It's our last big obstacle," he told her. "On the other side of those mountains is the San Juan. We're almost there."

Mary Ann tried to smile, but nearly six months on the trail had worn the smile right out of her. Were they really almost there? And where was there, anyway?

The wagons came to a stop, and Platte Lyman decided that they should camp for a few days and wait for stragglers. It would also give them the chance to get a head start on the road they knew they were going to have to build. It was inevitable—like the sun coming up the next morning, they would have to build a road.

* * *

Comb Wash
March 27, 1880

"Hello the camp!"

Ben looked up and saw George Hobbs riding up. Ben raised a hand in greeting. "How is your sister, George?"

George slid off the back of his horse. "She's much relieved for the supplies we sent, and anxious for us to arrive." He looped the reins over the back of his horse. "It's the most amazing thing, Ben. When Harvey Dunton left Montezuma and came back with us, he gave my sister his sack of wheat. After she used up what she had, she turned to his sack and began on it. Time and time again, she thought she had used the last of it, only to find a bit left. Ben, that sack just kept on refilling itself until I got there with supplies."

Ben was astonished. "That is truly a miracle," he said. "Amen."

* * *

Comb Wash
March 29, 1880

Everyone had caught up to the main group, and the road ahead was clear enough for them to proceed. The signal came to roll out, and they went as far as they could, to the point where Comb Wash ended at the San Juan River. They had expected to ford and continue on from there, but the spring rains had swollen the river to far beyond its normal levels, and it rushed too quickly for them to cross in safety.

"It looks like we'll have to go up and over the ridge here," Platte Lyman said.

Ben stepped back and looked upward. The mountain rose steep and tall, covered in slick rocks and boulders. He felt tired just looking at it.

"We have to break out of the wash," Platte said. "I wish we didn't have to go this way, but I can't see any other choice."

Ben thought about the options for a few moments and realized that they didn't really have any. They simply could not cross the river. It was far too great a risk that they would get swept away in the current.

It would be yet another impossible dugway. Ben rubbed his face. How many roads had they built? How many dugways had they constructed and blasted? He'd lost count. The urge to get to the San Juan drove him on, day and night. He had been called to perform the work. He knew it was the Lord's task for him, and he was determined to do it, whatever the cost. But he had to admit to himself that he felt worn down. It seemed almost too much to create one more road. And adding to the challenge, they were out of blasting powder.

He thought for a few more minutes. "How will we do it?" he asked at length.

"That's what I was hoping you could tell me," Platte replied with a smile.

Several of the men met together the next morning to discuss the situation. They decided to pile loose rocks on the outside edge and chisel grooves into the mountain on the inside edge. The grooves would hold sand to act as traction for the inside wheel, and, hopefully, the rocks would keep the wagon from going off the side.

The men began carting rocks and placing them. For five days they worked, carrying thousands of rocks and fitting them together with precision. They had no mortar. Only the careful placement of the stones, like a jigsaw puzzle, would ensure that they stayed intact.

"We'll be using the road in the morning," Ben told his family that night over the fire, his hands and back aching from the hard work. It took all he had to remain upright when he so badly longed to fall over into his bed.

"I'm worried about the animals," Thomas said. "It's been six months since they had enough to eat. They barely survived the wind and snow. I'm surprised we didn't lose more of them than we did. How are they going to make it up that mountain?"

"I don't know," Ben replied honestly. He'd had the same thought many times. In addition, the harnesses were fraying from the constant strain. Would they hold? He had no way to tell.

* * *

San Juan Hill
April 2, 1880

"Pull! Pull!" Ben whipped the horses and snapped the reins for all he was worth. Seven teams of horses were hitched to his wagon, each pulling with their might. Slowly they moved forward, fighting gravity and the rocks beneath that caused them to stumble. The lead horse on the right fell to his knees.

One of the men grabbed the horse's bridle and urged him
back up. They continued on, weary and sluggish. Ben could
see the muscles straining on the horses' backs. They were starving. He was pushing them too hard, but he had no choice. If
he let up on them, the wagon would slide backwards, perhaps
endangering his family—and that wasn't a risk he could take.

Finally the wagon crested the mountain. Ben urged the
horses on until they were out of the way, then climbed down
and began to unhook them so they could be hitched to the
next wagon in line.

"I hate to do this," he whispered to the animals. "But we need
your help."

The horses' ears twitched. They heard him, but he didn't
know if they believed him or not.

A commotion came up behind him. He turned to see Jens
Neilson's wagon coming over the top, one of his oxen dead in its
yoke. The other animals were making up for its loss, dragging its
body along regardless. The men at the top took hold of the dead
animal and hefted it the rest of the way, unhooking it as soon as
they were able and laying it to the side.

Jens spoke with sorrow. "That ox has given its all, from the
moment we started on this trip. I'm sorry to be the cause of its
death."

"There's nothing you could have done," Ben told him.

"I know." Jens turned and prepared the remaining oxen to
bring up the next wagon. Ben helped him, wondering how many
animals they would lose on that hill.

The trail became spattered with blood as the animals
repeatedly fell to their knees in an attempt to keep their footing
on the mountain. This went on for two days, until everyone
reached the top. Ben felt sick with fatigue. He had spent those
two days helping to pull the ropes that anchored the wagons,
harnessing animals, and doing all that he could to bring
everyone to the top in safety. He felt obsessed. They were so
close. They had to make it the rest of the way.

* * *

San Juan Valley
April 6, 1880

Sarah urged her horses to go just a little faster. She could see
something up ahead, and was almost certain it was the valley
floor.

Sure enough, a short time later the wagon leveled out and
broke out of the mountain. The San Juan Valley was just ahead.
Some distance away, she could make out a sod house, standing
proud and alone on the prairie.

Relief went through her from head to toe. "We're there," she
whispered, squeezing the reins tightly as though she could
somehow communicate to the horses that they didn't have to go
much farther.

* * *

The sun set as the long line of wagons pulled to a stop.
Many of the Saints were crying, so relieved to have reached
their destination at last. Mary Ann couldn't keep the tears
wiped away and eventually gave up trying. Sarah looked around
her with curiosity. She couldn't see much to be excited about.
How would they possibly make a home for themselves in such
a forsaken place?

The Harris family was overjoyed to see them. They poured
out of their home and peppered the travelers with questions.

"Shall we stay here for the night?" Platte asked the group.

"I'm not taking one more step," one woman replied. "You
might as well build my cabin right here. I've gone as far as I'm
going to." Many of the others echoed the sentiment. Her words
were spoken with a touch of humor, but it was obvious that she
meant every word.

Teams straggled in for several days. Some of the wagons just
barely made it to the valley. They were falling apart, held

together only with bits of leather and a lot of prayer. Many of
the people literally collapsed when they arrived. It had been a
long, difficult journey. They had built their own roads over two
thirds of the way, and faced every sort of danger. Now they
would have the challenge of making a home for themselves, out
here as isolated as anyone could imagine.

Sarah was only too glad that she didn't have to make her home
here. She would stay long enough to help get Mary Ann settled,
and then she was on her way back home to Cedar City. How she
would get there, she didn't know, but she would find a way.

CHAPTER TWENTY-FIVE

Bluff, Utah
April 7, 1880

This is our land," Ben told Mary Ann, pulling the wagon to a stop. "The brethren pulled numbers out of a hat, and this is the lot we were assigned."

Mary Ann looked around, searching for something positive to say. Dreary and barren, there were no trees, no tufts of grass, not even a rabbit merrily bouncing across it to cheer her up. She was too tired to be inventive. She glanced over at Ben, ready to make a caustic remark, and saw the look of hope on his face. He wanted her to like it—she could see that plainly. He had worked so hard to bring them there, and he would be crushed if she sounded disparaging. She smiled, and said the first thing that came to her mind.

"It's ours, Ben, yours and mine. That means I love it."

He smiled warmly and reached across the wagon seat for her. She came willingly into the circle of his arms, resting her head against his shoulder. "We've got to get some crops in the ground, first thing. But right after that, I'll build you a cabin. We'll make a home here, Mary Ann. It may not be fancy, but it will be ours."

"That's all I've ever wanted, Ben," she murmured into his coat. "Just a home. With you."

* * *

Bluff
April 11, 1880

Mary Ann and Sarah kept themselves busy while Ben plowed the soil nearby. They entertained the children, mended clothes, drew plans for the new cabin in the dirt, and at night slept in the wagon boxes just as they had on the trail. But this time it was on their own land—sixteen acres of it, ready for a field—and that made all the difference.

They also had a city lot for their house a mile away, but for the time being, they preferred to camp on the acreage. Mary Ann enjoyed the feeling of ownership and felt that they'd live on the city lot soon enough—she might as well take advantage of the field now before planting season.

The Rowley's lot had a beautiful tree growing on it, broad and towering—a perfect shade tree—and the Saints gathered there for church their first Sunday in the San Juan. Mary Ann felt a twinge of jealousy when she first saw it. She would have loved a tree on their property. But the land had been assigned randomly, and she knew she had no one to blame.

She was enjoying Platte D. Lyman's sermon when suddenly she heard a gasp behind her, and turned. A couple of Indian braves were riding up to their little gathering. She grabbed Ben's hand, and his other arm immediately went around their girls, who sat to the side.

Platte Lyman and Kumen Jones went forward to speak to the Indians. Mary Ann glanced over at Mary, Kumen's wife. Her face grew pale and her eyes were wide, but she didn't move or make a sound.

Mary Ann couldn't hear what was being said, but after a few exchanges, the Indians rode away, and Platte and Kumen returned to the meeting. She exhaled and leaned against Ben. He laughed quietly and stroked her hair. "Maybe they just came to welcome us to the neighborhood," he whispered.

"I don't know why they came," she whispered back. "I'm just glad they're gone." She looked over at Sarah, who sat nearby. Her sister's face mirrored the relief she herself felt. A moment later the meeting resumed, as though nothing at all had taken place.

"Is that what we're to expect?" Mary Ann asked Ben as the meeting closed. "To have Indians appear from nowhere, at any time?"

"We'd better be prepared for it, at least," he replied. "Who knows when they'll show up again. But those two braves looked friendly enough."

Nothing had happened during the meeting, but still, Mary Ann was on edge. Who was to say that all the Indians they would meet in the future would be so accommodating? Part of their mission was to befriend the Indians, but she just didn't know if she could do it.

* * *

Bluff
Mid-May, 1880

"I could use your help for a little while today, if you don't mind, Ben," Platte Lyman said, leaning up against the wall of the cabin Ben was building. Ben straightened his back and looked at his friend.

"What do you need?"

"I'm digging a well, and I'm now deep enough that I need a man on top."

Ben nodded, looking around at his unfinished project. "Let's make a trade. You help me here for an hour, and I'll come to your place and help with the well when we've finished."

"It's a deal." Platte took off his hat and hefted one end of the heavy cedar log while Ben grabbed the other. They lifted it into place, and Ben slathered it with mortar, filling in the chinks. Hyrum and Thomas showed up a short time later to help. Ben had already cut the logs to the right length, so they made good progress putting up the walls.

He had left the bark on to save time. Mary Ann said she didn't mind leaving the bark on, she just wanted a roof over her head, and he meant to take her at her word. He stepped back to survey the effect. He liked the bark on the logs. They gave the wall texture.

An hour later the walls were high enough that they were ready for the roof. "I hate to leave it now," Platte said. "Let's go ahead and finish up. There's still time for my well."

The men redoubled their efforts and put a cribbing of tree limbs and willows for a roof. Then they threw a foot of dirt on top. Without a sawmill anywhere nearby, the floor would be made of clay, tamped down firmly and allowed to harden.

"That will do for now," Ben said, wiping his forehead with his handkerchief. "The girls won't have to sleep outside tonight. Now, let's get that well done, Platte."

Platte led the way to his property, and Hyrum and Thomas came along too.

"Having a well will sure beat taking the water out of the river," Hyrum said as he moved a shovel of soil off to the side. The sun was making them uncomfortably warm, and they had been digging for some time. "Rachel's getting tired of having to wait for the sediment to settle before she can take a drink."

"I'm looking forward to clean water myself," Platte replied. He wiped his hands and surveyed the mound of dirt they had removed from the earth. "I think we've done all we can for today, gentlemen. Thanks for your help."

"I'll be back first thing in the morning," Ben told him.

"Thanks, Ben. I appreciate it."

Ben walked slowly back to the cabin, stretching his back as he went. He had already worked hard to get the crops into the ground. Once the land had been cleared and planted, he had given himself the task of chopping down aspen and cottonwood trees. The men traveled forty miles to Blue Mountain to get the wood, as there wasn't any to be had nearby. A lot of hard work went into getting the trees loaded and transported to Bluff. But now Mary Ann would have a cabin. She had slept in the wagon long enough. He wanted her to have a real bed.

* * *

Bluff
Mid-May, 1880

"It looks very nice, Brother Perkins," Sarah said as she looked around the cabin. The materials used were simple, but she could tell that he had put a lot of thought and care into the building. One large room held the fireplace and the table. Over in the corner stood a large bed, with a smaller one nearby. Off to the side was a door that went into another room. Sarah walked over to it and put her head inside.

"This is a room for your use the rest of the time you're here," Ben said from behind. "I hope you don't mind sharing with Mary Jane and Delia."

"Of course I don't mind," Sarah told him. She went farther into the room and noted the bed frame that had been built large enough to hold her and both girls comfortably. "Thank you."

He nodded and stepped back into the living area, where Mary Ann admired the fireplace.

"Thank you for putting my rocking chair by the hearth," she said.

"Where else would I put it?" Ben replied with a smile. "This is your spot, no matter where we live."

"Sarah," Mary Ann called out, "come and see the fireplace."

Sarah walked over and studied it closely. Ben had worked meticulously to fit all the stones in place.

"Building the road up San Juan Hill gave me some practice," Ben joked. "It wasn't much different."

Sarah helped Mary Ann bring their things into the house. Ben carried the larger items, then left to go help the men. They were having a hard time building the irrigation canals. The ground was so sandy, it seemed impossible to create strong enough earth walls to contain the water they would run in from the river.

By late evening everything had been arranged to Mary Ann's content. Sarah sat back and watched her sister walk around the cabin, moving this thing to one side or picking up a book from one end of the shelf and placing it on the other.

"Everything looks beautiful, Mary Ann," Sarah told her. She smiled to herself even as she said the words. It was good to see her sister getting settled in a place of her own after giving up her house in Cedar City and living on the trail for so long. Mary Ann deserved to have everything just right.

"Didn't Ben do a wonderful job with the cabin?"

"He did," Sarah agreed. "Especially given how hard it was to get wood."

The little girls were getting cranky, so Mary Ann and Sarah put them to bed. As Mary Ann placed them on their mattresses, she commented to Sarah, "I can't wait to climb into bed myself. The feather ticks were comfortable enough in the wagon, but they should be so much nicer on real bedsteads."

"Why don't you go to bed?" Sarah suggested. "I'll finish up the dishes and the sweeping."

"Would you?" Mary Ann's voice sounded hopeful.

"Of course. You climb in."

Sarah picked up the broom and got to work, laughing at the look of delight on Mary Ann's face as she climbed into bed and started to relax. "A real bed," she heard her sister murmur before she fell asleep.

* * *

Bluff
Late May, 1880

"What are we going to do?" Samuel Rowley asked. "The irrigation ditches have washed out again."

"We'll keep trying," Kumen Jones said. "We have to find a way to make this work."

The men were all tired and discouraged. Their crops were perishing in the heat.

They knew the land was fertile—they could sense it as they dug it up and sifted it through their fingers. But without water, even the most fertile land was useless. Ben stuck his pitchfork into the ground with frustration. He had to be able to bring in a crop. His family was depending on it.

The men got back to work, trying to repair the ditches. Ben had come to the conclusion that the canals had not been surveyed properly. Perhaps the Saints had been in too big of a hurry when they first arrived in the San Juan Valley. Everyone anxiously started to get their crops in the ground to fend off starvation, and they hadn't thought things through as carefully as they ought to have done.

Ben couldn't say that he blamed them, though. He wanted to get established right away, as well. What was done, was done—they would just make the best of it. But without water, all would be lost.

* * *

Bluff
June 4, 1880

Sarah rose from her knees, wiping tears from her eyes. She didn't know just when she had made the decision to be baptized. It had come slowly, creeping in when she least expected it, carried to her heart on the wings of the hymns the Saints sang at night around the campfires, shown to her in the calm faces of the people as they faced their challenges with courage. It was spoken to her soul on similar quiet nights—evenings full of the energy of the universe that flowed all around her, bringing her to her knees in humble gratitude for all that she had been given, prompting her to seek the answer to her prayer.

Finally she had the answer. The gospel as taught by the Mormons was true, and she would be baptized a member. She walked into the house and closed the door, eager to tell her sister.

"Sarah! Do you mean it?" Mary Ann grasped her sister by both hands.

"Yes. I'm going to be baptized."

"That's wonderful! Ben, isn't that wonderful?"

Ben looked up from his chair, where he whittled some pegs to fix the fence that enclosed their garden. "That is wonderful, Sarah. Congratulations."

"When did all this happen?" Mary Ann asked.

"I can't really say. It just . . . did." Her emotions wouldn't have allowed her to share her words, even if she did have them. Her heart was so full, she could barely breathe.

Once the decision had been made, Sarah didn't want to wait another minute. She came up out of the waters of the San Juan River on June sixth, the ordinance performed by Charles E. Walton, a member of their party.

"I can't describe how I feel," she told Mary Ann later that night. "It's as though I've finally come home, even though home is miles away. I resisted. I fought it. But slowly the message seeped into me, and I drank it up."

"I'm so happy for you." Mary Ann pulled her into a hug. "I've wanted this for so long."

"Thank you for teaching me," Sarah responded. "And thank you for not pushing. I had to figure it out for myself. You know how stubborn I am."

"Yes," Mary Ann said, laughing. "I know."

PART FOUR

THE SACRIFICE

CHAPTER TWENTY-SIX

Bluff
June 20, 1880

Sarah stood alone on the dirt path, her arms wrapped around her body to ward off the chill that had come up in the air. The night sky was beautiful, full of bright stars and a crisp crescent moon. She could see why several of the Saints proclaimed it the most beautiful spot on earth, but she still longed for the green of Wales.

She closed her eyes for a moment. How far away Wales seemed now, much farther than just an ocean or a half world away but a lifetime ago, like a dream that lasted only her first eighteen years of life. Surely no place on earth could be that green, that peaceful, and that serene. She had been a different person then, what seemed a hundred years ago.

Somewhere out in the desert, a wolf or coyote howled, and she jumped. The wildness never ceased to astonish her. Even though she slept safe at night behind thick walls, anything could happen, from a hungry animal wandering by or an Indian looking for bread. She was not yet used to either.

"Sarah?"

The voice frightened her, coming out of the darkness so close on the heels of the howling sound, and she turned, her hand over her heart.

"Brother Perkins! You startled me."

"I'm sorry." Her brother-in-law approached along the path, his eyes roving up toward the moon where her own eyes had been a moment before. "It's a lovely night."

"It is." They stood a moment in silence, watching the last wisp of an angel-hair cloud drift across the sky.

"I wonder if I might have a word with you." Ben nodded toward the path, and Sarah fell into step beside him.

He didn't speak again for a few moments, and Sarah wondered what he could possibly want to say. He had never sought her out before. When they spoke in the past, it was always on a chance encounter, while driving the wagon, or in Mary Ann or the children's presence.

They reached the end of the path and the large rock that had been placed to mark the turnoff to Ben and Mary Ann's home. Ben motioned with his hand for her to sit, and she did, gathering her shawl a bit more closely around her.

He shifted his weight back and forth as he stood in front of her, and glanced around as though making sure they were alone. Finally Sarah could endure the suspense no longer.

"Is something bothering you, Brother Perkins?"

He laughed, a short sound that came out like a bark in the stillness of the night. "Bothering me? Indeed, I should say so."

"If I've done something to offend you or Mary Ann—"

"No, Sarah. You've done nothing. In fact, far from it." He looked off into the distance again. "I am troubled by a far greater thing."

She waited a moment, ready to open her mouth again when he spoke.

"Several years ago, when I received my patriarchal blessing, I was given some curious counsel." He took a deep breath. "At some point in my life, I should enter into the practice of plural marriage."

Sarah gasped, although inwardly. Poor Mary Ann. She knew her sister loved Brother Perkins with all her heart. How would she bear sharing him with another woman?

"I didn't give much thought to it at the time. Mary Ann is a wonderful woman, and I've been very happy with her.

Indeed, I love her deeply. But as of late, the urgency to heed this commandment has been pressing on my mind to where I can scarcely bear it."

Ben's face creased with grief, and Sarah could see the difficulty he had in controlling his emotions. Although the light from the moon and stars shone with faint light, it only served to illuminate his anguish, and she didn't know what to say.

"Sarah, you're a very good woman, possessed of sterling qualities that I've come to greatly admire during this trek. If you were ever inclined to enter into a plural marriage, I hope you would . . . consider me as your first choice." His words came out in a rush, spoken all in one breath as though he had to get it out as quickly as possible.

Sarah's heart caught in her throat. What did he just say? Surely she had misunderstood him. "What?" she said after a long moment, hoping he would correct himself.

"I would like to take you as my second wife." He turned and looked her full in the face for the first time since their odd conversation began. "I see I've surprised you."

"Yes," she answered, a little more loudly than she had intended. "You've surprised me a great deal."

"I hope I've not offended you."

She shook her head. She was shocked, stunned, shaken. "I feel honored that you would choose me," she told him, standing up from the rock and turning toward the house. "Please forgive me, but I'm rather tired."

He reached out and caught her elbow. "Sarah, wait."

She stopped, the feeling of his hand on her arem foreign.

"I know this is a hard thing I'm asking. I would never put you or Mary Ann in this position if I didn't truly believe it the right thing to do. But the Lord has revealed to me that the principle of plural marriage is true and right, and He has shown me that you are to be my next wife." He rubbed his hand across his face. "Please think about it, Sarah. Pray about it and see if the Lord won't show you, as He has done me. I care for you a great deal, and would do my best to be a good husband to you. Think about it. I don't need an answer tonight."

"I'm afraid I don't have an answer to give you tonight."

Sarah walked toward the house as quickly as she could, nearly breaking into a run but holding back the urge. Mary Ann sat by the fireside rocking the baby, and glanced up at Sarah's entry.

"Did you have a good walk, Sarah?"

"Yes. It's a lovely night out." Sarah paused in the doorway to her bedroom. So much weighed on her mind, so much that she wanted to say to her sister—but she couldn't. "I'm rather tired. I'll see you in the morning."

She could see the concern on her sister's face but couldn't stay in the room another minute. She sank down on her side of the bed and stared at the wall, her hands pressed together between her knees. Her sister's husband had just proposed marriage to her. It almost seemed laughable. This man, whom she looked upon as a brother, wanted her hand.

She pressed her fingers against her mouth, trying to stifle the sob that would escape. Her little nieces slept peacefully in the other half of the bed, and she didn't want to wake them up. How innocent they seemed, lying there with their soft brown curls spilled over the pillow. Sarah longed to be that innocent again, to feel safe and protected. Tonight she felt very vulnerable, very alone.

Several of the women in their group were plural wives, or the first wives of polygamist husbands. She rarely heard a word spoken against the practice, and all those she knew seemed to be happy. But it still seemed wrong to her. Weren't they taught to be faithful to their spouses, to love and live and work with each other, cleaving only unto each other? But under the new law of marriage, if a man saw another woman and wanted her, all he had to do was marry her, and suddenly his desire for her became appropriate. Her thoughts were bitter.

Sarah shook her head. She knew those men were good and decent. Their motives didn't appear lustful. Hard to imagine, in the world they lived in, that a man could be married to more than one woman and retain his morals.

The restored gospel was an oddity and a wonder. So many of the teachings rang true in her heart, reaching places deep within her that she hadn't known existed. But others, like plural marriage, clanged discordantly within her. It didn't make sense that one part of the gospel seemed so right and others, so wrong. Could they truly be part of the same religion, part of one great truth?

Her thoughts flew to Tom Wilcox. He was deeply in love with her, had wanted to marry her, and would have given her a happy life. But he could not have given her the gospel—he was not a religious man.

She sighed. Did she have to trade one for the other? Did she have to give up the idea of being the only wife of a good man in order to follow the Lord? There were many Latter-day Saint men of good standing who had not entered into plural marriage. Many were attractive, prosperous, and would make admirable husbands. But none of them had asked for her. Ben had.

She changed for bed quickly and slid beneath the covers. The warmth of her nieces' bodies had not reached her side, and the sheets were cold.

After what seemed like hours, the front door opened, and she heard Ben's footsteps enter the house. His voice, low and mellow as always, greeted Mary Ann and engaged her in conversation. Although she could not hear the words, she knew they were talking about her. Did Mary Ann know he would propose to her tonight? Her eyes opened wide at the thought. Had Mary Ann been privy to the whole thing? She couldn't imagine her sister so willingly sharing her husband with someone else, all the while seeming so oblivious. She felt sure Mary Ann knew nothing about it. But she would soon.

* * *

Ben couldn't go in the house. He knew Mary Ann waited up for him, as she did every night when he was away. She would be sitting by the fire, rocking and knitting, perhaps reading, until he came in.

Such a good woman.

He couldn't face her just yet.

He looked toward the cabin. The room where Sarah slept with Mary Jane and Delia was shrouded in darkness. Not a single light flickered from within. His daughters would be asleep now. Was Sarah?

He could only imagine how his proposal had sounded to her ears. It must have been a shock to her. So many emotions had flickered across her face, the strongest one being fear.

"Lord, help me through this," he breathed.

When he had received his patriarchal blessing so many years before, he had been surprised by the commandment he received to take another wife. He had agonized over it for hour upon hour, trying to make sense of it in his head. Ultimately, his head had not mattered—he could not deny the witness he had received. He couldn't say the principle made sense to him. He couldn't even imagine how he was to go about supporting two wives—he barely had enough to care for one. But the Spirit had whispered to his heart that it was the right thing to do, and again when he contemplated Sarah—his sister-in-law, of all people, his own wife's best friend.

Oh, the pain it would cause Mary Ann! She had been so true and faithful to him in the years since he brought her to Utah. She had braved the ocean crossing and come to a new land, purely out of love for him. She traveled through that rough wilderness and came down a hole he himself blasted through a rock, never complaining and scarcely ever admitting her own discomfort or fear. She had stood by him through everything, holding him close to her heart when he felt he could no longer go on. He loved her so much that at times he feared it would overcome him. He felt like he had taken all that love and trust and thrown it back in her face.

But how could he ignore a command from God? The words had been spoken to his heart almost as a trump. For some reason he could not fathom, he should take another wife, and that wife was to be Sarah.

Right now, Sarah was in the house, hopefully thinking on his words. Mary Ann waited for him by the fire. His stomach twisted within himself. He had to go and talk to Mary Ann. He had to tell her what he had done. He didn't know how she would accept it, or if she would at all. But he couldn't put it off a moment longer, as much as he wanted to.

He walked briskly to the house and stopped with his hand on the doorknob. He breathed another prayer, asking God to help him with the task ahead, then he pushed his way through to face his wife.

Just as he knew she would be, Mary Ann sat at the fire. She held Naomi on her lap, the soft face turned toward her mother as she took deep, peaceful breaths.

"Let me take her," Ben whispered, scooping his daughter out of Mary Ann's arms. He crossed the room to the corner where the child's cradle sat and lowered her in, careful not to disturb her in transition. Naomi didn't stir, but snuggled down into her blankets like a chick in a down-filled nest.

"Sarah seemed troubled tonight," Mary Ann remarked from the rocking chair. "I fear I've been asking too much of her lately."

Ben pulled a chair from the table and placed it near his wife's, where the warmth from the fire touched his face and hands. "She has been a good help to you."

"Indeed she has. Perhaps too much. She looked tired when she came in."

"You look tired too, but never more beautiful."

Mary Ann smiled. "You always did know how to compliment me."

Ben leaned forward and put his elbows on his knees. "I need to speak with you."

Mary Ann seemed to sense his mood. Her face grew serious, and she shifted to face him directly. "What is it?"

He spoke slowly, trying to find the right words. "You recall my telling you that I was commanded in my patriarchal blessing to take another wife?"

"I remember that."

Ben couldn't look at her. He turned away, the gentleness of her voice almost harder to take than her railing would have been. "The Lord has told me that it's time."

"I see." Her flat, almost non-existent tone gave nothing away. "I've been expecting this since you told me." She rocked silently in her chair for a moment, then stopped. "We just got here. It seems so sudden, even though I had warning years ago."

"I know it's sudden. I'm sorry, Mary Ann."

She began to rock again, the blades of the rocker starting a rhythmic motion on the floor. "Who have you chosen?"

He stood and grabbed the back of his chair for support. His throat constricted, and he could barely breathe.

"Ben? Are you all right?"

He nodded, although he felt it was a lie.

"Who have you chosen to be your second wife?"

"Sarah." He forced the word out around his dry tongue.

"Sarah? My sister?"

He nodded again.

The rocking stopped suddenly, and for a moment the house echoed still, eerily quiet. The noise resumed, as rhythmic as before, but with more purpose, more speed.

Ben turned and looked at his wife. Her lips were pressed together, and her hands were clenched on the arms of the rocker. "Mary Ann—"

"Why?" she whispered. "Why my sister?"

"She's a righteous woman, Mary Ann. And she's who the Lord has chosen."

Mary Ann's feet came down with a thump. "I know she's a righteous woman, Ben. But why my sister? Of all the women in this world, why my sister?"

"I don't know." He reached out to touch her hair, but she turned her head away from him. "Mary Ann, you know I wouldn't hurt you for the world."

"I had prepared myself for a stranger, for a woman I hardly knew. You would build her a house far away from mine, and I could pretend the whole thing didn't exist. I could do that, Ben. I could love you and care for you and pretend that there wasn't some other woman out there, also loving you and caring for you." Mary Ann's voice was quiet, but far from soft. "You've taken that blissful ignorance away from me."

Ben stepped back, shaken not only by her words but by the look on her face. She looked angry, but also scared. There was a strange new gleam in her eye he had never seen there before.

"You asked her tonight, didn't you? That's why she came in here looking as she did."

"Yes, I did ask her."

"What did she say?"

"She was very startled. The idea had never entered her mind."

"Did she give you an answer?"

"No."

Mary Ann started rocking again. Her eyes drifted to the fire, and she didn't look at Ben again. "Go to bed, Ben. You've got a busy day tomorrow."

"Mary Ann, I can't leave you like this."

"You need to."

"But—"

"I need time to think, I need to be alone. Please, just go to bed."

Ben turned and walked over to the bed. His fingers felt stiff as he unbuttoned his coat. Mary Ann sat quietly except for an occasional sniff. He lay down and pulled the blanket up over his shoulders. He wished things were different, that he could have found a way to tell Mary Ann without breaking her heart. Or, better yet, that God had not chosen him for such a difficult calling. How could a man endure the suffering of, not one, but two of the most precious women in his life? He would do anything for Mary Ann, up to and including giving his life for her safety and happiness. Why, now, did he have to be the cause of her grief?

Only the strength of his testimony was more powerful than the love he had for his wife. He would willingly take back the proposal and pretend the whole thing had never happened if it weren't for the fact that he knew God had commanded him. He lay awake long into the night, staring at the darkness of the wall in front of him and listening to the rocking of the wooden chair—a sound that never ceased until the rooster crowed the next morning.

* * *

Bluff
June 21, 1880

Mary Ann's hands shook as she added oatmeal to the boiling water over the fire. The children were hungry, and Ben would soon be in from the barn, wanting his breakfast as well. As dearly as she would have loved to shut them all out, she knew she had obligations to fulfill.

Obligations. Duties. That's what it all came down to. She had come with Ben on the trek across southern Utah because of a sense of duty to her husband as he followed the call that burned so brightly in his heart. She had felt that glow herself and had come willingly.

But to see the spark in his eyes was something to behold. She had never seen anyone so alive with the fire of their testimony. He wasn't sure why he was supposed to join the San Juan mission, but when they'd reached the Hole in the Rock and saw what they would have to do, he told Mary Ann that he finally understood why he had come. He had unique talents that could get the Saints down that cliff—and he did it. Mary Ann still marveled at the road the men had built, sticking out of the wall of the canyon as it did. Only a project overseen by the hand of God could have seen that kind of success. An undertaking with any other purpose would have crumbled and fallen into the abyss below.

She didn't doubt that her husband was a man of God. She knew it as surely as she knew that the gospel was true. She could not doubt that his call to plural marriage was genuine. Although she didn't understand the principle fully, and felt opposed to it on many counts, she had felt the Spirit burning in her heart that night so many years ago when he'd told her that he would someday be entering into a plural marriage. The Lord would make a way for it to all work out. He would comfort and succor her as she tried her best to support her husband.

Mary Ann grabbed a long-handled spoon and began to dish up bowls of the thick gray oatmeal mixture. She had overcooked the cereal, and the children would be disappointed in their breakfast. They wouldn't complain—she and Ben had raised them to be grateful for what they had. But their faces would show their disgust as they tried to shovel each spoonful into their mouths. She took a taste and grimaced. She'd have a hard time eating it, too.

Although the sun had just begun to rise, sounds of stirring filled the house. The baby was growing restless in her cradle, and Mary Ann could hear Sarah softly talking to Mary Jane and Delia in the next room, no doubt braiding their hair and helping them get dressed before seeing to her own needs.

Sarah.

Mary Ann tried to turn her thoughts aside, but the hurt and anger filled her heart anyway. She stuck the spoon back into the oatmeal pot. No one could eat such a mess.

She had grown closer to Sarah in the last year than she ever would have imagined. They had shared common hardships and fears as they set off on the trek. Sarah had been a patient and kind sister, doing her share of the work and often more, trying to help her sister any way she could. She had nothing for which to fault Sarah—no idle word of gossip, not a moment lacking in faith. She had nothing to hold against her sister . . . nothing but the fact that her own husband wanted to marry her.

Mary Jane and Delia came out of the bedroom, neatly dressed in their faded calico. Sarah followed behind, much more slowly, tucking the last remnants of her hair up into a bun. She didn't meet Mary Ann's eyes, but instead went to the cradle and scooped up the baby. Catherine climbed up to the table, taking up her spoon and pulling her thumb out of her mouth to make room for her breakfast.

Mary Ann passed around the oatmeal bowls and looked at her own with contempt. She couldn't do it. She could not pass her own misery on to her family. It wasn't their fault she had overcooked the food. They shouldn't have to eat such slop. She rose quickly and grabbed the tin of sugar from the box in the corner.

"It's a treat, children," she told them, sprinkling a liberal amount on each bowl. Not much remained of the precious white substance. A scant inch settled in the tin when she was done. But she didn't care. It didn't matter. At that moment, on that morning, nothing seemed to matter.

Sarah finished changing the baby and came to the table. Her own bowl had been sweetened, just like the children's, and she looked at Mary Ann in surprise. Mary Ann pretended not to notice her sister's glance. She would be gracious. She would hold herself together.

Ben came in a few moments later, rubbing his hands together to shake off the morning chill. He looked around the room and must have sensed the tension in the air, for he said nothing to either sister, but instead sat down between two of the children and ate his own breakfast, raising his eyebrows in surprise at the sugar.

"It's a special treat," Mary Ann answered his unspoken question. "The children haven't had one for so long."

He nodded and scraped the last bit from his bowl, thanked Mary Ann, and went back outside, telling the older two children to put on their shoes quickly and come out to help with chores.

Once the noisy feet had gone outside and the baby lay down on her blanket to play, Mary Ann turned to face her sister.

"I might as well tell you, Sarah. Ben spoke to me last night and told me that he proposed to you."

Sarah's hands stopped in the motion of washing a bowl. "He did?"

"Yes." Mary Ann pulled out a kitchen chair and sank into it, exhausted from the effort of keeping up appearances in front of the children. She felt old all of a sudden.

"Mary Ann, I never sought his attention," Sarah spoke in a rush. "His declaration came as a surprise to me."

"I know." Mary Ann reached out and plucked a thread from the tablecloth. "You've been nothing but a kind sister-in-law. But nonetheless, he has chosen you for his second wife, so I have to surmise that his feelings for you are somewhat more than brotherly."

Sarah took another few swipes at the bowl, but her eyes were not on her work. "How do you feel about this, Mary Ann?" she asked after several seconds passed.

"How do I feel?" Mary Ann laughed. "How do I feel? Now, that's a very interesting question. It's not every day that a wife is asked how she feels about the other women in her husband's life."

"I'm not another woman," Sarah protested. She dropped the bowl back into the wash pan and turned to face her sister. "Nothing has happened, Mary Ann. He asked me a question, that is all."

"That's all?" Mary Ann rose and crossed the floor, her face in Sarah's. "He asked you to share with him a life that he has only shared with me. He is taking away a portion of himself and giving it to you. My children will do without a father for a period of time so he can spend it wooing you. And you think that's all?"

"That's not what I meant," Sarah said softly. "I meant that his actions toward me, and mine toward him, have been above reproach."

"I don't doubt that," Mary Ann retorted. "I know my husband well enough to know that he wouldn't say or do anything inappropriate. But the fact remains that while he's been married to me, he's been thinking about you."

"I gave him no answer," Sarah said. She turned back to the sink and resumed washing the dishes. "And I don't see how I could answer him now. This has been far too painful for you, and I can't put you through this any further."

"You would do that?"

"Of course I would. You're my sister."

Mary Ann sat back down, feeling as though the wind had been knocked out of her. A moment ago she had been filled with so much hurt and anger, she hadn't thought there was room for anything else.

But now Sarah offered an olive branch, and the fury left as quickly as a bolt of lightning.

That was not the answer to the problem, though. She knew that immediately. Ben believed the Lord had told him to marry Sarah. If she stood in the way of that union, Ben would hold it against her forever. He might not be angry with her outwardly, but he would be thinking about it, and it would be a wedge between them. All she could do was hope he would change his mind when Sarah told him no.

CHAPTER TWENTY-SEVEN

Bluff
June 26, 1880

Sarah, may I speak with you a moment?" Ben came up alongside her as she carried a basket of eggs toward the house. The chickens had been especially ornery that morning, and their temper matched Sarah's perfectly.

"Of course, Brother Perkins. What do you need?" She kept her tone purposely cool.

"Have you had a chance to think about my proposal?"

"I've thought of very little else," she answered. "It has been on my mind constantly."

"I know I'm not your idea of a dashing husband," he said. "When you first arrived in Utah, Mary Ann told me that you had been seeing a young man in Wales."

"Yes. His name is Tom Wilcox."

Ben nodded, looking out across the yard. "I imagine he's quite handsome."

Sarah pulled up a mental picture of Tom, all she had to remind herself of his laughing eyes and unruly hair. She smiled without meaning to. "Yes, he is."

Ben pulled a hand across his face. "Mary Ann tells me I'm handsome, but I don't know if that's the full truth or just love in her eyes when she looks at me."

Sarah looked at him for a moment, seeing him as though for the first time. She had never given much thought to whether or not he was handsome—as her sister's husband, his looks weren't important. But he was nice-looking, she had to admit—although she did not say so out loud. The expression on his face at her silence made her wonder if perhaps he hoped she would comment.

"Have you reached a decision?" he asked, low and hopeful.

She set the basket of eggs down gently on the ground. After all she had gone through to gather them, she didn't want a single one cracked. "Yes, I have."

Ben nodded. "I can hear by the tone of your voice that the answer is no." His own voice was hollow and a little bit sad.

"I can't hurt Mary Ann this way," she said. It seemed like such a simplistic reply to answer the hurt look on his face.

"Sarah, I love your sister deeply. I would never do anything in the world to hurt her. When the Lord first told me to ask for another woman's hand in marriage, I didn't want to do it. Such a thing was out of the question. Why would I want anyone else when I have someone like Mary Ann?"

Sarah nodded her understanding. She had wondered the same thing many times since the other night.

"Slowly, over time, I came to a full understanding and appreciation of the Lord's purposes for us. I gained a testimony of the divinity of plural marriage, when done as ordained by the Lord and at His command. Men did not bring it about, Sarah. Such a plan, if conceived by a man, would surely send all those who entered into it straight to Hell. But God's way is not our way. Things that seem strange to us make perfect sense to Him. And I began to see that this was bigger than me, bigger even than Mary Ann. We had to go beyond ourselves and what we wanted in order to accomplish the greater good."

Ben looked down at the ground and stepped in the dirt, making a random design of footprints. "It took me a long time to understand and accept this, Sarah. It certainly did not happen overnight, and not easily. But by the time the Lord told me He had chosen you for my second wife, I had come to a place in my heart where it made perfect sense."

"But why me?" Sarah asked the question that had been festering in her mind for days. "Why has the Lord chosen me?"

"You are a sterling woman," Ben said. "You have the strength and the courage to stand by me in whatever the Lord chooses to allow to happen to us. You have a tremendous faith, a kind and willing heart. You are an example to me, Sarah. You would be an excellent helpmeet."

Sarah didn't know quite what to say. She had never heard her qualities laid out like that before, and for a moment wondered if he was serious. But he showed no sign of mocking her. His eyes were sincere.

"Excellent helpmeet, you say?" she asked, a light touch of humor entering her voice at such a far cry from Tom's proposal. Tom's had been full of passion and yearning. Ben's was sedate and conversational.

Ben searched her eyes with his. "Not quite what you were hoping for?"

She smiled. "A helpmeet can be good. But I'm not ready to make this kind of decision, Brother Perkins. I feel in my heart that the testimony you've born is true. I may not understand the principle of plural marriage, but there are many things I don't understand. I'm thinking of Mary Ann. I love her dearly, as I know you do."

Ben stooped down and retrieved the egg basket. His fingers brushed against Sarah's as he handed it to her. "Please make me a promise, Sarah. Don't make this decision final until you have earnestly sought the Lord in prayer."

He bowed slightly in farewell and went into the barn. Sarah stood a moment longer and listened to him soothe the cow as he milked her. A moment later, an old and dear Welsh song broke from his lips.

She smiled. Ben was a good man. But so much remained that she didn't understand, and she could not—*would not*—break Mary Ann's heart unless she had an overriding reason to do so.

* * *

Bluff
June 27, 1880

Sarah removed her bonnet as she stepped up to the Rowley's house and knocked on the door. Ann opened it a moment later, shielding her eyes from the sun.

"Sarah!" she exclaimed. "Please, come in."

Sarah stepped into the cool interior of the house and sat in the chair Ann offered.

"How are you?" Ann asked. Sarah took a deep breath, not knowing what to say or how to begin. She knew that she needed to confide in someone. Ordinarily that person would have been Mary Ann.

"Brother Perkins spoke to me the other night," Sarah said, letting the words come out slowly. "He asked me to become his second wife."

Ann didn't say a word, but she put her hand over her mouth.

"I told him I would think about it. Indeed, I've never thought about anything so long and so hard in my life. I didn't sleep at all after he asked me. But the next morning, I got up and saw Mary Ann. She looked as though death itself had tried to take her. I promised her I would not marry her husband."

"But . . . ?"

"Brother Perkins spoke to me again yesterday. He seems determined that I say yes. I told him my answer would have to be no, that I could not hurt Mary Ann this way. He asked me to pray about it."

"You're leaving to go back home in a few days, aren't you?"

"Yes. Thomas and I are going back to Cedar City on Thursday. Hyrum and Rachel are taking us."

"Perhaps once you're no longer in Bluff, Ben will change his mind about wanting to marry you."

"Perhaps." Sarah thought about it for a moment. "No, I don't think he will. This is something that he wants, very much. The odd thing is, he wants it badly, but he seems reluctant to do it at the same time. He wants to follow the will of the Lord, but it seems to be hurting him terribly."

"That shows great strength of character," Ann said. "You would be blessed to marry a man with that sort of determination to obey the Lord's commands."

Her words came as a surprise. "Ann? Do you think I should say yes?"

"What I think has nothing to do with it. It's your decision— one that you need to make with the Lord."

Sarah shook her head. "I don't see how I could marry my sister's husband. It doesn't make sense to me. I have thought on it, hour after hour. How do I know if this is what the Lord truly wants?"

Ann sat back and regarded her friend. "How did you know you were supposed to be baptized?"

Sarah thought for a minute. "A little bit at a time, the things I was being taught began to sound true, and I realized, it's because they are true. Then the Spirit touched my heart and whispered to me, telling me that I had found Christ's gospel at long last."

"You'll get your answer to this question the same way," Ann told her. "Put your trust in the Lord. You were given the Holy Ghost when you were confirmed. Use that gift to guide you now."

Sarah stood. "Thank you, Ann. I appreciate your words."

Ann smiled and gave Sarah a hug. "Will you come say goodbye before you go?"

"Of course I will. You've been a true and dear friend."

* * *

Bluff
June 28, 1880

Sarah kicked at the dirt beneath her feet as she walked, not caring about the cloud of dust that rose and clung to the bottom of her skirt. The bottom four inches of her petticoat were always covered in rec powder, anyway—what did a bit more matter?

She had been to meet with the Church leaders who were assigned to the small gathering of Saints in the Bluff area. They had spoken with her at length, answering her questions. They explained to her that the Lord desired each of His daughters to hold the keys of the kingdom, and that without the sealing ordinance of marriage, those keys would not be theirs. Because many of the male saints had been killed by mobs or taken by illness, there were many more righteous women than men. How could God deny His daughters the fullness of their blessings, all for lack of enough men?

The leaders each bore a solemn and convincing testimony of the truthfulness of the practice of polygamy, and she knew, by looking into their eyes, that they believed the words they spoke. Yet she couldn't find that belief in her own heart. She knew they were men of God, but the words they spoke and the testimony they bore were foreign to her, even more foreign than the red rocks when she was so used to the green and rolling landscape of Wales.

One man and one woman, joined together under God, brought together by love or at least by mutual respect, pledged to serve each other and to care for any children that would come into the union. One man and one woman—that's how she had been raised. She believed it. She had seen her own mother and father in such a marriage, and they were happy. How could God, so wise and loving, ask His children to do something that was so unnatural? Sarah had every intention of giving her whole heart to the man she married, and expected him to do the same in return. How could he do that if he was married to someone else as well? How could that be called fidelity?

Sarah walked on and on, barely paying attention to her surroundings until she was far away from the settlement. The sun had set long before, and the sky cast a purple cloak overhead. Soon the stars would be out. Sarah walked all alone, but she was not afraid. She felt as though someone sheltered her, listening to her thoughts and drawing a protective veil around her so she would remain in solitude until the tumultuous questions inside her were answered.

She knew God lived. She had known it her entire life, and had tried to follow Him since she had any understanding of what that meant. Just recently she had embraced the Mormon faith and thrown in her lot with them, for good or for bad. She knew it was the right decision. But to take her devotion to such an extent—she couldn't imagine it. She walked until she found a large boulder and sat down on it, pulling her knees up to her chin.

Her bags were packed. Hyrum, Rachel, and Thomas would be by at first light to collect her. Her goodbyes had been said, all but those to Ben and Mary Ann and their children. She would see them in the morning as she left. But what would she say to Ben? No matter how she thought about it, it all came back to her love and devotion to Mary Ann. She loved her sister with all her heart. She couldn't bear the distance that had been between them since Ben's proposal. Mary Ann's heart had been broken at the idea of another wife—surely it would destroy her to have it actually take place.

Sarah pushed herself off the rock and walked back to the house. She would tell Ben no. That would be her final answer. Something deep within her heart felt troubled by her decision, but she ignored it. She could not hurt her sister any further than she already had. She would go home and forget all about Ben Perkins.

* * *

Bluff
June 31, 1880

Sarah gave each of the little girls a hug and kiss, then turned to the wagon. She didn't want them to see her crying, but it became harder by the minute to hide the tears that welled up in her eyes. She loved her nieces dearly, and she didn't know when she would be seeing them again. Now that the road had been cleared, it would not be as difficult to travel back and forth, but it still would not be easy.

She climbed onto the seat, holding her skirts with one hand and the wagon bow with the other. She felt an arm on her elbow and glanced over her shoulder. It was Ben, helping her into the wagon.

"Please, Sarah," he said in a low voice. "I've promised Mary Ann we'll come for a visit in about a year. Spend this time thinking."

"I have no other answer to give you," she said. "I can't imagine that a year would make any difference."

"The Lord is insistent," he told her. "I will ask you again. In a year," he added, holding up his hand to stave off her reply. "In a year."

Sarah waved as the wagon began to pull away. Her face smiled brightly, but her mind was whirling. Ben was certainly being persistent. But she couldn't imagine her answer would be any different in a year than at that moment. Her sister's happiness was the most important thing to her. And while she knew that Mary Ann loved her, she also knew that Mary Ann rejoiced to see her go.

CHAPTER TWENTY-EIGHT

Bluff, Utah
Mid-September, 1880

Mary Ann had tried to put the whole episode with Sarah out of her mind. Every day she made a conscious effort to focus on the here and now and not think about the past, or about the future. She concentrated on loving her children and mending her fractured feelings toward Ben.

At first, she had been angry with him for not discussing his choice of Sarah for his second wife. Only after Sarah left did she begin to realize that Ben had tried many times to broach the subject with her, and she had refused to listen. She had known on some level what was coming, but didn't want to hear the words come out of his mouth.

She knew he had not given up the idea. As badly as she wished it, it would not go away so easily. Every so often, Ben would quietly tell her that he didn't want his dinner, and she knew that he fasted. Why exactly, she didn't know. Was he hoping the Lord would remove the commandment? Or that Sarah would change her mind? She didn't ask him. It was a private matter between him and the Lord.

But she badly wanted the Lord to tell him that he had done enough, that no more would be required. Hadn't Abraham been released from his heart-wrenching commandment? But even as she had the thought, she knew it was not possible in her own life.

God had made a command, and Ben would strive to fulfill it at all costs. It was part of why she loved him. She never dreamed it would be part of why she hated him.

* * *

Bluff
Mid-September, 1880

That summer had been long and difficult for the Saints in Bluff. They still fought daily against the elements and the river. They were treated to a visit from Erastus Snow and Brigham Young Jr. who had come to visit the San Juan mission and congratulate the people on their progress. The apostles promised the missionaries that they would have increased blessings if they would continue in their dedicated efforts. The men had been close to despair as they tried to make the river bend to their will, but the words of the apostles gave them the motivation to keep working at it until they got it right.

After returning to Salt Lake City and making their report, Elder Snow and Elder Young wrote a letter and sent it to the San Juan Saints. Jens Neilson read it to the assembled Saints at their next gathering.

> *After viewing the facilities for settlement on this river and for grazing and timber in the country, we feel to congratulate you on being the pioneers in opening up this region for civilization, and for establishing of practical missionary labor among the Utes and Navajos, this being central and neutral ground between them . . .*
>
> *. . . There are small predatory bands of renegade Indian tribes to prey upon defenseless persons, as well as lawless adventurers from among the whites. We therefore deem it a matter of common prudence (that) your temporary dwelling should be in close proximity to each other, and where practical we would recommend that you build in the*

form of a hollow square, and close up spaces between your dwellings with a stockade . . .

The climate and soil upon the stream we deem are all that could be desired. Your chief difficulty will be how to arrange your water sets, flood gates, wing dams or other contrivances for controlling the water of this fluctuating stream, but experience gained by a few failures will enable you to accomplish it. Let none be discouraged or abandon the enterprise . . .

Let no man think of scattering or locating families upon farms or claims isolated from their brethren, or abandoning the posts to which they have been appointed . . . and where it is necessary to seek employment on the railroads or elsewhere to provide needed supplies, let not each man start out on his own volition and operate singly, but let working parties be organized.

Jens lowered the epistle and looked out over the assembly. "Brothers and sisters, the apostles are men of God who have been sent to guide us. I propose that we do as they have asked, and build a fort to protect ourselves."

"Ben, what of our cabin?" Mary Ann asked. "It's too far out to be included in the fort."

"We shall build another." He answered quickly, without hesitation.

"Just like that?"

"Just like that. Mary Ann, the brethren want us to be safe. I want it as well. I don't mind rebuilding."

Mary Ann shook her head. "You're an amazing man, Ben Perkins."

He took her by the elbows and looked deep into her eyes. "I would do anything for you, Mary Ann. Anything."

She knew he meant what he said. But she couldn't ask for the one thing she wanted more than all else.

* * *

Cedar City
Early June, 1881

The year passed quickly for Sarah. The trip home had been much more pleasant, now that the road had been cleared, although the inclines were still frightening. Sarah's parents were delighted to see her, and welcomed her back with joy.

Sarah continued to work at the Davis house, learning more about the strange intricacies of American cooking, and her English improved daily. She took long walks with Kate and Richard, played ball in the yard with Evan Edward and Gwilym, and consulted with Jane about hairstyles. To the outward eye, she led a normal life. Inwardly, she was a confused bundle of nerves.

For whatever reason, Ben would not accept her answer of no. He had commented that God was insistent. Did that mean she had no choice in the matter? Would he continue to ask until she finally gave in and said yes? She had been taught the principle of agency while the elders were preparing her for baptism. She had made the choice to refuse Ben, and yet he persisted. Why couldn't she exercise her agency and tell him no, once and for all?

She decided not to think about it, but six months had gone by with a portion of every one of those days spent thinking about it. Her determination to put it from her mind didn't seem to be working. Reminders came at the oddest times—while at church, while reading the scriptures, while she prayed. It kept coming back and coming back.

"God," she prayed one night. "Please, take these thoughts from me."

But they wouldn't go away. Ben had asked her to think about it, and that thinking was becoming all-consuming.

"I can't hurt Mary Ann," she said aloud one afternoon while out in her father's fields.

Neither can Ben, came the thought into her head.

"But why is he so insistent?"

She waited for another thought to come, but it didn't. Instead the answer came all in one piece. She shook her head, surprised that she hadn't seen it sooner.

Ben simply loved God. He hadn't chosen that path for himself—he chose it because God wanted it for him. He couldn't act based upon his feelings for Mary Ann. It was a relationship between him and the Lord, not between him and Mary Ann.

Sarah was grateful for the definition, but it didn't help her. If anything, her thoughts became more consumed with confusion. If she didn't come to an answer soon, she knew she'd go mad.

* * *

Cedar City
October, 1881

Perhaps it was because she dreaded it, but the year passed more quickly than any other year in Sarah's life. She received a letter from Mary Ann saying that she'd had a new baby, a little boy named Daniel. Their trip to Cedar City had been delayed, but they would be arriving in the middle of October, only a few days away now. They could be there at any time. Sarah had thrown her nervous energy into cleaning the house until even her fastidious mother told her she could stop. Everything sparkled from stem to stern, and now Sarah's hands were idle, giving her too much time to fret.

The morning after she thought she couldn't stand the suspense a moment longer, the Perkins' wagon pulled up in front of the Williams' home. Mary Williams bustled out the door, her skirts trailing out behind her. She snatched Daniel out of Mary Ann's arms, hugged and kissed them all around, then took Mary Ann by the elbow and led her into the house, leaving Ben alone by the wagon. Sarah turned to go back inside, but he called out to her, just as she knew he would do.

The time they had spent apart had been hard on Ben. He looked older, and she couldn't help but notice a few wrinkles where there had been no wrinkles before. He reached out and took hold of her fingertips.

"Sarah."

He had simply spoken her name, nothing more. But she heard the question in his voice, knew that more was coming.

"I have been thinking about it, Brother Perkins. I shall have your answer before you leave again for Bluff."

"What have I done to you?" he asked, almost to himself rather than her. "Your eyes are haunted. They always looked so bright before. How could I have done this?"

His voice was anguished. She looked into his eyes and saw again the pain that lingered there.

"And how could I have done this to Mary Ann?" he continued. "She has been kind to me, always kind. But I don't deserve it."

Sarah felt a strange sensation deep within, as though she wanted to comfort him in some way. She had never seen him so upset, and it moved her to tears.

"And now you're crying." Her head came up at his words. "Sarah, I would leave you alone if I could. I'm sorry my attentions are hurting you."

"That's not why I'm crying," she told him.

"Then why?"

"You look so sad."

"You're crying for me?" He sounded incredulous. "All these tears?"

She nodded, unable to say more.

"That's a wonderful gift," he said after several seconds. "Thank you." His own voice sounded thick, as though he would cry too.

"They'll be wondering where we are," she said, motioning toward the house.

"We'd best have a reason," he replied. He handed her a small suitcase and a bunch of wildflowers. "The girls picked these for your mother. They were growing along the road just outside Cedar."

"She will love them."

He grabbed a larger valise from the back of the wagon, and the two walked up to the house, their shared secret lingering between them. As they stepped over the threshold, Ben turned immediately to Mary Ann, and Sarah focused on getting to know her new nephew. But their eyes met once during dinner, and Sarah knew his thoughts had not left her at all.

* * *

Cedar City
October, 1881

Sarah walked alone through the fields that belonged to her father. Out there she was truly alone, except for the comforting love of God's spirit, and she could speak to Him with her heart and know that He heard.

The Mormons certainly were a curious lot. She smiled a bit, thinking of how they had set out on the journey across southern Utah without giving it a second thought. They just packed up and went. They encountered some hardships along the way, but that didn't deter them. They knew what God wanted them to do, and they did it.

And now, for Ben to ask her to enter polygamy . . . . She shook her head. It was impossible.

But suddenly a thought entered her head with such force that for a moment she couldn't see the trees that stood not six yards in front of her—the entire world went blank. Then she understood, and tears began to form in her eyes.

Do you believe that I am?

She nodded her head, unsure how to answer a voice that came from within and without at the same time.

Then keep my commandments.

She swallowed hard. "But Lord, how . . . ?"

It doesn't matter how. All will be made right.

How much longer she stood in the field, Sarah didn't know. Time didn't exist as she replayed that short conversation over and over in her mind. It didn't make sense. But a conviction began to grow in her heart. It didn't matter if she understood the principle of polygamy. She had been asked to do it by a God she trusted. He had promised all would be made right, and that had to be enough for now. Like those Saints who threw everything they had into the back of a wagon and headed off into the desert to settle the land, she now knew what God wanted, and she would do whatever it took to heed His call.

* * *

Cedar City
October, 1881

Ben was in the barn. Sarah entered the shadowy building slowly, her heart pounding.

"Brother Perkins?" she called out, knowing he was inside but not able to see him at first.

"Here, Sarah."

She walked over to the horse stall where he stood.

"The horse has thrown a shoe. I'll have to take her to a smith in the morning."

She nodded.

"It's amazing to me how many shoes a horse can go through."

She nodded again.

"And harnesses! They're made out of leather, but you'd think they were thread, with how often they break."

She continued to nod.

"Sarah, you're killing me. Please say whatever it is you came in here to say. I can't take another minute of this."

"I will marry you." She whispered the words, not sure if he heard her.

"What?" he asked, leaning forward.

"I will marry you."

He let out a breath of relief and closed his eyes. "Thank you, Sarah." He took a step closer and pulled her into his arms before she realized what he was doing. Her first instinct told her to step back, but she remained, relaxing into his hug.

It didn't feel like a romantic embrace—instead, it felt like friendship, and she could allow that.

"Somehow, we'll make this right for everyone," he told her. "There will be a way." He kissed the top of her head, then held her out at arm's length. "I promise you, Sarah, I will do right by both you and your sister."

She nodded, not knowing how he would accomplish it, but knowing that he would try his best.

CHAPTER TWENTY-NINE

Cedar City, Utah
October 27, 1881

Mary Ann had not said a word in two days. Sarah waited for her sister to bring up the subject, but Mary Ann wouldn't speak to her. She exchanged words with her parents, brothers, and sisters, but would not even look at Sarah.

No one noticed but Ben.

"She's hurting," he told Sarah when she asked him. "I've wounded her terribly, Sarah. She may never forgive me."

Sarah leaned back against the wall. She knew she was doing the right thing by marrying Ben, but could not handle the grief she caused her sister. And her parents—they didn't know yet. But Ben was taking her to the St. George temple the next day, and they planned to tell Evan and Mary that night. They both thought it would be better that way.

"Has she given her permission?"

Ben sighed. "She gave it, but with tears in her eyes."

Sarah ducked her head quickly. It would be a long night for all of them, but for Mary Ann especially.

The little ones were tucked into bed, and Ben thought it best that they tell Sarah's parents immediately. She agreed. Her stomach churned, but she had to get it over with as soon as possible.

"Mother, Father, I need to speak with you," she said, standing near the door. Evan and Mary looked up. Mary Ann sat near the fire, not looking at Sarah at all.

"We've . . . that is, I . . ." Sarah couldn't go on. Her voice failed her.

"It's all right, Sarah. This is my task." Ben stood up and faced the Williams. "I've asked Sarah to become my second wife, and she has accepted. We'll be going to the temple in the morning."

The room fell completely silent. Sarah looked from one face to the other, trying to read her parents' expressions. Mary Ann's face wore a solemn mask.

Finally Mary drew in a long breath. "Please tell me that you did not say . . . what I just heard you say."

"It's true, Mother Williams." Ben looked apologetic, but his voice held firm.

"No, it can't be true." Evan had come to life. He rose from his chair, towering over Ben. "You cannot do this thing."

"The Lord commanded it."

Evan turned to Sarah. She flinched under the powerful fury in his eyes. "You would take your sister's husband?"

She opened her mouth to reply, but no words came out. Her mother sobbed in her chair, and Sarah could not form words around the tightness in her chest.

"How could you do that? How can you run off with your own sister's husband?" Evan was yelling now, storming around the room.

"Father Williams, she is obeying the command of the Lord." Ben stood his ground, although his father-in-law was nearly a foot taller and could easily take him in a wrestling match. "She has done nothing wrong."

"Nothing wrong, you say?" Evan whirled on Ben. "How can you believe such nonsense? You honestly think it's right to marry two sisters out of the same home, pit them against each other, sit back and enjoy your spoils? What kind of man are you, Ben Perkins?"

"I'm only a man who is trying to be obedient. It's not my desire to hurt either one of them."

Evan turned back to Sarah. "If you leave this house and return to it a plural wife, I will not be here to greet you when you return." He took his hat off the peg by the door and strode out, slamming the door behind him.

"Mary Ann?" Mary asked, her sobs finally under control.

"Yes, Mother?" Mary Ann's voice was completely calm.

"What do you think of this?"

Mary Ann didn't answer. Instead she stood and went into the spare room, closing the door behind her.

"I hope you're satisfied, Sarah," Mary said, turning hateful eyes on her daughter. "You set your cap for your sister's husband, and now you've ruined this family."

Sarah turned and ran out of the house. She flung herself on the ground underneath a small stand of trees at the edge of the fields and wept. She had known her parents would be angry, but she had never expected them to treat her like a Jezebel who had come to steal away Mary Ann's husband with wanton words and actions. Nothing could be further from the truth.

She heard a step beside her and knew that it was Ben.

"They are treating me like a . . . like a . . ." She couldn't say the words aloud.

Ben sat on the ground beside her. "I'm sorry," he said. "I never expected them to react that way. I thought they would be angry with me, not you."

"I thought they knew me better than this," she whispered. "Don't they know my heart?"

"The Lord knows your heart," Ben answered. He put his hand on her shoulder. "Sarah, I admire your integrity above all else about you. If your parents can't see the light of virtue that shines through your eyes, they are simply blind."

She turned and looked at him in the moonlight. He seemed so unsure, sitting there with his hair rumpled, his eyes filled with worry. He looked like a little boy.

"Promise me," she said, her eyes filling with tears. "Promise me that the Lord will make it right."

"He will make it right," Ben echoed. "He always does . . . in His own due time."

* * *

Ben did not come back in the house that night. He sent Sarah in, kissing her forehead and telling her to get some sleep. He knew she wouldn't, though. He felt tired, but could not enter that house, not while the accusing words spoken by Sarah's parents still hung in the air like daggers on strings. For them to think such things of Sarah—it was unpardonable and ridiculous.

He wondered if Mary Ann slept yet, but he doubted it. He could go in and see for himself, but he knew her well enough to know she wanted to be alone. He longed to wrap his arms around her and tell her of his love, but she would push it away. He had to show her, a little at a time, over the rest of her life, in order to regain the trust he knew he had shattered.

He gasped and sat down on the bale of hay that sat just outside the barn. Of all the things he regretted, breaking Mary Ann's trust was tearing at him most. She used to look at him with eyes filled with so much love, he would almost cry at the devotion of such a good woman. She always knew when he was upset, and would often come over and sit near him, not saying anything, but showing that she cared. She had never questioned any of his decisions, even though he had given her plenty of reason. She had faced that dugway with faith and determination, saying that if he had done it, it would work. She had so much faith in him. He had broken that faith.

He buried his head in his arms and willed the sun to come up. The darkness that surrounded him made his aching worse.

* * *

Cedar City
October 28, 1881

Ben slowed his team to a plodding walk as they entered Cedar City. It was midnight, and they were sneaking into town under the cover of darkness. Sarah sat next to him, feeling like a fugitive from justice. They had to return quietly. If anyone found out they had just been married, they would be arrested.

Ben pulled the wagon up to the home of his sister Naomi. She had agreed to take Sarah in for the next two weeks, until it was time to return to Bluff. Sarah would be going with Ben and Mary Ann, but she was not welcome in her parents' home any longer and needed a place to stay. Naomi had gone with them to St. George and now climbed out of the back of the wagon to open her front door. She went inside and disappeared.

Ben helped Sarah down from the wagon and led her around the rear of the house, where no one from the street would see them. They entered the back door and stood in the hallway.

"Sarah, I have to go and see Mary Ann," Ben said, reaching out and taking her hand. "She needs me right now."

"I wouldn't have it any other way," Sarah answered truthfully. "Please, take care of her. Make sure she's all right."

Ben wiped away the tear that ran down Sarah's cheek. "I will." He tried to smile. "You'll be safe here with Naomi. She won't tell a soul."

Sarah nodded. "She's very kind."

Ben took a step closer and pulled Sarah to him. She felt his arms go around her back, felt the strength in them. She wished she had some strength of her own. She felt alone, abandoned, like she had done something terribly wrong and yet extremely right, and Ben was the only one in the world who knew how she felt.

He tightened his grip as though he could read her thoughts. "It will be all right. I'll go and see Mary Ann. I'll speak with your mother. I'll do everything I can to set things straight. They can't reject you forever, Sarah. They just can't."

"I'm trying to believe that." She laughed wryly. "No matter how long it takes them to come around, it will feel like forever to me."

Ben nodded. "I know. And I'm sorry."

"It's not your fault, Brother Perkins. You're only doing what the Lord told you to do."

A smile appeared around the corner of Ben's lips. "I'm your husband now, Sarah. Do you think you could call me Ben?"

She thought about it for a moment, and shook her head. "I don't know."

He laughed, a little too loudly for that time of night. She reached up and placed a finger on his lips. "You'll wake up the house."

He caught her hand before she pulled it away, and held it for a moment. "I'll be back tomorrow," he promised.

She closed the door behind him. A moment later she heard the horses walk away from the house. There went her husband. She was a married woman now. She took a deep breath. Whatever the Lord brought her way, he would also bring to Ben and Mary Ann. Their fates were now forever linked.

* * *

Cedar City
October 29, 1881

The day stretched on and on. Sarah wondered where Ben was. Did he succeed in talking to her parents? Did they still hate her? She didn't want to think about Mary Ann, but the question loomed, bidden or not. How did Mary Ann fare?

Ben came late that afternoon, slipping in through the back door. He crossed the room and kissed Sarah's cheek.

"Your mother accepted my presence in the house, but she isn't ready to let you back in," he told her. "I don't understand that at all. Aren't I the wolf who came into the little flock of sheep?"

Sarah shook her head. She had no explanation for him.

"Mary Ann said exactly three words to me today. I think they were yes, no, and yes."

"At least there were some yeses in there," Sarah offered.

Ben smiled. "There is hope for us after all."

"What did my father say?"

Ben leaned forward and put his elbows on his knees. "Your father has not come back to the house yet. He sent word to your mother that he went to work at a nearby mine and will return after we've left for Bluff."

Sarah stood up and turned toward the fireplace. "I have to speak to them, Brother Perkins. I can't stand this division in our family."

"Would you like me to drive you over there?"

"Yes, please."

"You'd better wait until nightfall," Naomi said from the doorway. She held a hot loaf of bread in her hands, wrapped in a towel. "Ben, have some supper with us before you go."

"I will, thank you."

Sarah tried to eat, but toyed with her food instead. She was sick inside to think about facing her mother, but it had to be done. She could not return to Bluff without first trying to patch things up.

* * *

Cedar City
October 30, 1881

"Are you sure you want to go in alone?" Ben asked.

Sarah looked at the front of the house, imagining what might happen once she stepped inside. It would be a comfort to have him with her, but she had to do it alone.

"I'll be all right."

Ben shook his head. "Very well. I'll be waiting."

Sarah took his offered hand and climbed down from the buggy. Although Naomi's house was not far away from her parents', the road trip had been dusty, and fine gray silt covered the front of her dress. She took a moment to shake the folds of calico, and walked toward the door with resolution.

She knocked once, then pushed open the heavy wooden door. Mary Ann sat inside by the fireplace. She didn't look up as Sarah came in. Her eyes looked tired and red, although they were dry.

Sarah glanced around for the children, but they must have been put to bed early, as they were nowhere in sight. That was good. It took the edge off the discomfort she felt. How she would have hated to have such a conversation in the children's presence!

"Mary Ann, can I talk to you for a moment?"

Mary Ann said nothing, but she turned her head and looked at her sister. Sarah faced the fire, trying to find a safe place to look that would keep her from the wrath she saw in her sister's eyes.

"I've come to talk to you," Sarah said.

"Why? So you could gloat?"

Sarah sank to her knees in front of her sister. "No, Mary Ann! I don't want to gloat! I know how much this has hurt you, and if it weren't for the fact that I truly feel it is right, I never would have done it."

"You told me you would not accept his proposal."

Sarah bowed her head. "I know. I made that promise in haste. I hadn't taken the time to study it out or pray about it. I haven't gone about this wisely, and I know that. I'm sorry, Mary Ann, and I'll do anything I can to make this up to you."

"You can get out of this house."

Sarah raised her head. Mary Ann's eyes glowed like embers taken from the fire. "What?" Sarah asked, hoping that she had heard wrong.

"Leave this house."

Sarah slowly pulled herself to her feet. "All right, I'll go. I know I've hurt you, and I'm so, so sorry. I don't blame you for wanting me out of your sight."

Mary Ann stood and looked Sarah in the eye for a long, silent moment. Then she drew back her hand and brought it hard across Sarah's face.

Sarah took a step back, holding her cheek. There was nothing more she could say or do. She turned and left the house, closing the door quietly behind her.

Ben sat in the wagon, looking out across the vista, and hadn't heard her exit the house. She stood a moment to compose herself, and wiped her eyes with her handkerchief. She got the square of linen tucked away just as her new husband turned and saw her. She mustered up a smile and joined him on the seat.

"How did it go?" he asked.

"As I expected," she answered truthfully. "Please, take me back to Naomi's."

CHAPTER THIRTY

Cedar City, Utah
October 30, 1881

Mary Ann sank into the chair and buried her head in her hands. She had no idea what had come over her. She had never struck another soul in her life, and yet she had not been able to restrain herself.

The house was still. Her mother and the children were in bed, and Thomas was out on a job. The only sound was the crackle of the fire. Glad for the quiet, she still wished for something else to happen to take her mind off the empty churning inside her.

Ben and Sarah were married. They had actually gone ahead and done it.

Ben had told her last night that they had gone through with the ceremony, and she wasn't surprised. But the stark reality remained that her husband was no longer hers alone. She would now have to share him with the one person she thought she could trust above all others—her own sister.

She wrapped her arms around herself and began to rock. She had stood by Ben through those rough first years as they worked themselves day and night to get their family established, to build a home and find paying jobs. She had mended his clothes, cooked his meals, born his children, and suffered their loss as well. Didn't she deserve to stand by his side as a jewel in his crown?

But now that place of honor would be shared with another woman who had not endured near so much as she, who had not earned the right.

She shook her head. She knew it was not a contest, and that the Lord knew of her sacrifices and suffering. Surely her efforts would not go overlooked. But it was more than that—so much more.

She refused to allow herself to think for a moment longer. She took up her knitting and began to plan what she would do the next day. She would make bread and teach the children more of their letters and numbers. After that she would read them a story and let them each pick a button out of her mother's sewing box. Maybe if she kept her mind focused on her children, she would forget how very alone she felt on that night.

* * *

Ben sneaked back into the house under the cover of darkness. Mary Ann closed her eyes and pretended to be asleep, although she hadn't dozed off once in the three hours since she went to bed. Ben walked quietly across the room to the side of the bed, and she could sense him looking down at her.

"Mary Ann?" he whispered.

She didn't respond.

He bent down and kissed her cheek, so lightly that she almost could have imagined it. He walked away just as quietly. A few moments later she heard him settle down in the rocking chair. She waited, expecting him to come back, but he didn't. He would give her some space. She nodded into the darkness. That was just as well. She didn't trust herself to hold her tongue.

* * *

Cedar City
November 1, 1881

Sarah put her bonnet on her head and tied the strings under her chin.

"Where are you going?" Naomi asked.

"To see my mother."

Naomi grabbed Sarah's hand. "You can't do that, Sarah! She'll throw you out in the street."

"I have to try, Naomi. We leave for Bluff in the morning."

Naomi shook her head. "You're braver than I would be. After the way they treated you—"

"I believe I would feel the same way they do."

Naomi looked at her with wide eyes. "You would?"

"I don't agree with everything my parents have said. I certainly never set my cap for Brother Perkins, and I didn't chase him down. But I know I've hurt them. I'm not angry, Naomi. Really."

"Go, if you must. But don't say I didn't warn you."

Sarah walked the mile to her parents' house in the daylight. But she wasn't with Ben, so there shouldn't be any danger. As she walked, she thought of all the things she wanted to say, but couldn't. Her chosen words would have to be short, if allowed to speak at all. She had already been to the house twice, only to be told that her mother would not see her. She wasn't even sure if she would get in again.

Thomas opened the door when she knocked.

He had been her ally through the whole misery. Kate had been shocked and kept to her room. The younger children didn't know what to think. But Thomas had been with them on their journey to Bluff. He knew they had done nothing wrong. He might not have had the testimony to back up their assertions that they had been commanded of God, but he knew that they had acted appropriately during the trip.

"Can I see Mother, Thomas?" she asked.

Thomas looked over his shoulder. "She's in the kitchen. Why don't you just go on back? If we tell her you're here, she's bound not to let you in."

"Thank you," Sarah said. She walked softly into the kitchen, removing her bonnet as she went.

"Mam?" Mary sat at the table with a bowl of string beans in front of her. "Hello, Mother," Sarah said, sitting down and taking up a bean. She snapped it and pulled off the string, then put it down. No other beans lay on the table, and she realized that her mother had been sitting there, staring at her work but not doing it. It was very unlike her.

"Mother, I've come to tell you goodbye. I leave for Bluff in the morning with Brother Perkins and Mary Ann."

Mary said nothing.

"It was a lovely wedding ceremony," Sarah continued. Her voice sounded hollow in the silence of the room. "I wish you could have been there."

Mary's hand came down and hit the bowl, scattering beans across the table. "You wanted me to come to your wedding, Sarah? How could I have done that?"

"I know it was a foolish wish."

"And now you come here and want me to congratulate you on your marriage." Mary stood up and went to the cupboard, pulling out an old quilt and two pillows. She turned and threw them at Sarah. "Here is your wedding present."

Sarah clutched the so-called gift to her chest as she walked back to Naomi's house. Thomas had given her a kiss on the cheek as she left. The other children were nowhere in sight. She would have loved to see them one more time, but Kate probably had them in her room, hiding them from Sarah.

She had not gained her mother's favor, but at least she had finally spoken to her. Sarah had to take that as a good sign.

Later that night Ben came over. "Are you all ready to go?"

"As ready as I can be, I suppose."

"Thomas helped me gather up the things from your room. I have them all in the wagon."

"My books and everything?"

"Everything."

"Thank you, Brother Perkins. I thought I would have to leave them behind, or have another unpleasant scene with Mother if I tried to collect them."

"I don't deserve all the credit. Thomas helped me."

"Yes, but you thought of it."

"Actually, Mary Ann thought of it."

Sarah blinked. "Mary Ann?"

Ben smiled. "Yes. She said you would want your things."

Sarah sat down on the couch, her knees suddenly feeling weak. "Has she forgiven me then, Brother Perkins?"

Ben sat down next to her. "She understands, Sarah. She doesn't like it, and she's not happy. But she understands."

Sarah leaned forward and buried her face in her hands. Ben put his arms around her and held her tightly while she sobbed.

"I can't tell you how much that means to me," she said when she could speak. "I thought she hated me."

"She doesn't hate you, Sarah. She's angry. She's also been angry with me, and I've deserved it. You haven't."

Sarah wiped her eyes. "I'm ready to go to Bluff now. Knowing that there's even a chance to make things right with Mary Ann, I believe I can do this."

CHAPTER THIRTY-ONE

Back to Bluff
November 2, 1881

Ben came by with the wagon first thing the next morning. Mary Ann already sat on the driver's seat. She started to scoot over to make room for Sarah, but Sarah held up her hand. "I'll ride in the back with the girls. It will be safer that way."

"Hi, Aunt Sarah," Mary Jane said as Sarah clambered in the back. She was echoed by Caroline and Delia. Naomi offered a wave of a chubby fist. Mary Jane leaned over and put her head on Sarah's shoulder. "I'm glad you came back here to ride with us. I missed you."

"I missed you too," Sarah replied, a lump forming in her throat.

Ben urged the horses forward, and the wagon rolled down the street. Sarah watched as her home became smaller and smaller in the distance, not moving her eyes until she couldn't see it at all.

They drove until noon and stopped to make lunch along the trail. Mary Ann moved around the fire, her actions quick and precise as she fixed plates for everyone. Sarah took a deep breath.

"Mary Ann."

Her sister looked up.

"Thank you for asking Thomas and Brother Perkins to get my things. It means a lot to me."

Mary Ann nodded without reply and continued preparing lunch.

Sarah sighed inwardly. It wasn't what she had hoped for, but the first step had been taken.

* * *

Bluff
Mid-November, 1881

The Perkins' arrived in Bluff at night, not by design, but by chance. Ben drove the wagon to a cabin Sarah had never seen before.

"Where are we?" she asked.

"This is our new home. The brethren asked all the Saints to build their cabins more closely together, in a fort." Sarah looked around. They had done just as they had been asked to do. She could see houses around on all sides.

"But what of the lovely house you already built?"

"It's still there. Perhaps someday we will return to it."

He carried Sarah's belongings into a room near the back of the cabin, and Sarah instinctively knew he had built it just for her, even though she had not given him a positive answer at the time he created it. It was set off in the corner of the house, far away from the area where Mary Ann kept her things, and Sarah immediately appreciated that. Mary Ann would want to feel like she had a place to herself.

"This room is yours for the time being," Ben told her. "I'll build you a cabin of your own as soon as I'm able."

She opened her mouth to protest, but shut it again as quickly. It was more than she had anticipated, but she knew it would be a necessity. She slept poorly that night, staring at the walls and unable to keep her thoughts cheerful.

Mid-morning of the next day, Mary Ann was out visiting a neighbor when there came a knock at the door. Sarah crossed the hard-packed earth floor and opened the door.

"Sarah! You've come back!" Ann Rowley greeted her with enthusiasm. She gave her friend a hug, then put her at arm's length and looked her in the eye. "And did you return a bride?" she asked quietly.

"I did," Sarah whispered.

"How is Mary Ann taking it?"

"Poorly. But so would I, in her place."

"You're a good sister, Sarah. She can't stay angry forever."

"No, but she aches." Sarah looked at her friend more closely. "I see there's to be another Rowley."

Ann laughed. "We think it will arrive near Christmas time."

The two friends visited for a while. Ann filled Sarah in on all that had taken place in Bluff over the last year and a half. Sarah was impressed with the growth of the town, but saddened to hear that they still struggled to irrigate the crops. All too soon, Ann had to leave.

"Please, come see me as often as you like," Ann told Sarah. "Perhaps if tensions run high and you would like some space."

"I appreciate that." Sarah walked Ann to the front door.

"You'll find a way, Sarah. I know you will." Ann gave her another quick hug and was off.

Sarah closed the door behind her friend, wondering just what that way would be and when it would come.

* * *

Bluff
November 23, 1881

The days passed slowly for Mary Ann. Sarah kept largely to herself, not speaking much but to talk to the children in a friendly voice. She helped even more than usual around the house, and Mary Ann couldn't fault her for taking up too much of Ben's time. She took care to leave the room if Mary Ann wanted to discuss something with Ben, and she never asked him for anything. Mary Ann could see that Sarah was terrified of intruding on their family.

Mary Ann appreciated that, but at the same time, felt bad that her sister felt so unwelcome.

She thought many times of offering a hand of friendship, but something inside her always made her pull it back. She didn't know if it came from pride or fear. She was reluctant to reach beyond her own hurt. She acted politely toward Sarah, but the wall that she had built around her heart galvanized, and she couldn't see a way around it.

* * *

Sarah came in one afternoon, tears streaming down her face. Mary Ann forgot her anger for a moment. "Sarah, what's the matter?" She had rarely seen Sarah so upset and wanted to know the cause.

Sarah handed her a letter from Evan and Mary that had just been brought by the riders. They had written to apologize to Sarah for all they had said and done before she left, and begged her forgiveness. They told her that she was welcome to come to their home at any time.

Mary Ann read the letter through and turned to Sarah. "Do you forgive them?"

Sarah nodded. "I found very little to forgive."

"They said some terrible things to you, and I didn't stop them."

Sarah looked at her sister, surprise in her eyes.

"I've regretted it, Sarah. I shouldn't have let them speak to you like that." The words were hard for her to say, but she knew she must.

"Don't think about it another minute, Mary Ann."

"But—"

Sarah reached out and touched her sister's shoulder. "You have no need to apologize."

Sarah moved off to help the girls, and Mary Ann returned to her own chores. She felt humbled by Sarah's acceptance. She didn't know if she would be that charitable under the same conditions.

* * *

Bluff
May 5, 1882

Sarah waited until she was sure. She wanted it to be true, but didn't know what Mary Ann would say. She put off talking to her for some time, but knew she must, before it became completely obvious. Mary Ann had just put Daniel down for his nap and sent the girls out to play.

Sarah took a deep breath. "Mary Ann," she said, saying a quick prayer in her heart, "I'm going to have a baby."

Mary Ann didn't turn from her task of kneading bread, but her hands grew still for a moment. Sarah held her breath, waiting for her sister to speak.

"Are you sick yet?" Her question was asked softly.

"No, I feel all right."

"When will it come?"

"In the fall, I believe."

Mary Ann kneaded for another minute.

"What did Ben say?"

"I haven't told him yet."

"You haven't told him? Why on earth not?" Mary Ann turned and looked at her sister in surprise.

"I wanted to talk to you first."

Mary Ann nodded. She turned back to the dough, flipping it one way and then the other. "He will be thrilled. He's a wonderful father."

"Yes, he is."

Mary Ann didn't say anything more, but she thought about it all day long. That night after supper, she picked up a book. "Why don't you take Sarah for a walk, Ben."

* * *

Sarah was surprised. Mary Ann had never encouraged Ben to spend time with her before. She must want Sarah to tell him about the baby.

They walked for a short time, the wind blowing gently around them. Ben reached out to take her hand as they stepped over some wagon ruts, and didn't loosen his hold when they got to the other side.

"Brother Perkins, I have something I must tell you," she said.

"What is it, Sarah?"

She took a deep breath. "I'm . . . I'm going to have a baby."

Ben stopped mid-stride and turned to look at her. "A baby? Truly?"

"Yes."

His face filled with wonder and delight. "I'd let out a whoop and a holler except I'd wake up the neighbors," he said. "Oh, Sarah." He grasped her hand tightly and led her around the corner of a building, then took her in his arms and held her. "A baby. I can hardly believe it."

"I think it will come in September," she told him.

"September? Sarah, it's already May. Why didn't you tell me?"

"I wanted to speak to Mary Ann first."

Ben's face grew solemn. "How did she take it?"

"I'm not sure. She wasn't angry, I don't think."

"I'll talk to her." Ben held her closer. "How do you feel?"

"I'm all right."

"Sarah, you don't have to be afraid to tell me anything—anything at all. I want to know what's going on with you. You've hardly spoken since we arrived in Bluff."

"I know." She shrugged. "I don't want to do anything to offend Mary Ann."

"I don't either. But you're my wife too. If anything is bothering you, I want to know it. Promise?"

"I promise."

Ben let her go, and they started walking back toward the house. He took several steps and began to laugh. "A baby! This is good news. I guess we'll need to get to work on that second cabin, eh?"

* * *

Sarah went straight to bed when she and Ben returned from their walk. Mary Ann set her book down and waited for Ben to join her by the fireplace. He crouched down by her chair and took her hand in his.

"Sarah told me," he said unnecessarily.

"Are you pleased?" she asked.

"I'm very pleased. But you knew I would be."

Mary Ann nodded, a slight smile on her face. "I knew."

"How are you?" He reached out and touched her hand.

Mary Ann thought about it for a minute. She had been trying to digest the news all day. She had known it would happen sooner or later. But now that it had, she didn't know what to think.

Ben's eyes were alight with joy, but also concern. She reached out and gently touched his face. "If you're happy about it, that's all I need to know."

He buried his face in her skirt. "Thank you, Mary Ann," he whispered. She ran her fingers through his hair, wanting so badly to just be happy for him without all the attending sorrow.

CHAPTER THIRTY-TWO

Bluff, Utah
Early July, 1882

Sarah found it more and more difficult to move with each passing day. It seemed to her that as soon as she shared her news with Ben and Mary Ann, she suddenly lost the ability to hide her condition, and it wasn't long before she waddled.

"I feel like a duck," she told Ann, who rocked little Maggie Elizabeth Rowley to sleep.

"You'd best get used to the feeling," Ann told her with a smile. "I've carried so many children, I might as well grow feathers to go along with the waddle."

"You do have a beautiful family."

"We feel very blessed." Ann tucked a blanket more closely around Maggie's small shoulders. "They're all so different, but so wonderful, each in their own way."

"Thank you for letting me come over here. I try not to be under Mary Ann's feet. It can be a little . . . hard."

"You've made some tremendous sacrifices for your faith," Ann said. "It's bound to be hard."

"Will it all truly be worth it?" Sarah asked.

"Sarah, let me tell you a little story. When we lived in Parowan, let's see, this would have been 1874, before you came to Utah. Brigham Young established what was called the United Order. Have you ever heard of it?"

Sarah shook her head.

"Everyone in the community shared their property alike. We would bring anything we had to a central location, and it would be redistributed so everyone would have the same amount of any given product. It was a means of teaching the people how to truly be one, to be unselfish in all their dealings—a beautiful concept, and we agreed to follow this counsel. We deeded our property over to the Church, and also our teams, wagon, and everything else we had. We meant to be faithful.

"Too soon, greed took over. The people found it impossible not to be selfish with what little they had. It's difficult to scratch a living out of the dirt, and then to turn it over to the Church so that others could use it as well. It was asking too much of many of the members. The United Order in Parowan disbanded within a year. Samuel received fourteen bushels of potatoes in recompense for all he had put in."

"But he gave horses, a wagon," Sarah protested. "And what of your land?"

Ann smiled gently. "It came as a shock, certainly. We wondered what had become of our things, and would have liked to have them back. But let me share what Samuel did. He went to work for some of the other men, and earned enough money to buy us a new piece of land, and new horses, and new wagons."

"But you gave up that home to come here," Sarah exclaimed. "Didn't you feel that you had given enough?"

Ann thought on that for a moment. "How do you know when you've given enough? I can't say I have the answer. Perhaps when the Lord stops asking. Then we'll know we've done all we should."

Sarah shook her head. She could hardly imagine the trials Ann had been through.

"I tell you this story to illustrate a point. You asked if our sufferings would be worth it. My answer is, yes. I can't explain it. But with all we've been through, we have come to know of a surety that we are God's children. You cannot exchange that knowledge for gold or silver, for teams or land."

"Sometimes when Mary Ann looks at me, she seems unbearably sad," Sarah said. "I hate to cause her so much pain."

"She's coming to know God, just as you are," Ann said. "And someday, you'll both be grateful for it."

* * *

Bluff
Late August, 1882

Sarah stepped over the threshold and into the cabin Ben had constructed just for her. It sat within the fort, as the apostles had recommended, and only a short distance away from the Rowley's. She appreciated the thoughtfulness Ben had shown in building her cabin close to Ann's.

It took a moment for her eyes to adjust to the dimness inside. She blinked a few times, and as things came into focus, saw a bed in the corner and a fireplace on the opposite wall. A shelf with kitchen items hung over the wash basin. It looked much like Mary Ann's cabin, but, she noticed immediately, opposite. Where Mary Ann's fireplace was on the north of the cabin, hers was on the south, and so forth. She smiled and shook her head. Perhaps Ben tried a little too hard to keep the sisters separate and individual.

She heard steps outside and turned to face the door, which stood open. Ben stuck his head inside and smiled at her. "Do you like it?"

"I do, very much."

"It doesn't have a second room on the back, like Mary Ann's, but I thought later . . . with children . . ." His face turned a little bit pink.

"Yes, perhaps later."

He relaxed against the door frame, obviously relieved that she understood what he was too shy to say.

"Truly, it's a lovely cabin." She turned around again, nodding her head. "I'll be very happy here."

"I'm glad, Sarah. I'm sorry it took me so long to give you a place of your own."

"You've had a lot on your mind."

Ben shifted his weight. "I'd best get back to the ditches. Who knows if we'll ever get water flowing properly." He hesitated, then walked away.

Sarah sat on the edge of the bed, pleased to have a cabin of her own, especially now that the baby was so close to coming. But she couldn't help but feel alone as Ben walked back to the other house. It would have been so nice if he had stayed, even for just a minute. But then she felt selfish for wanting him to stay. He wasn't really hers, after all. He was Mary Ann's.

* * *

Bluff
September 28, 1882

The pains were coming more frequently. Sarah couldn't walk around the cabin anymore. She went outside, resting her hand on the door jamb of the new cabin Ben had built and finished just the week before. He had been pleased to complete it before the baby came. Sarah now knew he had done it just in time.

The Rowley's cabin stood only a short distance away. She focused on it, taking one step at a time over and over again until she reached the door. She paused for a minute to catch her breath, and raised her hand to knock.

"Sarah!" Ann took her hand and guided her to a chair. "How long has this been going on?"

"Since the middle of the night."

"You should have gotten help sooner."

"I don't know how long these things take."

Ann turned to Hannah, her daughter. "Run over to the Perkins' cabin. Tell Sister Mary Ann that Sister Sarah's time has come."

Ann helped Sarah back to her own cabin, and began to prepare everything that would be needed.

A knock came at the door, and Ben stuck his head inside. "Mary Ann is on her way," he told Sarah. "She's packing a bag of necessities."

She nodded, unable to speak.

Ben stood at the door another minute, clearly unsure what to do. Ann solved the problem. "Go help Samuel in the fields for a few hours, Ben. We'll let you know when you can come back."

"Very well, Sister Rowley," Ben said with a smile. He came in for a moment and pressed a kiss on Sarah's forehead. "Be well," he whispered.

Mary Ann came and immediately got to work boiling water and preparing everything else that they would need. The afternoon was long and hard, full of great emotion and overwhelming pain. By the end of the day, Sarah held a tiny form in her arms—a perfect and pink bundle.

"Someone, go and get Ben," Mary Ann called out.

"No need. He came back and has been pacing outside for the last two hours," Ann said good-naturedly. She opened the door and ushered Ben in, then tactfully stepped out of the cabin and pulled the door closed behind her.

Ben came into the room reverently, his hat in his hands.

"It's a girl," Sarah told him.

He took the baby into his arms and looked her over. She stared up at him, eyes dark and intense, amazingly open for being so new.

"Hello," he said softly. He looked over at Sarah. "She's so beautiful."

Sarah nodded. "Yes, she is."

"What do you want to call her?"

"I like the name Mary Ellen."

Ben nodded. "So do I." He swayed back and forth, holding his new daughter close to his heart. Then he reached out and handed her to Mary Ann.

Mary Ann breathed inward sharply. She closed her eyes for a brief moment, and opened them again. The baby looked around and yawned. "Hello, I'm your aunt Mary Ann," she said.

Tears rolled down Sarah's face, and soon Mary Ann was crying too. She handed the baby to Ben, and bent down to hug her sister. The two women held each other long and hard, crying into each other's hair, wetting each other's shoulders.

"I'm sorry." Mary Ann said, at last pulling back and wiping her nose on her handkerchief. "I've been so unkind to you."

"No, you haven't," Sarah told her. "You were dealing with your own pain."

"Will you forgive me?" Mary Ann asked.

"There is nothing to forgive. I'm the one who should be asking you."

"All you've done is follow the Lord. I know that, Sarah. It's just been . . . hard."

"I will do everything I can to make this easy on you," Sarah promised.

"You've been a good and faithful sister, Sarah. I have nothing to fault you for."

They hugged again, feeling the ache that had consumed them for so long begin to ease. They knew it would not be easy, but if they worked out their disputes together, surely there would be a way to bring meaning to their sacrifice.

EPILOGUE

After five years of living in Bluff, Ben relocated his children and two wives to Cedar City. Over the course of her life, Sarah moved to Teasdale, Mancos Colorado, back to Bluff, and then ended up in Monticello. Mary Ann usually lived in a separate town from her sister, and Ben traveled back and forth between the two homes.

In 1888, the local law enforcement decided to arrest Ben for practicing polygamy. When they came to collect him at Sarah's home, he sent Sarah up into the woods to hide, and dealt with the marshals himself by inviting them to sit down and have a bite of breakfast with him. He treated them so kindly that they decided to allow him to remain at home to bring in the harvest, as long as he would turn himself in when he was done setting his farm to rights.

He kept his word, and so did they.

Ben went to trial on December 18, 1888. At that time, he was sentenced and fined three hundred dollars. He went to the State Penitentiary in Salt Lake City to serve his time, along with several other Mormon men who had also been arrested for polygamy. Some of the men determined that they would dissolve their plural marriages after their release. But others, like Ben, were determined to live the principle—whatever the cost.

Three days after entering the jail, Ben was made a trustee and given the freedom to leave the jail occasionally to go to the forest and gather wood. On June 17, 1889, he was released from prison after serving six months, and excused from paying the three-hundred dollar fine.

From that point on, Ben periodically moved his wives to different locations in an attempt to keep them, and himself, safe from the law.

Mary Ann died October 11, 1912, in Monticello.
Benjamin died March 30, 1926.
Sarah joined them in Heaven on June 30, 1943.

* * *

In all the family history records written about Ben, Mary Ann, and Sarah, much is said about their courage, faith, integrity, and virtue. Ben was called upon to live a most difficult life, but bore his trials with humor and diligence. Mary Ann had to endure a painful burden when Ben took his second wife, but she had enough pure love for her husband and trust in the Lord to live the principle patiently—although at times it wracked her soul. Sarah showed great devotion to the Lord in her decision to marry Ben, and she never wavered from that devotion, counting her testimony as the greatest of all her possessions. She did her best every day to treat Mary Ann with love and kindness, anxious that she not add to her sister's burdens. Sarah never demanded anything from Ben, and worked as a laundress to feed her own children so Mary Ann would not feel that her children were doing without.

The descendants of both wives have left written histories about their growing-up experiences, and they express their profound appreciation for both of their mothers—and their father—for the choice upbringing they enjoyed. Mary Ann's children looked upon Sarah with respect, and Sarah's children were always grateful to Mary Ann for the love and kindness she showed to them. Truly, in a situation that would ordinarily be a hotbed for hatred and unkindness, these two women put their own feelings aside and strived for the good of the family, showing true charity and perseverance.

As a direct descendant of Sarah Williams Perkins, I am honored to claim this branch of my family tree.

Sarah and Ben Perkins

Sarah Williams, in about 1873

Mary Ann Williams

Sarah Perkins (far right) and her nine daughters.
(The author's great-grandmother, Sade, is third
from the left. Sarah's only son, Richard Leonard,
is in the background.)

Replica of the cabin where Ben and
Mary Ann lived within the Bluff fort.

Monument built to commemorate the Hole in the Rock Pioneers at the Bluff Visitors Center and fort.

Author with her father standing at the graves of Ben, Mary Ann, and Sarah in the Monticello Cemetery.

Benjamin Perkins   Sarah Perkins

CHAPTER NOTES

Prologue:

At the age of fifteen, Ben was asked to go to Blongloha and help in the rescue effort after a large explosion demolished the mine. In reality, when he arrived, they had already received enough help and sent the workers from the Treboeth mine home again. I embellished this scene for purposes of the plot. Andrew Morgan is my own invention.

After returning home to Treboeth, Ben asked his father to baptize him, and they performed the ordinance that night in the river Tawe.

The incidents surrounding the placement of the Perkins family in the poor house are based on fact, as is the persecution the family endured for their choice to become Mormons.

Chapter One:

The exact circumstances surrounding the courtship of Ben and Mary Ann are factual, but I have embellished them.

For some reason I have not been able to determine, Ben never did learn how to read, even after coming to America.

The song Ben and Mary Ann sing together is called "Guide Us, O Thou Great Jehovah," written by popular Welsh composer William Williams (1717-1796), with the first verse translated by Peter Williams (1722-1796). You can find this hymn in its entirety in the LDS hymnal, number 83. Ben and Mary Ann's duet is my own invention, although they did sing together frequently throughout their lives.

Chapter Two:

The facts surrounding the ocean crossing of Ben, Mary, Naomi, Joe, and John Evans are based on fact, including the great sickness of the passengers and Ben's care of them.

I do not have on record Ben's true feelings about being a collier (coal miner). It is possible that, in actuality, he enjoyed the work. But given the tone of his life history covering the time he worked in the mines, I sensed dissatisfaction, and I elaborated upon it.

Chapter Three:

The circumstances related in this chapter are all based on fact, as told in Ben's life history. Matthew is a fictional character. Names were invented for the other teamsters in the wagon train, and for Captain Forbes, who was not named in the original account.

Mary Ann—and later Sarah—hired out to do housework for ladies in the neighborhood, doing whatever they could to supplement the family income. Other girls in the community were sent to the mines, but Evan and Mary Williams felt strongly that their girls should be kept from such a life.

"Mam" is a term used by Welsh children, refering to their mothers.

Chapter Four:

There are discrepancies in the various accounts concerning Mary Ann's trip to America. Ben sent her the money, and she was prepared to go, but some accounts say that she came without her father's blessing, and others say that he gave his permission. For the purposes of this story, I chose to use the version that felt the most right to me.

The other details of this chapter are factual, including the journey across the United States on the new Transcontinental Railroad.

The circumstances of Ben's travels across the continent and becoming a teamster are correct, including Ben hitching up the wrong oxen. Streaking the oxen with mud was my invention, as were Ben's methods of saying hello to Mary Ann once he finally got her alone.

The Deseret News article is quoted verbatim.

The wedding of Ben and Mary Ann and the sealing of William and Jane occurred as written.

Chapter Five:

The argument between Evan and Thomas about Thomas' chosen profession is based on fact, although embellished somewhat.

Evan did belong to a Druid society, which met every so often outside in the middle of the night, and he frequently took Sarah with him. He gave up those meetings after a time.

The circumstances surrounding Evan going to Russia are factual, although there is some discrepancy as to exactly when he left and just how long he was gone. Thomas' efforts to stow away on a boat, and his eventual success, are factual, although Mary's attempt to find him by going to the docks is my own invention.

I have been unable to discover what happened to Evan's wages. I don't know if he brought them home with him, or if he tried to send them to his family, but was unable. The histories simply show that the family suffered in his absence.

Chapter Six:

Mary Ann lost her second child—a little boy named William—after only a few short hours of life. The cause of his death is unrecorded and may even be unknown, so that passage is my invention. Brother Thurston brought his infant daughter Caroline Cordelia—nicknamed Delia—and let Mary Ann keep her for a time. Whenever he would return to collect Delia, she would scream and hang on to Mary Ann. He eventually gave up and allowed Ben and Mary Ann to raise her. She became one of their children in every respect.

Evan did return from the Russian mines with a severe case of asthma, which weakened him considerably.

Chapter Seven:

I have embellished the relationship between Sarah and Tom Wilcox, although it is based on fact.

Richard Jones is my own invention.

Evan's health had deteriorated, and he was told by his doctor to take the ocean voyage, and that it would either kill him or cure him. In fact, the Williams' made the attempt to immigrate twice, but were held back the first time because of Evan's health. For the purposes of this story, I left out that first attempt.

Tom's proposal is based on fact, although embellished.

Chapter Eight:

The lifestyle described in this chapter, as pertains to Ben and Mary Ann, is based on fact, although much of it is conjecture.

In reality, Tom Wilcox decided to follow Sarah to America. He earned his passage and sailed for New York six months after she left. He was there working for train fare to Utah when he received a letter from her saying that she had decided not to marry him. For plot simplicity, I chose to have them end their relationship in Wales.

Sarah's Methodist minister was very concerned and made her the gifts mentioned in this chapter.

Chapter Nine:

The events described in this chapter are based on fact, including Tom Wilcox following them to the boat and Evan having a difficult time making it. Sarah did indeed lose her hat in the ocean, and solved that problem by tying her handkerchief over her head. They stayed at Castle Gardens and had a look around the city, overhearing someone refer to them as "foreigners."

The circumstances of Hugh Griffin picking up the Williams family and taking them to his home are based on fact, with one exception—his name was really Joseph Matthews. I changed his name to avoid confusion, as many of the characters in this book have similar names.

I have found no documentation as to why Ben and Mary Ann had to wait two weeks until they could come and meet the family. I have conjectured that since Ben hired out, he had a job that he could not leave immediately.

Chapter Ten:

The incidents surrounding breakfast in this chapter are from Sarah's own history. She had never seen a baking soda biscuit or a banana before, and her confusion is quite understandable.

The party did travel in the manner indicated in the book, sleeping under the stars at night.

Chapter Eleven:

The call to the San Juan was issued much in the same way mentioned here. It is not known when Ben learned of the plan to settle the San Juan. His finding out about it in advance is my own invention.

Chapter Twelve:

Ben and Mary Ann did ask Sarah to accompany them on the trip to San Juan. Thomas Williams, long away at sea, returned sometime during this period, although the exact date of his arrival in Utah is not known. He did volunteer to go along on the San Juan mission, even though he was not a member of the Church.

Chapter Thirteen:

George Hobbs told his story to Ben and Mary Ann much the way it is recorded in the histories. While I have no knowledge that a special friendship existed between George and the Perkins, I have created it for the purposes of the book.

Chapter Fourteen:

It was understood that the missionaries who were called to the San Juan were leaving permanently, so they sold their homes and land.

It is a recorded historical fact that Sarah drove the wagon to the San Juan. What has not been recorded is exactly why she needed to. Surely, with Ben and Thomas both along on the journey, she wouldn't have to handle the team herself. But history does not tell us why Thomas didn't drive the second wagon. It has even been speculated that perhaps the Perkins family had three wagons, and Thomas drove the third.

But the writings plainly state that the wagon was given into Sarah's care six miles out of Cedar City, and gives no possible answer as to how the wagon would have driven itself those first six miles. Given that many of the single young men on the journey were called to herd the cattle, I chose to use that as the reason for Thomas' absence, and left it at two wagons.

Chapter Fifteen:

While Sarah drove the wagon on the flat lands and over minor inclines, I have to believe that Thomas or Ben took over for her when the wagon needed to pass through a difficult patch. There are no records as to exactly who drove the wagon on those treacherous roads, but if Sarah had done it, that fact would have been recorded somewhere, certainly in her life history.

I have no verification that Sarah learned how to harness the team herself. That is my own invention.

Chapter Sixteen:

In the recorded histories, there is some discussion as to just what happened when the missionaries reached Escalante. Some sources say that the shopkeepers in town jacked up their prices, knowing that the missionaries would pay whatever they asked. Others have defended the shopkeepers, saying that they were honest people who wanted to support the Church's expansion into the San Juan territory. Not having actual documentation of what the missionaries were charged for their goods, I have chosen not to enter the debate.

The friendship between the Rowleys and the Perkins has been fabricated Since they traveled in the same company all the way to San Juan, and both built homes there, it's very likely that they were at least well acquainted with each other—if not good friends.

The scouting party proceeded much as written. Although I was not able to include all the details of the scouting parties and their finds, I would encourage you to read them in the accounts listed in this book's bibliography—especially *The Incredible Passage* by Lee Reay. The scouts had many life-threatening and faith-promoting experiences, and their stories will inspire you.

Chapter Seventeen:

The scouts returned with an unfavorable report. However, when they met with Silas Smith to discuss their findings, the meeting was held in private. For the purposes of the plot, I wrote that the meeting was held in public. After the decision was made to go forward, the people bore their testimonies and spontaneously burst into song with "The Spirit of God," which was written by William W. Phelps (1792-1872), and can be found in its entirety in the LDS hymnal, number 2.

Chapter Eighteen:

Due to the lack of forage for the animals, it was decided to split the group up so that all the animals wouldn't fight over one patch of grass. As written in the book, half camped at Dance Hall Rock, and the other half at the Hole in the Rock.

Chapter Nineteen:

It is not documented just how Ben came up with the idea to create the road that hung from the side of the cliff. I believe it was inspiration.

Chapter Twenty:

Elizabeth Decker had her baby while camped at Dance Hall Rock and named her Lena Deseret.

Coal was discovered as the missionaries blasted in the cliffs. Until that time, they had been burning shadscale, which is a type of bush, and a large armful of it only burned for a few minutes. They felt blessed to find the coal.

The story of the scouting party is told much as George Hobbs related it in his personal account.

The descent down the hole is represented much the way it is documented in the histories.

For years, historians contended that the first wagon down the Hole in the Rock was driven by Kumen Jones, and that Ben drove the second wagon. This mistake bothered Kumen throughout his life, and shortly before his death, he wished to set the record straight. I paraphrase his statement, but his message was clear: Benjamin Perkins drove the first wagon down, and Kumen didn't want to continue to receive the credit for it.

In the first printing of this novel, I wrote the chapter to indicate that Kumen was the driver of that first wagon, just as the histories attest. But in July of 2009, I attended a family reunion where a portion of Kumen's journal was read aloud. I have made the change in this version and have placed ownership of that event back where it belongs, on the shoulders of Benjamin Perkins.

Chapter Twenty-one:

I found many different accounts of Stanford and Arabella Smith. Each account states that Stanford was upset that no one had remained to help bring down his wagon.
But there, the stories diverge. Some say that he told his wife to hold back on the wagon and was callous to the fact that she had been injured. The version I use in this story is the one found in Miller's *Hole in the Rock*, and is nearly verbatim of the story that has been passed down through their family as fact.

Chapter Twenty-two:

Each of the events depicted in this chapter are based on fact, including the half-frozen bees that were too cold to fly away.

Chapter Twenty-three:

The windstorm at Whirlwind Bench is a recorded fact. The statement by Platte D. Lyman that "it was impossible to be comfortable in bed or anywhere else" is found in his personal writings. The tipping over of the second wagon is my own invention.

Chapter Twenty-four:

I was unable to find documentation on just when it was that George Hobbs returned to camp, but have evidence that he was with the Saints when they entered the San Juan Valley. His return to the group in this chapter is my own invention. It was as good a time as any.

Chapter Twenty-five:

Immediately upon their arrival in Bluff, the Saints drew lots to determine which family would get which plot of land. There was not room for all the missionaries to stay in Bluff, so some continued on to Montezuma, including George Hobbs. The incident of the Indians visiting the church meeting and being convinced to leave by Kumen Jones and Platte D. Lyman is based on fact.

It was a hard task indeed to try to irrigate the land. For an in-depth look at the difficulty that the Saints had in performing this duty, see Blaine Yorgason's three-book series, *Hearts Afire*.

Chapter Twenty-six:

Sarah was baptized in the San Juan River on the date mentioned. She tells the story of her conversion and the impact that the missionaries made on her life:

> *The longer I lived among these people, the more convinced I became that Mormonism was the religion for me. . . .*
> *Many and varied are the experiences I have been called to pass through. While some have tested my courage severely, I have never doubted God's wisdom. . . .*

My testimony of the gospel is the most prized of all my possessions . . . .

As a girl there was something lacking in my life, I didn't know what it was, but the longer I lived among these people, the more I became convinced that Mormonism was the religion for me, and it came to me little by little, the things I had been wanting and didn't know I wanted.

The brethren from Salt Lake City did come to visit Bluff, then sent the letter, as partially quoted in this chapter.

Chapter Thirty-one:

The cabins, as built in the Bluff fort, were very small. The replica recently built to honor Benjamin Perkins is no larger in size than my living room—and I have a fairly small living room. However, I felt that Sarah deserved a room of her own, and so I fabricated its construction in this chapter. I have no knowledge as to whether Ben built Sarah a cabin of her own, but again, I thought she deserved one.

AFTERWORD

A Note About Polygamy

In 1843, the Prophet Joseph Smith received a revelation which would become section 132 of the Doctrine and Covenants. This revelation taught the principle of plural marriage, and the Lord commanded that his Saints begin to practice it.

Because the early Saints loved the Lord and trusted that He knew what was best for them, many accepted this doctrine and lived it—generally when called upon to do so by Church leaders. Others found it difficult to believe, and it caused many rifts in marriages and families. Because of it, some left the Church.

It wasn't easy to follow the practice, even for those who believed. Tempers flared and jealousies ignited. It would be truly difficult not to be selfish under these circumstances. Martha Cragun Cox, an early Utah pioneer, made the following comments in her personal writings:

> *Adopting the rules and regulations of my husband's family—an order already established—I had to submit to almost an entire reversal of my nature and habits. The greatest foe I had to meet was the hot Irish temper that had always swayed me when occasion aroused it. Many times the words of McCarty would be brought to my mind. "Remember in your plural home to speak no words when angry." When I disobeyed that injunction, it brought me sorrow.*

Yet despite the difficulty, she believed the principle to be true. She also says:

> *I had studied out the matter—I knew the principle of plural marriage to be correct—to be the highest, holiest order of marriage. . . . If the Lord would have manifested in answer to my sleepless nights of prayer that the principle of marriage was wrong, and it was not the will of Heaven that I should enter it, I felt I should be happy. But it only made me miserable beyond endurance when I tried to recede from the decision I had made to enter it.*

It would seem that a family built around a plural marriage would be doomed to failure. It was that way for men who entered into it without the proper mindset and the right spirit. But when a man took a second wife with the desire to be obedient to the Lord and keep the commandments—and his wives also had that desire—their lives were blessed for their efforts. Records exist of happiness in polygamous homes.

Many opinions circulate as to the reason for polygamy. To some, it was a Mormon meat market, instituted to fulfill the lusts of the men. But who could believe that the Lord would allow such a thing to take place in His Church? In other books of scripture, we get a taste of the love the Lord has for His daughters:

> *And also it grieveth me that I must use so much boldness of speech concerning you, before your wives and your children, many of whose feelings are exceedingly tender and chaste and delicate before God, which thing is pleasing unto God.* (Jacob 2:8)

And later in the same chapter:

> *And I the Lord delight in the chastity of women. And whoredoms are an abomination before me; thus saith the Lord of Hosts.* (Jacob 2:28)

One of my favorite scriptures:

> *. . . that our daughters may be as cornerstones, polished after the similitude of a palace.* (Psalms 144:12)

Surely a God who speaks so tenderly and compassionately about His daughters, and urges His prophets to do the same, could not condone an act which would, in essence, prostitute women.

After the Edmunds act of 1882, followed by the Edmunds-Tucker act of 1887, polygamy was considered a felony in the United States, and many of the Saints who were practicing it at the time had a tough decision: they could either abandon their other families and live only with their first wife, or they could go into hiding to avoid arrest. My own great-great-grandfather on my mother's side took the option of moving two of his families to the Mexican colonies, which story will be documented in another book.

President John Taylor went into hiding, and encouraged his councelor, Joseph F. Smith, to remove himself to the mission field. Julina Lambson Smith, wife of Joseph F. Smith, sent the following statement in a letter to the Women's Exponent in 1886, written while in hiding in the islands of Hawaii:

> *I have never felt that I have been guilty of any crime, notwithstanding the action of the courts. . . . It is not a question of any law with us, but a matter of conscience, of religious conviction, and of earnest and undying faith in the laws and purposes of God, a matter of happiness or misery, of life or death.*

However, the law would not be satisfied on this point, and the persecution of the Church became more than the Saints could bear. On October 6, 1890, a declaration was given by Church president Wilford Woodruff, which became known as the Manifesto. It proclaims, in part:

> *Inasmuch as laws have been enacted by Congress forbidding plural marriages, which laws have been pronounced constitutional by the court of last resort, I hereby declare my intention to submit to those laws, and to use my influence with the members of the Church over which I preside to have them do likewise.*
>
> *And i now publicly declare that my advice to the Latter-day Saints is to refrain from contracting any marriage forbidden by the law of the land.*

No one can truly comprehend the mysteries of God, but those who seek to do His will are blessed for their desires to be obedient. Many are the stories of polygamous families where love and joy prevailed, and the residents of such homes bore their testimonies of the strength that they found in living the principle righteously.

For many, plural marriage is a hot button of debate, a cause for the flaring of tempers and hurt feelings. To this day, the question of "Why?" is tossed about, with many offering their opinions. Especially amongst modern-day Mormon women, it is a subject to be met with utter disgust.

I was such a woman.

When I entered into this project, it was difficult for me to write the passages wherein Sarah decides to marry Ben. How could I take a situation which I find so difficult, and present it in such a way that I could accurately convey Sarah's change of heart?

It wasn't until I hit upon one fundamental truth—that Sarah wasn't converted to polygamy, but was converted to the Lord and wanted to be obedient—that I was able to forge ahead and complete the book.

I still don't know all the answers, but I feel as though I have grown personally by researching the lives of these incredible women . . . and that's truly a blessing to me.

Appendix I

Members of exploring party, Spring of 1879

Adams, James J.
Allan, Issac
Bayles, Hanson
Bladen, Thomas
Bullock, Robert
Butler, John
Butt, Parley R.
Dailey, Nielson B.
Dalton, John C.
Davis, James L.
    Mary Elizabeth Fretwell
        Edward Fretwell
        James H. Fretwell
        Emily Ellen
        John Orson
Decker, James B.
Decker, Zachariah B., Jr.
Duncan, John C.
Dunton, James Harvey
Dunton, James Cyrus
Gower, John
Harriman, Henry H.
    Sarah Elizabeth Hobbs
        Henry George
        Mary C.
        John Alma
        Lizzie Constance

Hobbs, George B.
Jones, Kumen
McGreggor, Adelbert F.
Nielson, H. Joseph
Perry, George E.
Smith, Albert R.
Smith, Silas S.
Smith, Stephen A.
Thornton, Hamilton
Urie, George
Wallace, Hamilton

The exploring party left Paragonah April 13th, 1879. Later at Moenkopi, the expedition was joined by Thales Haskell and Seth Tanner, who acted as guides and Indian interpreters.

Appendix II

Important Mission Assignments

Silas Sanford Smith
    Expedition Captain, Mission President

Platte DeAlton Lyman
    Field Captain, First Councilor

Jens Nielson
    Group Captain

George W. Sevy
    Group Captain

Benjamin Perkins
    Group Captain

Henry Holyoak
    Group Captain

Zachariah Decker, Jr.
    Group Captain

Samuel Bryson
    Group Captain

Charles E. Walton, Sr.
    Clerk

Jens Nielson
    Chaplain

George W. Decker and George Ipson
    Livestock Foremen

Charles Hall and family
    Ferry Construction and Operation

Appendix III

Original Mission Members

Agnell, Alma Truma
Barnes, Noah
Barney, Danielson B.
    Laura Matthews
        Onley Buren
        Sarah Elcea
        Alfred Alonzo
        Laura Mae
        Rachel Sophia
        Edison Alray (or Elroy)
        Malinda Eliza (or Eliza Melina)
        Betsy Maud
        Bird Ella
Barton, Amasa
    (only missionary killed by Indians)
Barton, Joseph F.
    Harriet Ann Richards
        Harriet Eliza
        Mary Voila
Bayles, Hanson
Bryson, Samuel
Butt, Parley R.
Butt, Willard
Cox, Samuel
    Sarah Jane (or Gane)
        Sarah
Dailey, Milton
    Mary Wilson
        Marion
        Madalene

Dailey, Wilson
>   Lorane Tilton
>>   Bade
>>   Belt

Decker, Cornelious I.
>   Elizabeth Morris
>>   Cornelious William
>>   Eugene Morris

Decker, James Bean
>   Anna Marie Mickelson
>>   Anna Lillian
>>   Nancy Genevieve
>>   Lena Deseret (born at 50 Mile Spring)

Decker, Nathaniel A.
>   Emma Morris
>>   Sarah Jane
>>   Alvin Morris (first baby born at Bluff)

Decker, Zachariah, Jr.
>   Emma Seraphine Smith
>>   Zachariah Nathaniel
>>   Louis
>>   Emma Constance
>>   Inez Gertrude
>>   Jesse Moroni

Decker, Zachariah, Sr.
>   George William

Dunton, James Cyrus
>   Eliza Ann Prothers
>>   James Albert
>>   Mary Alice

Dunton, James Harvey
>   Mary Ann Doige Barker
>>   Ellen Melissa Barker
>>   Medora Barker
>>   John Harvey

Dunton, Marius Ensign
    Emily Hadden
        Marius Alfred
Eyre, John Edwin
    Jane Anne
Eyre, William Naylor
Fielding, Hyrum Amos
    Ellen Agnes Hobbs
        Hyrum Amos
        Joseph Oliver
        Thomas Amos
        Ellen DeLecinn (or Delcena)
Goddard, William P.
    Anna Gilley Taylor
        Herbert
        Maud
Goddard, Sidney C.
Gower, John Thomas
    Harriet Jane Corry
Gurr, William Herbert (or Heber)
    Anna Hansen
        William John
Haight, Caleb
    Sarah Ellen Challerley
Haight, Issac Chauncey
Hobbs, George Brigham
Holyoak, Henry
    Sarah Ann Robinson
        Alice Jane
        Henry John
        Mary Luella
        Eliza Ellen
        Albert Daniel
Hunter, David
    Sarah Jane Urie

Hutchings, William Willard
  Sarah Agnes LeBaron
      Sarah Eliza
      Matilda Ellace
      Linda (or Lydia) Maria
Ipson, George
Jones, Kumen
  Mary Nielson
Larson, Mons
  Olivia Ekelund
      Moroni
      Lars
      John Rio (born on Grey Mesa)
Lewis, George
Lewis, James Harding
Lillywhite, Joseph
  Mary Ellen Wilden
      Joseph
      Benjamin
      Mary Eleanor
      Charles Willden
      Jeremiah Lawrence
      John LeRoy
Lyman, Amasa Mason, Jr.
Lyman, Edward Leo, Sr.
Lyman, Ida Evelyn
Lyman, Joseph Alvin
  Nellie Grayson Roper
Lyman, Lydia May
Lyman, Platte DeAlton
Lyman, Walter Clesbee

Mackelprang, Samuel William
 Adelia Terry (or Perry)
   William Samuel
   Adelia Estella
   Margaret Ann
   Lydia Cornelia
   Minerva
Mickelson, Erasmus
Mickelson, Peter
 Harriet Emily Decker
   Don Alvin
Morrell, George
Mortensen, Peter Andrew
 Hannah Mariah Smith
Nelson, Peter Albert
Nielson, Jens
 Kirsten Jensen
   Hans Joseph
   Margaret
   John
   Francis
   Lucinda Diantha
   Caroline
   Hyrum
Nielson, Jens Peter
Pace, James Wilkerson
 Hannah Caroline Sevy
   Margaret Melinda
   Frank
   Preston D.
   Roy
Pace, John Hardison
 Pauline Ann Bryner
   Elizabeth Mary
Pace, Wilford Woodruff

Perkins, Benjamin
  Mary Ann Williams
    Mary Jane
    Catherine
    Naomi
    Caroline Cordelia Thurston
Perkins, Hyrum
  Rachel Maria Corry
    George William
Redd, Lemuel Hardison, Sr.
  James Monroe
Redd, Lemuel Hardison, Jr.
  Eliza Ann Westover
    Lula
Riley, James Henry
  Sarah Ipson
    James Morton
Robb, Adam Franklin
  Sarah Permelia Holyoak
    Alburtis
    William Heber
Robb, George Drummond
  Caroline Jones
    Mary Ann
    Ellen
Robb, John
  Sarah Edwards
    Ellen
    Sarah
Robb, William
  Ellen Stone
    William
Robinson, John Rowlandson

Rowley, Samuel
    Ann Taylor
            Mary Ann
            Samuel James
            Hannah Eliza
            Sarah Jane
            Alice Louisa
            George Walter
            John Taylor
Sevy, George W.
    Margaret Nebraska Imlay
            George F.
            Rueben Warren
Smith, John Aikens
    Emily Jane Bennet
            Emily Jane
Smith, Joseph Stanford
    Arabella Jane Coombs
            Ada Olivia
            Joseph ElRoy
            George Abraham
Smith, Samuel
Smith, Silas Sanford
Smith, Silas Sanford, Jr.
    Betsy Williamson
            Ann Clarinda
            Silas Sanford
Smith, Stephen Augustus
Stevens, David Alma
Stevens, Roswell
Stevens, Walter Joshua
    Elizabeth Kenney
Taylor, Edmund
Taylor, Warren
Topham, John
Urie, George
    Alice Jane Perry

Walker, Joseph
Walton, Charles E., Sr.
   Jane McKetchnie (or Jane Hatch)
      Francis Magnolia
      Charles Eugene
      Leona Jane
Webster, Francis
Westover, George Henry
Westwood, George
Williams, Sarah
Williams, Thomas
Wilson, Henry
Woolsey, Joseph Smith

AUTHOR'S NOTE:

Some discrepancies occurred when comparing different sources that listed the names of the participants in the San Juan Mission. For the purposes of accuracy, I cross-referenced the lists and included all names found here. There will be some confusion as to the spelling of some of the names, as well as the birth order of some of the children, but I did my best to produce an accurate listing, based on the information available to me.

RECOMMENDED READING

Miller, David E. *Hole in the Rock: An Epic in the Colonization of the Great American West*, University of Utah Press, 1966

Reay, Lee. *Incredible Passage Through the Hole in the Rock*, Meadow Lane, 1981

Yorgason, Blaine. *At All Hazards*, Shadow Mountain, 1997

ABOUT THE AUTHOR

Tristi Pinkston is the author of two published novels, *Nothing to Regret* and *Strength to Endure*, both set during World War II. She has been critically acclaimed for the realism of her novels, which uplift without being preachy. She also recently released *Agent in Old Lace*, her first contemporary mystery. She's also the author of four as-yet-unpublished novels, some of which are based on the  true-life stories of her ancestors, as is *Season of Sacrifice*.

Tristi has been married to Matt Pinkston since 1995, and together they have four children: Caryn, Ammon, Joseph, and Benjamin (who was named after Benjamin Perkins). She home-schools these children and considers it a joy to watch them learn and grow.

Tristi enjoys reading, watching good movies, scrapbooking, and taking long naps.

Tristi has been a member of LDStorymakers for over five years. She is a regular presenter at the LDStorymakers Writers Conferences, has presented at the League of Utah Writers monthly meeting as well as the Spring Workshop, was featured at the ANWA yearly conference, and gives firesides regularly to promote the cause of literacy.

You can learn more about Tristi by visiting her website and blogs at:

www.tristipinkston.com
http://members.families.com/tristipie/blog
www.tristipinkton.blogspot.com